"WHAT'S CLOSE OFF THE PORT BEAM?" KEN asked, moving his fingers lightly up her waist, then down again. Ingrid felt each touch to her marrow.

"Not much . . . a few boats a mile or more off," she said.

"And what's to starboard?" he asked, his hands playing sensuous games against her skin.

"Nothing much," she said. "A few points of land, hazy and purple in the distance." Thank goodness, she thought. She hadn't been keeping much of a watch, her attention focused entirely on the sensations Ken's fingers aroused.

"Good," he said, and slid one hand under her chin. "Because I just remembered I like to live dangerously and this time," Ken said, "I'm kissing you for real. Last time I didn't know who you were, but this time I do." He brushed her lips again, his tongue tracing their shape, flicking at their soft parting.

She forgot to search the water for dangers, forgot everything but him. Closing her eyes against the dazzle of the sun, she felt his mouth fully cover hers.

Yes, she said silently against the velvet touch of his lips. Oh, yes . . .

WHAT ARE *LOVESWEPT* ROMANCES?

They are stories of true romance and touching emotion. We believe those two very important ingredients are constants in our highly sensual and very believable stories in the LOVESWEPT line. Our goal is to give you, the reader, stories of consistently high quality that may sometimes make you laugh, sometimes make you cry, but are always fresh and creative and contain many delightful surprises within their pages.

Most romance fans read an enormous number of books. Those they truly love, they keep. Others may be traded with friends and soon forgotten. We hope that each LOVESWEPT romance will be a treasure—a "keeper." We will always try to publish

LOVE STORIES YOU'LL NEVER FORGET
BY AUTHORS YOU'LL ALWAYS REMEMBER

The Editors

LOVING VOICES

JUDY GILL

BANTAM BOOKS
NEW YORK · TORONTO · LONDON · SYDNEY · AUCKLAND

LOVING VOICES

A Bantam Book / July 1994

If you would be interested in receiving protective vinyl covers for your Loveswept books, please write to this address for information:

Loveswept
Bantam Books
P.O. Box 985
Hicksville, NY 11802

ISBN 0-553-44455-7

Published simultaneously in the United States and Canada

Bantam Books are published by Bantam Books, a division of Bantam Doubleday Dell Publishing Group, Inc. Its trademark, consisting of the words "Bantam Books" and the portrayal of a rooster, is Registered in U.S. Patent and Trademark Office and in other countries. Marca Registrada. Bantam Books, 1540 Broadway, New York, New York 10036.

PRINTED IN THE UNITED STATES OF AMERICA

OPM   0 9 8 7 6 5 4 3 2 1

To Hairless Joe and his Egmont Harem
February 1993

ONE

Ken Ransom muttered a curse as he knocked over a lamp while trying to find the ringing telephone somewhere to the left of his bed. The phone shrieked again as he clamped his hand over it. He snatched it up, uttering a rough "Hello."

There was no reply.

"Hello?" he said again, and added impatiently, at the continued silence, "Who is that? What do you want?"

He heard a muffled sound, then what could have been a gulp, followed by a pleasant female voice, slightly garbled. "Oom! Kem Ranthom?"

This was getting ridiculous, Ken thought. His sister, Janet, must have had some kind of brain fever, finding him an apartment in her building of overly friendly singles. It was bad enough, women knocking on his door at all hours of the day with pies and cakes and cookies and casseroles, "welcoming" him, "looking after" him in Janet's absence. If they'd now started phoning him in the middle of the damn night, he was in serious trouble. And so, for that matter, was Janet.

He was there to relax, rest, think—and heal if possible—and he couldn't do it if he was constantly answering the door and, it now seemed, the phone. The number, though, was supposed to be unlisted.

"Who wants him?" he asked cautiously.

"Um . . . momma," she said. Or he thought she said.

"Momma? Not mine you aren't. At least I don't think so, not unless someone's been lying to me for a long, long time."

"Sorry," she said, and he heard humor bubbling in her voice. "I wasn't claiming to be your momma. This is Ingrid Bjornsen. I was asking you, in my own quaint way, to be patient. To wait a moment. I had my mouth full."

"Of what?"

His question startled Ingrid, and she blurted out her answer. "Apple," she said. Because his abrupt manner made her nervous, she continued babbling like an idiot. "I hadn't expected you to answer so quickly, you see, and Golden Delicious apples are much too good to rush, so I finished chewing before I spoke and, if the truth be known, I'm not absolutely certain I expected you to answer at all, which might explain my utter rudeness in taking a bite of my apple even as I dialed."

"You phoned me," he said pointedly when she finally paused for breath. "Why wouldn't you have expected me to answer?"

Feeling more and more like a fool, Ingrid wished she could simply pretend she'd gotten a wrong number and hang up. If he hadn't been Janet's brother, she would have. It was clear he really hadn't wanted to take this call any more than she'd really wanted to make it. Janet had that effect on people, though. Somehow she got them to do things. It made her a formidable executive of the Volunteer Bureau. "I, um, more than half expected an answering machine," she said.

"And got me," he said. "How disappointing for you."

"*I'm* not disappointed. If you are Ken Ransom?"

"I am. What can I do for you?"

"Why, nothing! Nothing at all. I'm here to do something for you, as I'm sure your sister explained. I'm your Living Voices volunteer, and I do apologize for the lack of one—a voice, that is—when you first answered.

"I'd have called a lot earlier," she went on, as his silence seemed to invite, "but I was late getting in after work because one of my kids went missing and his parents quite naturally called me at once. The search took some time, and I had to ask a replacement to do my usual Living Voices stint. When I did get home and found your sister's message saying that she would drop your file off at the church office so I could be sure to call you today, there was no time to dash out and get it. My parents needed me to help a friend by filling in for some missing woman at a dinner party. I had to shower and change and run. I just got home again. Father Ralph at Saint Justine's sent the envelope to my house because it was marked 'Personal and Urgent.' I hope it's not too late to call, but your sister assured me you're as much of a night owl as I am."

She fell silent, waiting for him to comment. Some quality in his silence told her the truth. She moaned softly, clapping her hand to her brow.

"You don't have the faintest idea of who I am or what I'm talking about, do you?" she said. "I'm sorry! I feel like a dope. I imagine I sound like one too."

"No, you sound like an angel. A slightly demented one, speaking in riddles I don't understand, but that's okay. I like to hear you speak."

She moaned again. "I'm sorry I bothered you, Mr. Ransom. I'd never have put you on my list if I hadn't thought you wanted me to call. This is . . . Oh, damn, I'm embarrassed. Good night. I promise I won't bother you again."

"Hold on!" Suddenly Ken didn't want her to hang up. "Are you with a charitable organization? What is this list?" He really didn't care about the answer. Whatever the group wanted, he could easily say no, though more than likely he'd say yes, simply as the cost of hearing more of Ingrid Bjornsen's beautiful voice.

"The list of people I call, just to keep in touch."

He frowned, an ache beginning between his brows as it so often did now. "But . . . you don't know me from a hole in the ground. Why would you want me on your list of people to keep in touch with? Do you make a habit of phoning strangers?"

"Well, yes. I mean, that's what Living Voices is all about. We call lonely people and talk."

"Really?"

Since his sister had set this up, the woman on the other end of the phone could be anything from a nun to a hooker. Janet numbered both among her friends. Maybe it was time to find out which.

"Then this is something like phone sex in reverse?" he suggested. "What do you do when you don't have people dropping off names for you? Call numbers at random until you get a man interested in talking dirty to you? I'm game. Who goes first?"

Obviously unoffended, she laughed, and the warm,

delightful sound wrapped around him. It reverberated in his ears long after its tones had faded. Heat pooled in his lower belly and spread as she answered. "That would be a novel twist on phone sex, wouldn't it? But no, this isn't a random call, nor is it about sex, phone or otherwise. Your sister said you'd appreciate having someone to talk to now and then, preferably in the evening."

"My sister says lots of things. I've learned over the years that she usually has a purpose in mind, however obscure that might be. So I'm sure she had a reason for asking you to call me."

"Me too." She sounded as if she had her teeth clenched. "Janet," she muttered as if his sister were by her side, "I'll get you for this."

A strange feeling welled up in his chest. To his astonishment he recognized it as the beginnings of laughter, which had been in short supply in his life these past few months.

He chuckled. "I've said that a time or two myself. Do you think Jan's been trying to set us up?"

"I know it!" She made a sound that could have been a growl. He pictured a ruffled kitten and grinned.

"Suppose you explain to me what she's up to," he said, primarily to keep her talking. He hadn't been kidding when he'd said she sounded like an angel. He could listen to her voice all night. It lilted like water trickling over pebbles in a brook. He chuckled again. "That is, if you have her scheme figured out."

Ingrid liked the sound of Ken Ransom's chuckle. She also liked his looks.

Her gaze swept over the eight-by-ten head-and-shoulders photograph Janet had thoughtfully supplied of her brother.

Ingrid swallowed hard. She *really* liked his looks.

He had thick dark auburn hair that hung a bit too long around his ears. He was clean-shaven and had a square, masculine chin to balance his broad forehead. Though his unsmiling expression was a trifle aloof, with a hint of a challenge in it, his thick-lashed eyes held a greenish glimmer that made her suspect a good sense of humor lurked behind his serious facade.

"Explain?" she repeated. She couldn't explain. She wouldn't. Damn, damn, damn! Her supposedly good friend, who knew all about Ingrid's problem and knew the rules that Ingrid had made to minimize its effect on her life—"living in a phone booth," as Janet liked to call it—that friend had just set her up. Janet knew better!

Oh, she had Janet's scheme figured out, all right. Stupidity wasn't one of Ingrid's major problems. Jan's plot: Give Ingrid a sob story so she felt sorry for the guy, then let his sexy voice slide into her ear and charm her socks off. Worse, show her a picture of the man so she'd know what she was missing. Add to that mixture by making the man Janet's own lonely brother, far from his family, business, and social contacts, with the full knowledge that he'd react as every man Ingrid had ever called reacted to her telephone voice, then sit back and watch.

"Please," Ken said. "I feel more secure when I know what my little sister's up to."

Ingrid sighed. "Last week Janet asked me to give you a call because she was going to be away and was worried about you. I told her I'd put you on the Living Voice's list if she cleared it with you first. Since you obviously weren't expecting my call tonight, I can only guess she didn't tell you about Living Voices and what we do. That being so, of course you didn't agree to being called."

"That's right. I didn't. And no, she told me nothing about any of this."

"Then I'm truly sorry that I disturbed you. We only call lonely shut-ins who want our calls."

"Lonely!" Ken rolled onto his side, hooking the phone between his head and the pillow. "That figures." He didn't know which emotion was uppermost—annoyance or amusement over his sister's machinations. "Janet is convinced that I'm suffering from terminal depression. But believe me, I'm fine." He paused for a beat, then added, "And I don't need charity."

"That's good," Ingrid said crisply. "I'm not offering it."

He flopped onto his back, nearly dislodging the phone. He snorted. Sure. Right. "Then what, exactly, are you offering?" Cookies? Casseroles?

"Just time," she said. "And conversation. Janet asked me to call today. In fact she made a real point of it. She didn't say why, though."

"It's my birthday."

"Oh! Happy birthday, Ken." Her tone was warm enough to bathe in. He grimaced at his body's response to her voice and bent one knee to take the weight of the covers off his midsection. It didn't help, especially when that melodic voice went on. "I wish I'd known that. I would have sung for you. Would you like me to do it now?"

"Hell, no!" A bark of uncomfortable laughter broke loose. "I hate it when people sing 'Happy Birthday' to me."

"Oh, that's too bad. I sing at any excuse. Not well," she added with another soft chuckle, "but with great enthusiasm. What did you do to celebrate today?"

Dammit, Ken thought. He'd heard people address six-year-olds in that same tone of voice—*What did Santa bring you, sonny?* "Nothing," he said, and didn't care if he came across as truculent.

"Oh. I'm so sorry."

Her sincere-sounding commiseration, coupled with knowing that Janet had told her he was a "lonely shut-in," irritated him. "Don't waste your sympathy on me," he snapped. "My mother called and talked for an hour. She wanted to fly out—from Montreal if you can believe it—and cook dinner for me, bake me a cake. I quashed that notion, and fast."

Indeed, one of the reasons he'd moved from Montreal to Vancouver after getting out of rehab was to put distance between himself and his mother. He'd chosen the West Coast because, since his sister was based here, it kept his mother from following him. He loved her dearly, but she tended to hover. And he was determined to deal with this problem in his own way, at his own pace, without coddling.

"Then you've been alone all day," Ingrid said. "No wonder Janet insisted that I call regardless of what time I got home."

"I haven't been alone all day." He didn't want her thinking of him as needy in any way. "I've had plenty of company. But I didn't want it any more than I wanted a celebration."

"Most people love personal celebrations. Did you have birthday parties when you were a child?"

"Of course I did, but I'm not a child. And why celebrate another year in *this* life?"

"Tsk! Do I detect a note of self-pity there?"

Ken scowled. "Of course not! I'm simply stating a fact

as I see it. My life as I knew it is over. And I'm not madly enthusiastic about the one I've been left to deal with."

"What makes you think the one you knew is over?"

His frown deepened, and he rubbed at the stab of pain between his eyebrows. The smart thing to do would be hang up and try to get a few hours' sleep. Maybe when he awoke, the headache would be gone.

But if he hung up, Ingrid Bjornsen and her velvety angel's voice would be gone too.

"Do you really care why I think the way I do?" he asked.

Her simple yes wasn't what he'd been looking for. He tried again. "What are you, some kind of a shrink hired by this Loving Voices gang?"

Her soft spurt of laughter, accompanied by an emphatic no, was only a minor improvement. He wanted to say *Talk to me, woman. Recite poetry, read stories. Wrap me in your voice*. Instead he said, "I've had it with shrinks. I don't talk to them anymore, and Janet knows that. She shouldn't have sicced you or your loving voice on me."

"That's *Living* Voices, not 'loving,' " she said. "And I am not a shrink. Nor," she added, and her voice was crisp again, "did your sister 'sic' me on you. She thought she was doing you a kindness. However, if you'd rather not talk, that's okay with me."

Something final in her tone made him grip the phone tighter. "Wait! Ingrid? Don't hang up."

"Why?" she said. "Are you one of those people who feels empowered hanging up first? If so, feel free."

"No," he said.

When she didn't reply, he said sharply, "Ingrid?"

She remained silent, but he thought he could hear her breathing. Why didn't she speak? Was she chewing another bite of apple? His mouth watered. When Jan had asked him what he wanted in the way of groceries, he hadn't mentioned apples. He wondered if she'd had any sent. He'd give his best computer for a bite of that woman's apple.

Yeah, sure. That's what had gotten Adam so deep into it. He needed an apple-equipped woman like he needed another head. For a moment his nearly atrophied sense of humor poked itself through. Come to think of it, another head would be of benefit right about now.

"Are you still there?" he asked.

"I'm still here."

"Look, forgive me, okay? I didn't mean to be rude to you. None of this is your fault, and I shouldn't take it out on you." He swallowed. "I wouldn't blame you if you left me to simmer in my own bile. I guess you don't get many responses like mine. Otherwise you wouldn't bother, would you?"

He heard the smile in her tone as she said, "I forgive you, and I don't find it a bother. I enjoy doing this. People who don't get out much for one reason or another often appreciate a call." She paused, then added gently, "Appreciate a living voice."

As *he* did, Ken mused, so long as it was hers. Not that he was about to admit it and prove Janet right. "What do you normally talk about with these people you call?"

"Whatever they want to talk about."

He sensed that was an invitation for him to choose the topic. He didn't want to talk, though. What he wanted was for her to talk so he could lie there and bask in the warmth of her voice. But he couldn't very well tell her that.

"Are you lonely this evening?" he asked, then felt

his eyes bug out. What the *hell*? He hadn't meant to say that at all.

"Not now," she said cheerfully. "Not with you to talk to. Other times, though, I often feel that way. Do you?"

"No." Instantly he was ashamed of the ragged edge in his voice; ashamed, too, in a strange way, of the lie. Lie? Had it been a lie? He'd never thought of himself as a lonely person, just a frequently solitary one—of necessity. His privacy and the time alone he needed to think, plan, and create had always been as important as the social and business contacts that gave his life balance. But now he guessed that some of what he'd been feeling these last few months was loneliness. Without those social and business contacts, there hadn't been any balance. Or much pleasure either. He'd also learned how few real friends he actually had.

He cleared his throat. "You said you 'often' feel lonely. Why is that?"

"I don't know." He conjured up a mental image of her frowning, fair brows drawn together over a slim, narrow-bridged nose in a perfectly proportioned face. "I guess because I'm frequently alone and don't always like it. When it's late at night and the drapes are drawn, I envy those who have someone special, someone all their own to curl up with, to talk to, to share the events of the day with, or even just to discuss the late news. Then, having none of that, I feel very much alone."

He swallowed hard. "Yeah." The word came out in a rough whisper. He hadn't even meant to utter it.

Hearing her say she was lonely made him want to curl up beside her—around her—so she'd never feel that way again. Curl up and listen to her voice in his ear, feel her soft, pale hair under his cheek, breathe in the sweet woman-scent of her skin—

He broke off the thought before it could go any farther. For corn sakes! That was just plain nuts. He'd never even seen her. In all likelihood he never *would* see her. For all he knew, she was eighty-seven years old and had a warty nose and bristles on her chin.

"You too?" she asked, and her voice settled in his gut like a gulp of hot brandy.

"I was a bit . . . lonely before you called," he said, then groaned. Hell and damnation! Why hadn't he simply ended the conversation? Had he lost his emotional ballast along with everything else? "I wish I hadn't said that," he blurted out, making things much worse. He tried to control his runaway tongue, but it continued. "Now you're going to think of me as nothing more than another of your poor, miserable shut-ins."

"I don't consider you a poor, miserable anything," she said, and she'd gone all crisp again, even a touch tart. "How could I? You have a sister who cares enough about you to ask me to call you, a mother who wanted to fly several thousand miles to spend your birthday with you, and more company than you claim to want. Do you feel miserable?"

"No. Of course not." He did, but she was right. He shouldn't. There were people a hell of a lot worse off. He thought of the men who'd died when the scaffolding fell, the three widows, eight fatherless children. At least he had his life.

Trouble was, he didn't know what the hell to do with it.

"What do you feel, Ken?"

The question, put so gently, in a tone of such concern

that he sensed she truly wanted to know, made him feel even more sorry for himself. He couldn't speak for a moment. His eyes stung. For the love of Mike, what the hell was happening to him? He abhorred this tendency toward self-pity, loathed discovering it was still so close to the surface. He'd thought he was beyond that, yet there he was, on the verge of wallowing in it again.

He forced a laugh. "I feel . . . embarrassed."

"Embarrassed?" Ingrid asked as she gazed at his picture again. "Why?"

Lord knew he had nothing to be embarrassed about, she thought, running her gaze over his broad shoulders, the muscles clearly defined inside a polo shirt. A small tuft of chest hair showed in the V of the open collar.

"Why?" His sharp repetition of her question snapped her back to attention. "Because I don't make a habit of admitting my deepest feelings to people I don't know," he said crossly. "It must have something to do with your voice. I think it's mesmerized me." He sounded as if she'd set out to enchant him and he resented it.

"I didn't mean it to," she said. And she hadn't, but it was something she couldn't prevent. Most people opened up to her during her Living Voices sessions. Her phone voice was one of her few—lamentably few—assets, as her mother often reminded her. Though always kindly, always gently. But always.

"Anyway," she went on, "I apologize for making you say something you'd rather not have said, even if I did do it inadvertently."

"Was it so inadvertent?" he asked suspiciously. "Are you sure you're not a shrink?"

"I already told you I'm not."

"Then what are you?"

"Days, I run a day care at Saint Justine's, but for now I'm a Living Voices volunteer. A potential phone friend—that's something like a pen pal—who called to ask if you wanted to spend ten or fifteen minutes chatting to me or one of the other volunteers on a regular or periodic basis. If you don't, that's fine. I won't be hurt. We have lots of people who do want our calls."

"Ten or fifteen minutes?" He snorted. "That's hardly long enough for you to try to tell me how an architect is supposed to deal with sudden blindness."

Ingrid didn't want her heart to ache for him. She wanted simply to help alleviate his loneliness by making a phone visit now and then, the way she did with her senior citizens. She glanced back at his picture and shook her head. Who was she trying to kid?

"You've gone very quiet," he said. "Didn't you know I'm blind?"

"I knew."

"And? How does that make you feel?"

"Now who sounds like a shrink?" she countered, because she didn't have the faintest idea of what to say. Suddenly she wasn't sure what Janet had wanted her to give him, or what he'd be willing to accept. She was also unsure just what she'd expected to be able to provide. She did a damn good job as a clinical psychologist dealing with problem children; she brought light and interest to the lives of elderly shut-ins. However, Ken Ransom was no child, nor was he a senior citizen. He was a vital man in his prime, and somehow that made his problem worse in her mind.

"Answer the question," he said challengingly. "How does knowing I'm blind make you feel?"

"It makes me sad on your behalf," she said. "I'm sure

it won't be easy to adapt to being blind, even if it's only a temporary thing. If it proves to be permanent, then the adjustment will be a lot more difficult. I don't envy you."

"If that was pity, Ingrid, I don't want it."

"I wasn't offering it," she retorted. "I never waste my pity on those who carry around their own supply."

She expected, in the ensuing silence, to hear the angry smash of the phone as he slammed it down. His full-bodied laugh, when it came, both startled and delighted her.

"I like you, Ingrid Bjornsen," he said.

"Good," she responded at once. "Then I'll call you again if you'd like to talk with me some more. My next evening for calls is Wednesday. Do you want a Living Voices call?"

He was silent for a long moment, then he sighed. "Oh, what the hell. Now that my name's on your list, I suppose it would be almost impossible to get it off."

"No. Not at all."

"Bull." Scorn toughened his voice. "I know how hard it is to persuade any organization to delete something once it's entered into a data base. I once received a renewal notice every two months for three years for a magazine I'd never subscribed to in the first place. No amount of phone calls or correspondence convinced them I wasn't one of their subscribers. *Three years.*"

Ingrid grinned at his aggrieved tone. "A name stays on our lists," she said, "only until we're asked to take it off. I can delete yours right now if you want, and no one will call you again."

Of course not, she thought, especially since his name wasn't even on the Living Voices list yet.

"If my name's on there now, you might just as well leave it." He sounded as if he were bestowing a favor—grudgingly.

Ingrid laughed silently. He wanted the calls, all right. He just didn't want anyone to know he wanted them. She called several elderly men with similar attitudes. As long as they didn't admit having a need, the need didn't exist.

"It's no trouble," she said sweetly. "I run the data base and can erase your name in a nanosecond."

"No!"

"All right," she said, glad she'd called his bluff. "Would you prefer a woman to call, or a man?"

"A man?" he echoed. "Men do this?" He might have been saying "Men bear young?"

"Certainly. Several of the other volunteers are men, though they're all elderly. They might find it a refreshing change to talk to a guy who doesn't have World War Two stories to swap. Would you prefer that?"

Ken clenched his teeth. He would not. He wanted the Living Voice on his phone to belong to Ingrid Bjornsen—at least part of him did. The other part hated being nothing more than a name on a list of other shut-ins she'd give her time to, her ten or fifteen minutes, or whatever she could spare from her busy, varied life.

Why wasn't she so wrapped up in that life, with her own family, that she had no time for church offices and shut-ins? And why was she often alone in the evenings?

"Are you still there?" he asked, and heard her soothing, comforting murmur as she said "Of course."

She added, "If you need time to think about it, I can call Wednesday to see what you've decided."

He could decide right now. He knew he should put

an end to this call, should refuse all others because he *would not* become dependent on anyone, even for a thrice-weekly phone call. Nor was he exactly a shut-in. He could get out. He did. He just . . . didn't do it often. But she thought of him as a shut-in. That irked him.

Still, his delight in hearing her voice kept him clutching the phone, holding it to his ear as if it were some kind of lifeline. That voice of hers . . . it stroked over him like velvet, filling him with sensual pleasure. That, like smiles and laughter, had been in short supply of late. He ached for more of it.

He frowned so hard even the back of his head hurt, and just when he thought the headache might have subsided. Dammit, he did not want some strange man calling him. Or a strange woman.

Okay, so Ingrid was a stranger too. He tried to heed the message from his subconscious, but the desire to hear her voice again was too strong, and in only a moment it overrode all other considerations. Ingrid Bjornsen was the first human being outside his immediate family to spark his interest since the accident.

And the first woman to remind him so forcibly that he was still a man.

He wanted whatever kind of contact with her he could get.

Hang up, you damn fool, he told himself. *Hang up now!*

He would have, too, if he hadn't heard her draw a soft breath. Getting ready to say good-bye? Quickly he said, "Ingrid? I've decided."

"And?"

"I'm used to you now. I suppose you'd better be the one to call."

"All right," she said briskly as if they were about to conclude a business deal. Which, he supposed, in her estimation, they were. "What's a good time for you? I usually make my calls between six-thirty and eight-thirty, Monday, Wednesday, and Friday."

He did not want to be another name in a file to her. He did not want her to call him from some dingy church office and only three times a week.

"Look," he said, "why not just give me your number and then if I decide I want to talk to someone—sometime when the drapes are drawn and the doors are locked—I could call you."

Ingrid's mouth went dry as she thought of answering her phone some evening and hearing Ken Ransom's rich, darkly soft voice on the other end—Ken Ransom wanting to speak to her so much that *he* placed the call. But . . . if she weren't in, someone would answer her extension in the main wing. Someone such as her mother.

If her mother heard Ken's voice, she'd think—hope— he was interested in Ingrid personally. Her effusiveness would transmit every nuance of her unsubtle gratitude that someone, *anyone* who might be remotely eligible, was calling her daughter. It was one of the most humiliating situations Ingrid could contemplate.

"I'm sorry," she said quickly, aware the silence had gone on too long. "I can't do that. We at Living Voices always initiate the calls."

"Why is that?"

"Just . . . policy," she said. "Rules." Before he could argue, she said, "Good night, Ken. Sleep well. I'll talk to you Wednesday."

A knock sounded on her door just as she hung up.

Ingrid placed Ken Ransom's photograph face-down on the window seat, covering it with her sweater. She stood, shook the pins and needles from the leg she'd been sitting on, and went to the door.

Opening it, she stepped back. "Muh-muh-muh—" She broke off, drew a deep breath, and tried to relax her face, her throat, her chest, her mind. "M-mother," she managed to say. "Cuh-cuh-come in."

TWO

Phillipa Enderby frowned as she strode into Ingrid's suite. "Did I hear you on the phone?"

Ingrid nodded.

"But it's so late, dear, and I know you're tired. Why aren't you in bed?"

Ingrid laughed. "B-b-be . . ." She closed her eyes, gritted her teeth, and turned from her mother. Facing away from the calm, compassionate brown eyes under her mother's professionally coiffed dark bangs, she managed to say, "Because you're here. It wouldn't be p-p-polite to go to b-buh-buh—bed while I have c-c-c-company."

Her mother laughed dutifully. "I meant, why were you on the phone, instead of sleeping? When we left the party, you could scarcely get a word out, you were so weary. I was on my way to bed when I saw your lights on."

Ingrid smiled and waved her mother to a chair.

Phillipa accepted the invitation, smoothing her pink satin dressing gown over her slender thighs. She cast Ingrid a sidelong glance. "Now, wasn't that a nice party this evening, Ingrid? Aren't you glad we insisted you attend?"

Ingrid shook her head. She hated the social functions her parents found so necessary, and her mother knew it. As a politician's daughter, Ingrid was a dead loss, but they still persisted in dragging her along as frequently as she permitted it. Such as that evening. The occasion had been a dinner party to honor a visiting dignitary from Washington, D.C., and at the last moment the hostess, a good friend of her mother's, had required another female to keep the numbers even.

Or so the story had gone. Likely it had been a setup from day one, and they only sprang it on her at the last minute so she couldn't come up with the excuse of a prior engagement. Her mother never considered her Living Voices commitments as valid excuses, which was why Ingrid normally made her calls from the church office rather than from home. Unfortunately that night she'd come home earlier than usual, because she'd had to pass her calls on to someone else and thus had been trapped.

Her parents had undimmable hopes that if Ingrid were to meet "just the right man," her problem would disappear overnight and she'd turn into someone they could be proud of. They even saw the day care as "Ingrid's little hobby."

Often she thought it would be better to move out and get her own apartment on the far side of town, maybe in another city. Another country? She'd always thought the Falkland Islands sounded intriguing, or possibly Lapland.

But they'd both be so hurt if she did move out, she couldn't bear the thought. Especially when they'd gone to the trouble of having this self-contained suite built for her after her divorce. Besides, when the Senate was in session, or her parents were on one of their frequent trips, she had the whole house to herself—along with the staff of course.

"You seemed to enjoy your conversation with Braydon McGuire," Phillipa said.

Ingrid merely raised her brows and shrugged. She wasn't surprised her mother had noticed her spending the bulk of the evening in Braydon's company. She could, she supposed, have broken away at any time, but it had been easier to let things ride. As long as Braydon's attention remained fixed on her, no one had felt obliged to insist that she circulate, or worse, that other men be introduced to her.

Braydon had monopolized her most of the evening, requiring nothing more of her than the odd "Oh," and eyes widened in appreciation of his wit, charm, business acumen, and intelligence, all of which he expounded on in great detail. In that way he was very much like Ingrid's ex-husband, Ron, had been at the beginning of their acquaintance.

"He's very handsome, isn't he?" her mother persisted. "He reminds me, in a nice way, of Ron."

Ingrid nodded, busying herself by tidying her china mouse collection displayed on the tiers of a corner shelf. Strange how, despite the odds, she'd learned to love her little mice.

"I do wish you'd try to speak to me, dear. I've always disliked your answering questions with gestures, and your speech therapists over the years have all concurred. It's better for you to communicate normally. Or," Phillipa added with a smile Ingrid knew she meant to be kind, perhaps even teasing, "as normally as you are able. I'm your mother. No small speech impediment will ever change the way I feel about you."

Ingrid could have laughed, except she might have cried. That "small speech impediment" seemed pretty damned big to her, and while she knew her mother loved her, she was also horribly aware of a glimmer of Type-A-personality impatience behind the compassion in her parental gaze. Phillipa truly believed that if Ingrid would simply try harder, she could overcome her stutter.

"S-sorry," she said, still concentrating on her collection.

The mice were a symbol of how little real understanding there had ever been between Phillipa and Ingrid. The mice were a relic of her boarding-school days, when she'd been stuck with the unkind nickname of Mousie. Her mother hadn't understood that the other girls were being cruel; she'd thought it a sign of affection, accused Ingrid of being overly sensitive, and had begun giving her little mice as gifts.

"Look at me, dear, please," she said. Ingrid turned. "What did you and Braydon discuss for such a long time after dinner?"

"Him," Ingrid said, and yawned, making no attempt to hide her boredom with the subject. Or the man. "He talked. I listened." She only tripped a tiny amount on the *l* sound.

Phillipa misunderstood, perhaps on purpose. "That's

all well and good, dear, but it helps to be a good conversationalist too."

Ingrid tilted her chin, a spurt of anger enabling her to say quite clearly, "Helps what, Mother?"

"Why . . . helps a woman in a . . . in a social sense. Ingrid, don't you want to have friends?"

Just phone friends. They're the only safe ones. And children of course. Ingrid closed her eyes for a second and sat down on the window seat, placing herself between her mother and Ken Ransom's photograph, still hidden under her sweater.

She'd been hearing this same lecture, or variations of it, from her mother for the past twenty-nine years, with the exception of the two years during which she was married. Then she'd heard it from her husband, except that for *want to have friends* he'd substituted *want me to succeed in business.* Finally, he'd left her, and the last she'd heard, he had succeeded in his business with a wife at his side who could do the social scene without embarrassing him by stuttering.

"I have fuh-fuh-friends," she said, pinching her hands between her knees. "I'm hap-hap-hap—" She drew a deep breath and let it out slowly. "Content."

"But lonely."

Ingrid shook her head and smiled. "Not so very luh-luh-luh . . ." As she'd been taught, she stopped, rather than fighting the trapped sound, swallowed, breathed, and brought it out smoothly. " . . . lonely. I have y-you and Dad."

Phillipa leaned forward and patted her daughter's knee. "Me, and Dad, and your phone calls. Who were you talking to so late at night? One of your girlfriends?"

Ingrid hesitated, then nodded. It was easier than trying to explain, especially when she was tired and knew her stutter would be more pronounced. She tried, and failed, to stifle another yawn.

Phillipa smiled. "All right, then, I'll leave you to get ready for bed." She stood, then bent and kissed Ingrid's cheek. "Good night, darling."

Ingrid sat for some time after her mother had gone, then wandered into her kitchenette, separated from her sitting room by a half wall topped to the ceiling with an ivy-draped lattice. She made herself some herbal tea, took the cup with her, and, carrying Ken Ransom's picture, went into her bedroom. She put the photograph away, out of sight, and readied herself for bed.

Lying there, she sipped her soothing tea, staring out the window at the lights of the buildings on Point Grey, visible across the expanse of Vancouver Harbor. She wondered if one of them shone in the apartment where Ken lay, undoubtedly sleeping by now.

Did a blind man remember to turn off the lights before he went to bed? Did he think to turn any on before dusk? What must it be like to live in a world of darkness? He would feel isolated, alone. As isolated and alone as she had always felt, trapped in a world where it was nearly impossible to communicate her thoughts and feelings except over the phone, or to small children.

Oh, yes, she'd call him Wednesday evening. No matter what. As long as he wanted her to she'd make those calls.

Ken leaned back on the sofa, hands gripping his cordless phone, eyes open and staring into darkness in the direction of the phone. *Call me*, he said silently, trying to project into the ether a mental image of Ingrid Bjornsen lifting her telephone, dialing his number, listening to the ringing on his end. *Call me, Ingrid. Do it now.*

It was Tuesday evening. With a ragged laugh he shook his head. *Fool!* He stood abruptly in response to the chiming of his doorbell, for once grateful for the interruption. He concentrated on walking with confidence and poise across the room, not because anyone was watching but because he needed the practice, and opened the door.

"Hi, Ken." The perky voice came from somewhere not far below his eye level. Ken adjusted the angle of his head, hoping he was getting it right. "Remember me?" the woman said.

"I, uh . . ." He let his voice trail off lamely. Dammit, there were so many people in the building, two-thirds of them female, and he figured he'd met all of the latter in the past couple of weeks.

"Maddie from the third floor," she said, taking pity on him. "We met when your sister was showing you around the gym. I'd have been up a lot sooner, but I'm a flight attendant and I haven't been here a lot. I've brought you tofu candy as a welcome-to-the-building gift."

"Thank you. That's very kind." He didn't know whether to invite her in or to hold out his hand for the gift. As an attendant, she might be a friend of his sister, who was a pilot. He simply stood there feeling uncharacteristically gauche.

He remembered now. Maddie was the one who had kept him and Janet standing in the gym for nearly half an hour as she intimately detailed, for Ken's edification, the lives and loves of everyone in the building. No, she and Jan weren't friends, didn't even fly for the same airline.

He suspected that Maddie, despite her frequent absences, was the reason word had gotten around so quickly that there was a new man in the building and that he was, of all things, blind. *Helpless.*

There was nothing a woman liked better, he knew from a widowed friend, than a man whom she saw as being in need of womanly help, not necessarily including sex—but not excluding it either. His friend had been left with a three-year-old son to raise on his own, and women who wouldn't have noticed him before had stacked up on his doorstep with offerings of food and friendship, assistance and solace.

It would have been a lie for Ken not to acknowledge that women of all descriptions had been noticing him since he was about sixteen years old. Since this was a singles building, he supposed he must be considered fair game to any female with her hunting instincts astir. His blindness might even be seen as a bonus—until the novelty wore off.

Maddie now took his right wrist in a surprisingly strong grip and turned his hand over to place a flat box on it.

"Tofu's very good for you," she explained. "I hope you like the candies. I make them myself. They're very energizing. I work out a lot, as you can probably see—Oh! Oh, do forgive me. That was insensitive, wasn't it? It's just that you don't *look* blind."

While he sought desperately for something to say, Maddie went on enthusiastically. "That's the main reason I dropped in. I haven't seen you in the gym since that first time. You mustn't stay up here and vegetate, you know. A strong, healthy body makes for a strong, healthy mind. I'd be more than happy to guide you around if you're afraid of getting lost or bumping into things. How about right now? Or if you don't feel like working out, there's a great jam session going on in the gathering room and we could dance."

"I, uh," Ken said, but Maddie rushed on, not giving him a chance to refuse.

"Come on. It'll be fun. You might want to change your shirt first, though. You have a dribble of gravy right here." She twirled what felt like a long, tapered fingernail in a swirling motion down his chest.

He cringed and clenched his teeth as he shook his head. *Hell!* How many other times had he stood around chatting with neighbors, oblivious to the food he was wearing on his clothes? Humiliation burned his face.

"Ohhh . . . I'm sorry," she said in a sweet little-girl voice. "I didn't mean to embarrass you. It's not a very big stain, and I wouldn't have noticed, honest, if the light hadn't caught it just so." She traced its shape again. "Forgive me?"

He grinned and caught her hand, moving it off him. "Sure."

"Then prove it by letting me take you down to the gathering room."

"No." He dropped her hand. "I don't think so."

"How about the gym, then, to show, uh, guide you around the equipment?"

"No!" The idea of being "taken" or "guided" anywhere by this woman—any woman—rankled. It was bad enough going out with Chuck Middleton, his counselor, or teacher, or whatever he liked to be called, to keep him out of trouble, but a woman? He'd feel like a doddering old man being led around by a nurse.

He forced himself to remember that Maddie was simply being friendly and helpful. The least he could do was be polite. "Thanks all the same.

"I hope you'll excuse me," he added with a smile he knew must look strained and insincere. "I'm, uh—" He indicated the phone dangling from his left hand. "I'm expecting a call."

Conveniently the phone rang at that instant, startling him so that he nearly dropped it. Instead he dropped the box of candy, punched the talk button, and before anyone spoke on the other end, obeyed an impulse he'd never be able to explain.

"Ingrid!" he crooned. "Sweetheart. At last."

Ingrid gasped at Ken's greeting. "How—how did you know it was me?"

"It is?" He laughed, sounding as astounded as she felt, but his recovery was quick. His tone became low and smooth, deeply intimate. "I mean, who else could it have been but my angel? I've been waiting for your call for hours."

He dropped his voice even lower and continued. "I miss you so much, baby. I can't wait till you get here. I—listen, can you hold for just a second?"

Sweetheart?Baby? Ingrid repeated silently. He'd been waiting for her call for "hours"? It was Tuesday, for heaven's sake! She wasn't even supposed to call him till tomorrow. He *missed* her?

After a moment's thought she caught on. "Sure, 'darling,' " she said, laughing. "Don't be long, 'sweetheart.' You're trying to get rid of someone, aren't you?"

She thought he sounded chagrined. "Well, yes."

"Male?" She didn't think so for a second.

"No."

She laughed again. "Well, we both know what's left, don't we? What makes you so sure I'll help you?"

"I'm not. But will you? Please?" Apparently taking her chuckle for assent, he said, "Don't go away, honey. I'll be right back."

She listened to muffled voices as he excused himself, then heard him speak her name in a soft and distinctly sexy tone. At least that's the way it sounded to her. "Your . . . friend is still there?" she asked.

"No, but I'm glad you are. I'm also very, very glad that you called."

She managed a weak laugh and pulled herself together. His sexy tone meant nothing. He was likely no more responsible for it than she was for her telephone voice. It was simply the way he talked. To everyone. "So happy to be of service," she said.

"You're not mad?"

"No. Why should I be mad?"

"Most women would be, if they thought they'd been used."

"Possibly. But it wasn't exactly me you used, was it, but my name."

"That's true," Ken agreed. "It wouldn't have mattered who was on the phone, I'd have called the pope 'Ingrid.' "

She laughed, and her warmth came over the phone like a caress. He basked in it as he sauntered, phone in one hand, box of tofu candy in the other, back to the chair where he'd been sitting when the doorbell rang. He made it without error.

"The pope?" she asked. "He calls you often?"

"Only on Tuesdays," he said, turning and sitting. He leaned back, stuck his legs out before him, and crossed his ankles, feeling good. Better than good. Wonderful. "I really am sorry, you know. I guess I grabbed your name out of my mental hat because I'd been thinking about you when that woman showed up. She's a neighbor, but quite frankly I've had it with neighbors. I was sitting here willing you to call when she rang my bell."

"You were? *Willing* it?"

"Sure. It's called creative visualization." He laughed. "I only learned recently what it's called and that it's supposed to be an acquired technique. I thought everyone did it as a matter of course. I've done it all my life."

"Really? I'm totally impressed." He heard and appreciated the delicate amusement underlying her attempt at projecting awe. "You can force people to do things you want them to do, simply by willing it? Sounds like a dangerous talent."

"Not to me."

She laughed with him, and he enjoyed the blended sound they made. Their laughter was harmonious. "And does it work every time?" she asked.

He breathed steam onto his fingernails. "You called me, didn't you?" he asked, buffing them on his shirtfront.

"Well, yes, but I had to."

"See?" he said triumphantly.

"I had to"—he didn't know how a person could sound repressive through laughter, but she managed it—"because I thought it only fair to warn you that I probably won't be able to fit you into my schedule tomorrow. I called mainly to ask if you'd like to have someone else to talk to instead."

Ingrid listened to her own words and wondered if they sounded as false to him, wondered if he believed them any more than she did. *Face facts*, she told herself. *You phoned the man because you wanted to hear his voice again and didn't want to wait till tomorrow.*

"I told you," he said. "You or nobody. What's up tomorrow that you won't be able to fit me in?"

"I'm having an emergency conference with the parents of one of my kids. The only time the dad can make it is at seven o'clock. This means I won't have time for all of my calls, and since you're low man on the totem pole, guess who has to get bumped?"

"No problem for me. Besides, you could always call me later. I'd like that better anyway."

So would she, but she couldn't very well tell him that any more than she could tell him she was making this call from her bed with his picture propped on her upraised knees.

"Okay, then," she said, "we'll talk tomorrow after I'm home. It may be late."

"Can't we talk now as well?" he asked. "Tell me about your day. Did you lose any kids?"

She laughed. "No. And *I* didn't lose that one yesterday either. Though in a way, I suppose, it was my fault he went missing."

"How so?"

"We'd talked about sleeping under the stars and he took a blanket out into the backyard, planning to spend the night there. Trouble was, he lay down to try out his outdoor bed and likely fell asleep within seconds. He's one of those kids who violently resists naps, then is out like a light once you get him lying down. Anyway he didn't hear his mother calling. Panic throughout the land. He'd tucked himself in between the garbage cans and the garage wall so the 'wolves' wouldn't find him. That was my fault, too, I guess.

"I try to instill some self-sufficiency in the kids. Being aware of dangers and guarding against them as a way of life, on the principle that paranoia saves lives."

He chuckled. "Tell him for me that sleeping under the stars isn't all it's cracked up to be. The only time I tried it, it rained and soaked me and my sleeping bag before I could get into the tent."

"I'd tell him, but he wouldn't believe it. Ivan's an incurable optimist. He'd have to be, to expect wolves on East Second Avenue."

"How about you? Do you have much trouble with wolves?"

"None at all," she said, and was pleased when he obeyed the dictates of her very final tone and changed the subject.

"Tell me more about your kids, then," he said. "Talk about your day."

Ingrid wrinkled her nose. "Oh, Ken, no." Men never truly wanted to hear about preschool children and their antics, unless, perhaps, the children were their own. "My day, in detail, would bore you. You tell me about yours instead."

Ken clenched his teeth. "It was exactly the same as yesterday," he said shortly. "Except it had a few minor variations you don't want to know about." That she knew nothing about the day he'd spent yesterday didn't faze him. His days simply weren't worthy of discussion, and today . . . He still stung with humiliation thinking of the gravy dribbled down his shirt. He placed a hand over the stain as if Ingrid could see it through the phone.

"Some phone friendship this is going to be," she said gently, "if we both insist our lives are too mundane to discuss." He heard a smile in her voice, but for once it failed to lighten his mood. "Of course I care about what you do, Ken. That's why I call. Come on, talk to me. I'm your phone friend, remember?"

Her reminder slammed into his already smarting ego like a mailed fist.

"Right." He clacked his teeth shut on a surge of unreasonable hurt. "That's me. A name on a list."

"Ken . . ."

"A file pulled from a drawer."

"A *friend*," she said, but he didn't listen as rage built inside him. Illogical, unfair, inexplicable, it was nonetheless real, and it exploded from him like water through a ruptured dam.

"Dammit, don't try to tell me this is personal to you! We both know better!" He had to remember that. She used her angel voice on everyone she phoned. "You called because I'm a name on your list. Your mandate is to alleviate the boredom and loneliness of a group of poor, pitiable shut-ins, of which I am but one. How could I have forgotten?"

"Hey, that's not what—"

"Isn't it?" he snarled as he heaved himself to his feet. He strode around the room as if he could somehow escape his inner turmoil. "Oh, don't get me wrong," he said, the phone still pressed to the side of his face where sweat beaded. "I am infinitely grateful, my sweet lady of mercy, for your kindness and charity, and of course I want to share the details of my day with you. I've been lost without that fine oppor—"

"Ken! You don't have to tell me any—"

He swept over her attempted protest. "Of course I do," he said, wheeling for another pass through the room. He smashed into the love seat near the west windows and drove a fist into its thick upholstery. "Isn't that your purpose in life? To bring me out of myself? To save me from another day of solitary agony? To offer me an outlet for my hurt and anger and frustrations?"

He vented all three in another punch at the furniture while Ingrid said not a word.

"Oh, you insist?" he went on into her silence. "Do let me regale you, then, Ms. Bjornsen, with the various details of my fascinating daily life.

"I buttered two slices of toast and one shirt cuff. And I was wearing a short-sleeved shirt! I poured hot coffee on my left foot and ate lace-trimmed fried eggs for breakfast." He paced back the way he'd come—he hoped. "Then I listened to three game shows, one soap opera, and a PBS thing about cooking in medieval England. I think I fell asleep for a while during that." He ran into the back of another chair, circled it, found the corner of the stereo cabinet with one knee.

Rubbing the knee, he said, "I managed to nuke a frozen lunch entree, open the bag it's cooked in, and put it on a plate without mishap—then the whole thing slid off the plate as I carried it to the table. Cleaning it up took me until two P.M., but also took care of my hunger. There's something of an appetite depressant in wiping up spaghetti sauce while kneeling on cooked pasta you can't see.

"After that my teacher from the school for the blind came and took me for a nice walk. I practiced telling the difference between the cuckoo and the chirping bird that help people like me cross the street. I discovered—the hard way—that it's preferable to find the bumper of a car with my cane than with my shins.

"I slept again after the man left, then nuked another frozen dinner, which I managed to eat without spilling— except what ended up on my shirt. That's just one of the charms of being blind. You can never be sure of what you look like. Really a great way to build self-confidence. If I'd found the advances of the flatteringly large number of women who've come knocking on my door every day an ego booster, tonight's visitor shot that down by inviting me out, but only if I changed my shirt first because it had gravy on it.

"Oh, those sweet gals in this building! Each one determined and eager to be of service to the poor blind man on the twelfth floor. Clean the gravy off his shirt. Wipe the drool off his chin—"

"Ken—"

"It's my turn!" he barked. "After all, you asked. The next exciting episode in my action-filled day was listening to the inspirational books the blind-teacher brought me. When I got through the last one, I went on sitting here because it's so interesting to listen to the elevator come and go, wondering about the people riding in it.

"It was a wonderful day, as I'm sure you can imagine. Please try to control your envy and eager requests for more enthralling details."

She said nothing.

"Well?" he demanded. "Anything else you want to know?"

"Sounds to me as if you've pretty well covered it," she said evenly, irritating him even more. He ground his molars together and hammered a fist on the back of a chair. Dammit, he didn't want a saint on the other end of the line. He wanted a human friend. A loving voice.

He wanted a hug!

And that scared him half to death and tuned his anger to a fine pitch. "All right, then," he snapped. "If I've covered it to your satisfaction, good night."

"I'm sor—" she started but he didn't want to hear another word. He punched the shut-off button, then smashed the phone down and flung himself into a chair, breathing hard, wrapped in the kind of anger the hated school for the blind had been supposed to help him overcome.

He'd failed that lesson, too, he thought, rocking forward and burying his face in his hands. He hadn't learned to overcome a damned thing. He wanted to weep from sheer rage, but he'd already done plenty of that and learned how little help it was. He wanted to roar and curse and hurt something—or someone—but the only one there to hurt was himself.

His fury continued for all of three more minutes before it spilled away and remorse set in. He reached for the phone, found it immediately, then sat there with his hand on it while sick regret coursed through him.

He couldn't call Ingrid back. He didn't know how to reach her. His lifeline had been broken.

And he'd done it all by himself.

THREE

When the phone rang the next night, Ken sat listening to it. The machine would pick up. Let it. He didn't want to talk to anyone. Except . . . what if by some miracle it was Ingrid?

It wouldn't be, though. He wouldn't call anybody who'd bellowed at him the way he had her. And if it was her, he didn't want to talk to her. He wouldn't know what to say. He didn't want to hear her voice.

Just in case, he fumbled with the buttons on the answering machine and shut it off. He hoped. Yup. The phone continued to ring and the machine didn't pick up. Ingrid's warm, sexy voice didn't imprint on a tape he knew he'd have listened to over and over until it wore out.

He'd gotten the right button the first time. The minor triumph pleased him.

He ran his fingertips over the array of buttons again, reciting aloud the function of each as he stroked it. He was doing fine with buttons. That much of this new business of being blind he had aced. The answering machine, the telephone, the microwave oven, and the remote controls that took care of the TV and CD player.

Whoopee. All the essentials of life.

A feeling closely approaching defeat swept over him, nearly overwhelming him before he fought it off. If he could just feel those damned little bumps that were supposed to represent language in his Braille book, maybe he'd make some progress.

He went back to his probably futile studies and, with dogged determination, persevered for another twenty minutes.

He hadn't become an architect overnight, he told himself. He wasn't going to learn Braille overnight. He wasn't, he decided thirty seconds later, flinging the book from him, going to learn Braille at all.

Because he wasn't going to remain blind for the rest of his life.

There was no apparent clinical reason for his blindness. All the doctors said that. He'd suffered a severe blow to the head when the scaffolding collapsed, but his optic nerves were intact—at least as far as medical science could tell. Ergo it was, as the saying went, "all in his head."

What he had to do was get inside his head, the way he would if the problem were in his computer, and rewrite the message that had gotten screwed up.

He ground his teeth together. Was there an auto-exec.bat for the brain? A config.sys for the emotions? If so, how could he access it?

The phone rang again. He found it with a gratifyingly unerring placement of his hand, kept his palm on it, feeling the vibrations of its shrill tone in his bones. He didn't answer. If it was his mother, he was in no mood to sound cheerful so she wouldn't worry. It wouldn't be Janet, who was back in town for only a twenty-four-hour layover before heading out to Europe again. She, he knew, was catching up on her sleep.

If it was Ingrid . . .

But it wouldn't be.

It rang again probably an hour later. Ken still sat in his chair, a CD playing softly in the background while he searched his mind for the missing autoexec.bat that controlled his eyesight.

What if it *was* her?

On the sixth ring he picked it up. "Hello?" His voice came out in a strained croak.

"Oh, no!"

It was her. Even through the wail of dismay with which she greeted him, he recognized her voice. His breath whooshed out.

"This is Ingrid Bjornsen," she said, "and this time I *did* wake you up, didn't I? I can tell by your scratchy voice. I'm really sorry. I tried earlier, during my regular calling time, because my parent meeting got canceled at the last minute, but there was no answer then. Did you go out? Did you have a nice time? You really should switch on your answering machine when you go to bed, though, and unplug your bedroom ph—"

She broke off with a sorrowful sigh. "I'm doing it again, aren't I? Running off at the mouth without giving you a chance to say a word. I only do it when I'm nervous. I'll shut up. Right now. You can tell me to *hang* up, too, if you want."

Ken forced himself to breathe in. "No," he said on

his second, more controlled release of breath. "No, you didn't wake me." There was no way to control the grin spreading across his face, the elation flooding him. "And don't hang up. Please, whatever you do, don't do that. At least not until you've given me your number so I can call and apologize if I let my mental toothache get the better of me again."

"Ken, I'm really s—"

"If you apologize to me one more time for my bad behavior, Ingrid, I'll probably get mad all over again."

"I wasn't doing that," she protested. "I was apologizing for my own actions. I insisted you tell me about your day when you'd already said you didn't want to. I should have respected your wishes and I didn't, so I'm sorry. And I had no right to get you out of bed at this hour."

"I wasn't in bed and I couldn't have slept if I'd wanted to. I was just sitting here wondering how to justify the way I acted last night, if you ever did call me again, which I didn't think you would do." He sucked in another deep breath and exhaled it explosively. He laughed from sheer pleasure. "I'm so damned glad you did, I could listen to you run off at the mouth all night."

"Oh," she said, and he reveled in the breathless quality of the single word.

"So come on, mouth," he said teasingly. "Run on."

For a moment she was silent, then, sounding delightfully girlish and appealingly shy, she said, "Now I can't think of a single sensible thing to say."

Neither, now that she mentioned it, could he. The silence went on until he broke it. "Well, then, give me your number so I can call you the next time I need to apologize."

"I can't do that," she said quickly, too quickly, as if she'd been primed and ready to say it. As if she'd known he was going to ask.

"Why not?"

"I told you. It's policy. The rules say we initiate all calls."

"Policy," he said, "is normally just an excuse for continuing an illogical protocol when there's no real need, and you know what they say about rules."

"What? That they're made to be broken?"

"Yup."

"I don't like to break rules."

"No? I do."

"Now, where would we be if everyone did that?" she asked in a tone that made him envision an old-fashioned schoolmarm looking disapprovingly down her nose.

He grinned. "Ah, but I'm not talking about 'everyone,' but about me—" he lowered his voice, the way he had over the phone when he'd been trying to get rid of Maddie—"and you."

He heard her pull in a quick, shuddering breath and knew a moment's elation. Good. If she affected him, it was only fair that he could get to her once in a while.

"Are you flirting with me?" Ingrid asked, astounded. Lord! What the man's voice could do to her! How could she respond so physically to nothing more than a suggestive tone? And a picture of course. She turned Ken's photograph facedown.

"Who, me?" he said, all innocence.

"I wasn't aware this was a conference call."

"And if I were flirting with you?" he asked. "Would you flirt back?"

"Not a chance," she said, refusing to take up the

challenge so strong in his tone. It was a challenge she was ill equipped to deal with. "Not me."

"Why not you? Is that against the rules too?" Before she could reply, he went on, softly, silkily, and she felt as if his breath had stroked over her skin. "Trust me," he said. "Breaking a rule or two makes the game more . . . satisfying, when you win in the end."

"And do you always?" she asked, injecting coolness into her voice in an attempt to disguise the surge of excitement she felt. "Win?"

"Most of the time. Don't you?"

"I . . . don't play many games." They were playing one now, weren't they? Flirting. It wasn't something she'd ever done. She wasn't sure she knew how. But part of her was enjoying it immensely.

"And when you do play games, you always play by the rules," he said.

"When I know what they are. Why don't you explain them for me?"

"There are none. We can make up our own as we go along."

"I don't think so. I'm the product of a strict boarding school. I like rules, boundaries, knowing where I'm supposed to be and when."

"Not me. Give me anarchy every time."

"That, too, sounds dangerous."

His chuckle made her shiver in pleasure. "A little bit of anarchy makes life more interesting—as does a little bit of danger. Come on, Ingrid, be brave. Go for it. Break loose. Give a man your phone number. Try living life on the edge. Why, I bet you've never so much as gotten a speeding ticket. Or, even speeded in the first place."

She laughed. "You'd be right. I'm probably the most law-abiding person you'll ever meet."

"And that's another thing," he said. "When are we going to meet? In person, I mean."

Ingrid froze in alarm. "We aren't."

"What? Why the hell not?" he demanded, then gave a bark of laughter. "Don't tell me. Rules and policy again? Ingrid, Ingrid. You can't let your life be dictated by other people's regulations."

"I don't! Those rules, though," she said, improvising rapidly as she went along, "that govern what Saint Justine's volunteers do, make sense and they're for our own protection."

"Mmm." She knew he was smiling. "So you feel you need protection from me?"

"No," she lied. "Not you specifically. But—"

"But rules are rules," he finished for her, his singsong tone suggesting boredom.

It hurt, where it shouldn't have. She was used to men seeing her as a bore.

"Ingrid . . . are you married?"

"No. I was, but I no longer am. Are you?"

"Nope. And never have been, though I did have a long-term live-in relationship. That's over, though."

"She left you after your accident?"

Ken caught the horror in her voice and laughed comfortably. "No, no. It was over several years ago. She's married now and has two kids. Yours? Has he remarried?"

"Yes."

Something about the one, tight little word disturbed him. "What happened, Ingrid? It hurt you, didn't it?"

"Failure always hurts."

He had to agree. He hadn't liked it when his relationship with Ellen was falling apart. He, too, had felt like a failure. "It's also always a two-way street," he said.

"Not in this case. I was the one who couldn't . . . adapt. I couldn't be what he wanted. Needed, in a wife. I never fit in. When he realized I never would, he left me."

"Maybe it was the other way around. Maybe he was the wrong man for you."

She laughed. "Thanks for the vote of confidence, but that's not the way it was."

"What makes you so sure?"

"Because *he* left *me*. And his second marriage is quite successful, by all appearances."

"Your not having remarried yet means nothing," he said. "Unless . . ." He hesitated. "Unless it means something to you. Are you still in love with him? Still grieving the loss?"

"No," she said quickly. "I was young when we married."

He chuckled. "Honey, I think you're young now."

"I was a lot younger then. Only twenty-two."

"What happened? What exactly went wrong?"

It wasn't supposed to be this way, Ingrid thought. She was the one supposed to provide an ear, a shoulder, a friend. Nevertheless she answered him. "I told you," she said lamely, and repeated what Ron had told her all too often. "I just didn't fit in."

"Fit in with what?" he asked with a hint of impatience. "Fit in where? What made you feel you didn't?"

"I'm not comfortable on the social scene," she said, "and he's in a business that demands socialization. He's climbing up the ladder of a large international communications corporation. He needed a wife who could help advance his career by being amusing and charming and clever for all the right people at all the right times."

"Why? Isn't he good enough at what he does to rise on his own merits?"

His question surprised a gust of laughter out of her. Still laughing to herself ten minutes later, she said good night and reluctantly hung up the phone.

It was good having a phone friendship that worked both directions, she mused. It was even better having a friend who championed her. She smiled, recalling how Ken had immediately said that maybe Ron had been the wrong one, not she.

She gazed for several moments at his photo propped against her lamp, then turned out the light and snuggled into her covers. She liked Ken Ransom. Liked him a lot. Maybe someday she'd go so far as to let Janet say "I told you so."

Two nights later Ken again asked to meet her face-to-face. This time Ingrid's refusal wasn't so quick, but she made it anyway after a brief mental argument. Janet was her friend, wasn't she? It was safe to assume she'd eventually have to meet this brother of her friend, now that he'd moved here from back east. And if she did, the friendship would be over before it had really begun.

If only, if she ever did meet him face-to-face, she wouldn't have to watch him turn away before she'd managed to get out more than a conventional greeting. She sighed.

"Well?" Ken asked. "What are you going to do? Play by the rules or come live dangerously with me?"

The surge of pure sexual excitement his words generated both shocked and thrilled her. If he could elicit that kind of reaction over the phone, with nothing more than a mocking question she knew he didn't mean her to take literally, she'd be wise to go on pretending it was a Living Voices regulation that kept her from meeting her clients in person.

Come live dangerously with me . . . He hadn't meant it the way it sounded. He was probably totally unaware of the ideas his careless phrasing gave her. Living with a man again, being married, sharing a life, a bed, the feelings of completeness, of togetherness, of being a part of a whole. . . . And children of her own . . . Lord, how she longed for that!

But no. She ruthlessly suppressed the regret that boiled up to replace the excitement. Such longings had to be curbed.

Never again would she make herself that vulnerable to a man, set herself up for the kind of pain she'd suffered over Ron. She hadn't even, as several friends insisted most dumped women do, been able to console herself by dating a variety of men and repairing her damaged self-esteem.

She would always have wondered if another man would someday tell her scathingly, as Ron had, "Baby, if your family hadn't made it so worthwhile, I wouldn't have given you ten minutes, let alone two years."

"Ingrid?"

Her decision was the only one she could possibly make. "I can't meet you, Ken."

Now he sighed, loud and long and, she thought, mockingly. "All right. But what about calling every day instead of only three times a week?"

She could, she supposed, concede one point to him. "Okay. If that's really what you want, I'll call you every day."

"Late and from home."

"If that's what you prefer." Besides, a precedent had been set—and she had set it.

"I still wish you'd give me your number." He seemed determined to push for what he wanted. "A guy likes to do some of the courting himself, despite this being the nineties."

"What courting?" she asked, with a light laugh she would always be proud of. "A strictly over-the-phone relationship is what we have here, friend. No courting allowed."

"Oh, well." He sounded philosophical. "I guess I'll have to live with that. Since you're a woman who refuses to break the rules."

"And since you're a man who spends a large portion of his days fending off the advances of all those aggressive single women in his building, I'd think you would prefer it that way."

"Now there," he said, and she knew he was grinning, "you do have a point." He said nothing for a moment, then added, "But they don't feel like friends, Ingrid. None of them makes the darkness light. You do."

His simple statement touched her deep inside. "Good night, Ken," she murmured while she was still capable of speech. "I'll call you tomorrow."

She hung up so abruptly, she nearly dropped the phone, then sat and stared at her hand. It trembled. Her heart beat a rapid tattoo against her ribs and set up a thick hammering high in her throat.

She stared at Ken Ransom's picture for a long moment

before sliding out of bed and tucking it away in a drawer. It was crazy, this intensely physical reaction she had to nothing more than a man's photo, voice, and manner. She felt like a thirteen-year-old going googly-eyed and weak-kneed over some unattainable rock star.

He didn't know her. If he ever met her, those sexy green eyes would look anywhere but at her and he'd murmur an embarrassed excuse, then make tracks for elsewhere as fast as he could stride. She'd seen it happen time and time again, with all the men her parents arranged for her to meet.

Flirtations, even telephone flirtations, were not for the likes of her.

She thought about his voice, thought about the picture now safely out of sight, thought about the glimmer of teasing laughter in his eyes. She ached deep inside.

Maybe a telephone flirtation was exactly what she needed. After all, if a thirteen-year-old mooning after a rock star was in no danger, neither was she, just talking to Ken Ransom on the phone. If a young girl could enjoy an infatuation with no fear that anyone would ever expect her to act on it, why couldn't a twenty-nine-year-old woman luxuriate in a harmless telephone flirtation?

Oh, yes. She'd call him tomorrow. In the evening. Late.

And maybe she'd flirt right back.

Ingrid lay in bed Saturday night after a long, fascinating conversation with Ken, gazing at his photo and castigating herself. Dammit, why did she have to be so scared when it came to meeting the man in person? She'd faced plenty of fears in her life, stared them down, refused to let them dictate to her. But this one . . . It made her tremble inside almost to the point of nausea, and it likely wasn't even valid.

She felt, after nearly a week's worth of nocturnal conversations, that she really knew Ken. They shared several likes, a few dislikes, and had enough differences of opinion to keep their conversations peppery.

She certainly liked him and was more than mildly attracted to his voice and manner. Attractive, too, were his face, his strong column of a neck, his shoulders. She reached out and touched his picture, running a fingertip from his eyebrow to the solid block of his chin. What would it feel like, touching him for real? Was his hair as crisp as it looked? Would his voice have the same deep resonance that it had over the phone? Would those green eyes, assuming they could see, light up at the sight of her? What would those large, square hands, folded before him on a desk, feel like if he touched her? Did they have calluses, or were they smooth? She liked the feel of calluses on a man's hands.

She tossed her sheet off and flopped onto her back, hoping for a stray breeze from the open window to cool her suddenly hot body.

Ken didn't try to hide what she sensed was a genuine interest in her, a true liking, a meeting of minds. Could it become, ever, a meeting of hearts? Bodies? Maybe, if she could only find the courage to take that next step.

There was no real reason for them not to meet, besides her continued, obdurate refusal.

She'd called him initially as a favor to his sister. She'd called him the second time, and every subsequent time, as a favor to herself. It was wonderful having a man to talk to, one who didn't view her as a freak but who teased and flirted and made her smile, made her laugh, made her heartbeat quicken.

Wouldn't all of those feelings intensify with an in-person meeting? She squeezed her eyes shut. Maybe. And maybe not. If they did, that, too, would be wonderful. If they didn't, if he found her stutter so disconcerting that he cringed when she spoke, she was a big girl and could handle it. It would simply be another disappointment, and grown-ups suffered those daily.

Grown-ups who dared to take chances . . .

She groaned and thrust the picture away.

Oh, hell, who was she trying to kid? Quit dreaming, dummy, she told herself firmly. With a last, quick look at the picture she turned off the light.

But dream was exactly what she did—of Ken, of the two of them walking hand in hand through an unpopulated park. They talked and laughed, enjoying each other, then sat under a tree eating fresh strawberries and kissing until she ached with unfulfilled yearning, yearning that still coursed through her when she awoke Sunday morning.

His face filled her view as she opened her eyes. She blinked, startled, to find the dream figure so close and vivid. She lifted the photo from where she'd left it propped against her lamp, holding it at arm's length as she lay on her back and stared up at it. Those alert, expressive eyes seemed to call out to her. Would they, in their now sightless state, still be so penetrating, so clear, as if able to see right into her heart?

It was hard to remember that they saw nothing, that Ken's sole reason for asking her to come to him was because he was trapped by his blindness, lonely and isolated because of it. If his sight were intact, he'd have dozens of women he could choose from—all of whom were capable of carrying on bright, intelligent conversations, of entertaining a man, of captivating him and holding his interest—and not just over the phone.

Resolutely she arose, slipped the photo out of sight, and readied herself for the day.

Dreams were one thing, reality another, she reminded herself. In real life, there was no such thing as an empty park where two people could be alone without a world intruding.

She did not deal well with other people. And Ken, for his part, was still at the stage of learning how to walk in public without, as he put it, making an ass of himself by running into garbage cans and tripping over small children.

As she sat with her breakfast in a sheltered corner of the patio, a hummingbird dive-bombed her head, then hovered over the table, checking out her cranberry juice, its wings buzzing loudly. Moving slowly so as not to startle it, she tipped the glass, and the bird drank.

A breath of wind, laden with the scent of kelp, blew the little bird into a tilt. It fought back with an angry *chirrr* before adjusting its trim and sideslipping neatly into position at the rim of her glass.

It took what it wanted despite the winds of opposition.

She admired its determination, her gaze following it as it flew away, stopped to investigate a bank of pinks, then zoomed on into the woods where it undoubtedly had its nest.

Still staring at the woods, Ingrid frowned. The untenanted park of her dream had been the spacious grounds of her family estate. From the oyster-shell paths of the formal gardens to the hush of the small slice of forest, along the stream with its banks lush and green with a variety of ferns and mosses, peace hung over the place.

Would Ken enjoy a walk through the aromatic gardens and on into the fragrant forest? There was room here for two people to walk and talk uninterrupted. There'd be no unexpected small dogs darting out, startling a blind man so that he stumbled and felt foolish.

There'd be no people to ask Ingrid to speak.

Stupid, stupid, stupid! she berated herself. No people except Ken, and he'd expect her to keep up her end of the conversation.

No, it would never work.

She thought of the hummingbird battling the wind. She remembered phrases Ron used to throw at her, trying to force her to be something she was not. *No guts, no glory*, he'd say. *No pain, no gain*. And Ken . . . *Come live dangerously* . . .

What must it be like for a man, blind and alone, to spend a long, empty Sunday by himself? Wouldn't she, if she were locked up in a stuffy apartment, appreciate having a friend come and invite her out?

"Yes," she said emphatically, thrusting her chair back and jumping to her feet. "Yes, I would!"

"Oh, lordy, what am I doing here?" Ingrid muttered to herself, staring at the thick glass doors that barred her way.

She should have phoned first, shouldn't have run to her car so impetuously, but she'd been afraid to call. It would have given her time to think and . . . Now, though, she realized that she couldn't just march up to

his door, knock, and be admitted without having to deal
with someone else first.

She could see it now. She'd ring the bell. The
building's security man would answer. He'd ask who
she wanted to see. She'd tell him. He'd ask her iden-
tity so that he could announce her. She'd stumble over
something as simple as her own name, and he'd look
at her suspiciously, making her stammer all the more
as she tried to explain herself. By the time she got to
Ken's apartment, she'd long since have fallen apart, lost
every bit of the cool and courage that had carried her
this far.

Moisture slicked her hands. Fear dried her mouth.
Her heart pounded wildly.

She'd been crazy to think she could do this! She
jammed her shaking hands into her shorts pockets and
turned to go just as a sweat-covered bicyclist bounded
up the steps to the door, bike in one hand, helmet in
the other.

"Hi," he said. "You're the new tenant on ten, aren't
you? I'm Andy Gollen, on seven. Remember? We met
in passing at the main entrance to the gathering room
last week. Forget your key?" Before she could open her
mouth to answer, he rushed on, "Here, don't worry
about it." Handing her his helmet, he inserted two fingers into an impossibly tight pocket on one thigh. He
withdrew a key, which he slotted into the door.

He swung the door open and stood back to admit her.

She slipped into the elevator with him and his bike,
managing a smile and a nod in response to his observations
about its being a lovely day. He pressed ten for her and
seven for himself and, on the way up, continued his
friendly routine.

"Will you be at the barbecue Tuesday evening? Someone did remember to tell you about it, didn't they? It's posted on the notice board in the gathering room, but new people never remember to read the notice board. The barbecue's on the back patio at six-thirty, and everyone's welcome. Bring your own weenies or hamburgers and booze of course."

Ingrid nodded again as he stepped off at his floor.

She rode the elevator all the way to the tenth floor, then pressed the button for the lobby again, where she ran a finger down the list of doorbells beside the elevator.

K. Ransom, 1201.

Heart hammering hard again, this time with exhilaration, with anticipation, Ingrid rode the swift elevator upward, leaving her stomach behind.

She pressed the buzzer outside Ken's door, stood back, and waited.

Sunday-morning television—especially with nothing but audio—was the worst torture ever devised by broadcasting companies.

Ken poked the off button on the TV's remote control and stood, dropping the remote onto the table. A breeze blew into the apartment through the open balcony door, lifting his hair. He drew a deep breath and strode out. There he paced the length of the small balcony, feeling caged. Did he smell freshly cut grass? Did he smell the ocean? Or did he smell nothing but exhaust fumes, with wishful thinking providing the rest?

He wanted out!

So go out, he told himself, and felt his mouth go dry.

Coward. Gutless. *You can do it*. He heard Chuck Middleton's voice, encouraging him to go for it. Chuck had worked with blind people for years, counseling them, teaching them to get along in a world of sudden darkness. He knew the fears Ken suffered, had heard them a thousand times.

What he needed now, Ken thought, was to go out on his own, build up his confidence. What he had to do was to put to use the skills Chuck had given him, accept himself the way he was, and get on with life.

"Right," he said, returning to the apartment and slamming the door shut. "No more thinking about it. Today is the day you do it. Outside, Ransom. On your own."

He turned tightly so as not to lose his orientation and headed for the door, patting his pockets for keys and wallet.

Six deliberate strides took him between the recliner and the love seat and to the door. There he wrapped his hand around the top of his cane, leaning exactly where he'd left it the last time he'd come in with Chuck. He paused long enough to draw a deep breath and reached for the knob.

The doorbell rang.

He muttered a curse and propped his cane back where it belonged.

If it was one more woman offering him solace, he was going to barf.

He snatched the door open, smelled perfume—light and clean and pleasant—and made up his mind. The women in this building were going to have to understand he was not fair game.

"Ingrid," he said, sweeping one hand toward the source of the scent and encountering a bare upper arm.

"Sweetheart! I'd recognize that scent anywhere! I thought you'd never get here."

He clamped his fingers around that smooth, firm arm, drew the woman up against his chest, and bent his head while he curved his other arm tightly around her back. He heard a soft gasp of surprise and zeroed in on it. Covering a pair of warm lips with his own, he proceeded to kiss the woman as if she were a lost lover returned to him from an eternity in exile.

FOUR

Ingrid scarcely had time to take in the fact that Ken Ransom was a more potent threat to her in person than he had ever been when he was nothing more than a voice, a photograph, and a creature of her own vivid imagination.

He stood taller than she'd expected, with broad shoulders straining against the thin cotton of his T-shirt. His eyes, as green as the photo had suggested, retained all of that keen intensity she'd noted. He appeared to be staring right into her eyes, smiling in what could only be joy, speaking her name, saying something about perfume, while her tongue tried against too many odds to form a coherent word of greeting.

In the next moment he reached out and caught her arm and dragged her up against his chest, against the length of his body, saying something she scarcely heard through the roaring in her ears.

She tried to remain rigid as he swept her into his embrace, his arms folding around her. His head dropped, his eyes closed, thick dark lashes dropping like curtains, then his firm, smooth lips came down over hers.

When his mouth covered hers, amazement held her motionless, stiff, until the heat of his kiss melted her.

He kissed her, and need exploded within, need long unfulfilled and never fully explored. At his touch it leaped forth in a vibrant rush, weakening her even as it flooded her with a vast and secret power, a silent, exultant voice saying, *So* this *is why!*

For a moment thoughts tumbled wildly through her mind. Oh, Lord! How had he known it was her? Was his blindness a hoax? Had he and Janet both been trying to set her up? Why was he doing this? Why was she letting him? Heaven help her, why was she participating so avidly?

Because his kiss was perfect. No woman alive could have resisted. He didn't have to urge her to open her lips. Her startled gasp had done that, and he took full advantage.

As, after that one frozen moment, did she.

Her head spun as she slid her hands up over his bulging biceps to support herself against the weakening of her knees.

In the next seconds, as his grip shifted, pressing her more fully against his body—and his very evident arousal—she forgot to question herself or anything. She sighed into his mouth, sliding her hands higher over his shoulders.

They were hard, broad, made for her hands to explore, as was the thick hair brushing the back of his neck, curling around her fingers. His lips trailed over her face, and she took the opportunity to suck in a deep breath. As if he were loath to let her regain her senses, he swiftly reclaimed her mouth, capturing her exhalation.

She thought of struggling, but the notion fled as her fingers tunneled deeper into his hair and his tongue advanced, met hers, stopped to mingle, eliciting a soft moan. Hers? His? She didn't know, didn't care. One of his hands tangled in her hair, dragging on it slightly, tilting her face an inch higher as he deepened the kiss. She curved her fingers down his neck, inside his collar, and he released a low, growling sound of pleasure as he pressed into her ever more tightly.

Stop, Ken ordered himself as he drank in the flavor of this superbly responsive woman. *You can't do this*! He tried to stop, he meant to stop after just one more sip, but her bottom lip trembled deliciously as he swept his tongue across it, tasting her. He bent his head even lower as he tilted her head back. She was short, probably not even up to his chin, not the tall, rangy, athletic shape he'd long thought he preferred, but damn! she fit neatly against him. She felt good, felt . . . right in her curvaceous femininity.

Oh, hell, what if this was Maddie from the third floor? The thought intruded, but he squelched it. This woman's scent was not Maddie's. Her body was not one that worked out rigorously. What it was, was voluptuous, luscious, soft in all the right places.

Her hair smelled like a rose garden. Her mouth tasted of cinnamon. Her skin, when he finally managed to drag his lips from hers again and across her cheek, felt like rose petals. He felt and heard each ragged catch of her breath, then she sighed, tremulously, lowering her arms.

No! Please, he wanted to beg. He wasn't done yet. He needed more. He soothed her with long, firm strokes of his hands down her back, slowly tracking kisses over her cheek, her nose, her temple, her chin, the soft skin below her ear. He trailed one hand through her hair, finding it thick and silky, long, with little discernible curl.

As if she loved the sensation of his hand in her hair, she sighed again, a soft, shuddering sound, a hot, breathy sensation against his chest. He tilted her face up once more.

"We—" she began on a whisper, but he zeroed in on her mouth, unable not to kiss her just one more time. In seconds he was lost in the magic of it again.

Ingrid felt the last vestiges of good sense deserting her. Her fantasies, her dreams, paled in the bright glow of reality that was Ken Ransom, the potent torment that was his kiss.

He tasted tangy and sweet at the same time. His scent, different, unique, overwhelmed her. Even the sound of his breath, the feel of it against her cheek, captivated her. And his arms . . . They cradled her strongly yet gently, as if she were precious.

Nothing could have stemmed her response to this second assault on her senses. It flowed from her, hot and swift and total, as if it had only awaited him to trigger it.

She went pliant against him, clinging, relying on him to provide the support her liquid muscles could not. When his mouth left hers to make a new foray down her throat, she heard her own breathing, raspy, irregular, a complement to the frantic hammering of her heart. Her head fell back to give him more room, and his hand rose to cradle her skull with a tenderness that nearly brought tears to her eyes. She curved a palm around his jaw and drew his lips back to hers.

"Oh!" The sharp sound of the single word impinged only slightly, but the clatter of metal and china falling to the floor jerked Ingrid back to the world.

A woman wailed, "Oh, no! Look what I've done!"

Ingrid whirled. The woman, tall, lean, gloriously blond, as pretty as a girl on a chocolate box, stared at the two of them from within the elevator. A tray lay at her feet with three small white casserole dishes upside down, spilling red sauce and white pasta across the floor and into the carpeted hallway. Sauce spotted the woman's pink cotton slacks and a viscous stream of it slid over the instep of one sandaled foot.

"Oh, duh-duh-dear," Ingrid said, then clamped her lips shut.

"What happened?" Ken asked. His fingers closed over Ingrid's shoulders, and she glanced back at him. He looked as dazed as she felt, and for obvious reasons he kept her between him and the other woman. "Who's there?"

"Maddie," the woman replied in a taut voice. "I brought you some"—she glanced down at her feet again—"lasagna." She looked up again, her gaze sweeping from Ken's face to Ingrid's, a furious accusation there.

"I—I—" Ingrid wanted to offer to get something to clean up the mess, but the words wouldn't form. She closed her mouth again and wrapped her arms around herself to still the sudden trembling that came shuddering out from her insides. "I'm s-sorry," she managed to say to Maddie, the wave of her hand indicating the mess on the floor.

She wondered sickly how much right Maddie had to that stricken look, if Ken Ransom had ever greeted Maddie the way he'd just greeted her. Maybe he did that with all the women who came to his door. Maybe—

"Aren't you going to introduce me to your . . . girlfriend?" Maddie asked. Her eyes blazed fury at Ingrid.

Ken's hands tightened spasmodically on Ingrid's shoulders.

"I-I-I-I'm Ing-Ingrid," she said, to get him off the hook. Her voice was nothing more than a choppy, strained thread of sound.

"Yes," said Ken, pulling her back against him and curling a supportive arm across her chest, just under her chin. "This is Ingrid."

His voice, low and intimate, rumbled very close to her ear. She leaned into him, breathing in his scent, taking comfort in it, in the solidity of his body. It felt good. Too good. She stood erect, lifting his arm off her. His touch reminded her that she still burned all over, was trembling in the aftermath of that unexpected, unsought passion they'd shared.

"Ingrid, meet Maddie McKee, one of my neighbors." He smiled in Maddie's direction. "Did you say lasagna? Thanks, that's good of you. Now, see, honey"— he gave Ingrid a little shake—"you'll have to believe me."

He chuckled indulgently as he draped an arm around her again. "It wasn't easy reassuring her, Maddie, that I've had lots of help since moving in. Your arrival couldn't have been timed better."

"But I . . . *spilled* it!" The renewed glare suggested the spillage was Ingrid's deliberate doing.

"Never mind," Ken said. "Now that Ingrid's here, I won't starve."

Maddie's face threatened to crumple. "No."

"I'm sure the two of you will become great friends," he went on, "this being such a friendly building."

"Oh, sure." Maddie's doubts, Ingrid could see, were as strong as her own. The elevator began to chime a subdued but insistent *bong, bong, bong* as someone on another floor demanded its use.

Maddie released the button holding the doors open. They slid shut on her and her spilled lasagna, leaving Ken and Ingrid alone.

Ken kept his arm wrapped around Ingrid's shoulders and steered her through the door into his apartment. He shut the door, and as he found the lock without fumbling, she wondered again if he could see.

She sidled away from him but kept her eyes on his face as he slumped back against the door and let out a long, loud gust of breath.

"Whew!" He wiped at his top lip as if drying the mustache he didn't have. "I don't know exactly what to say now." He focused on a spot about a foot to her right and somewhat higher than her eye level. "But I guess I should start by saying I'm sorry. I don't know what came over me."

"Me . . . me either," she whispered, still staring at him. His face was as pale as hers must be. As she spoke, he fixed his focus so that it appeared he saw her. A muscle jumped spasmodically in his temple, under a lock of mussed, dark auburn hair. Hair she'd mussed with her fingers. They tingled as she remembered every sensation.

"That, uh, that was unforgivable," he said. "Grabbing you, kissing you like that. But I've had it up to here"—he made a slicing gesture across his throat—"with neighbors determined to take over my life for me. I thought you were another one, and I wanted to show them all that their . . . attentions weren't needed. I acted purely on impulse. It wouldn't have mattered who was at the door, she'd have thought *I* thought she was Ingrid."

He paused to draw a deep breath and let it out in a rush. "But I shouldn't have kissed you so, uh, thoroughly, or gotten so carried away. I don't know what happened to me, except—" He broke off with a helpless shrug and wiped a hand over his face. He grinned, a stunned but sheepish grin, appealing and oddly boyish. "Boy, did I get carried away."

"Me too," Ingrid whispered. She cleared her throat and watched his gaze swing toward her face again.

Humor started to dance in his eyes. "Still, I started it and I'm sorry."

"It's okay," she said, and then didn't know what else to say. He didn't seem the slightest bit surprised that she'd arrived, unheralded, at his door.

"I suppose you know who I am," he said. "Do you think you could introduce yourself? I mean, I should be on first-name terms with a woman I've kissed with so much enthusiasm.

"I'm . . ." she began haltingly, still whispering, terrified her voice was going to betray her at any moment, break up and come out in miserable little sputters. Terrified that when it did, his face would take on the distant, closed look she'd seen too often, a look strangers adopted to disguise their embarrassment at having to wait for her to complete a simple statement.

She didn't want Ken Ransom to be a stranger to her. She wanted him to be a— She refused to complete the thought.

"I'm . . . Ingrid," she said.

He laughed, and his teeth, she saw, were very white. His face had lost its pallor. "Hey, that was a neat bit of ad-libbing out there! Thank you for going along with me on it. Ingrid is a name I just pulled out of the air. I have a friend of that name, and she's been on my mind a lot, but the game's over now, the enemy thwarted, and I'd like to know who you really are."

She fought the buildup of tension, tried to reply, and made only a small, helpless sound that angered her. She clenched her teeth, clenched her fists, and wished mightily that Ken were not between her and the only means of escape she could see.

What a fool she'd been, coming to him.

"Do you live in the building?" Ken asked when the woman of the delicate scent failed to respond. He momentarily pressed one hand to his eyes in embarrassment. "I hope not," he said, beginning to realize the folly of that impulsive kiss. Hell, he'd been all but groping her, and another couple of minutes of kissing, he would have been doing a lot more.

Jamming his fists into his pockets, he frowned and answered his own question. "Of course you don't live in the building, or Maddie would have recognized you. She knows everyone and is willing to talk about their lives in intimate detail to anyone who'll listen.

"As she'll talk about you and me and what she saw," he added, and shook his head. "Jeez, I really am sorry."

"Wasn't that the whole idea?" Ingrid murmured. "I thought—" She stopped and stood with her mouth open, replaying her words in her mind. She heard their smoothness, the lack of hesitation, the perfect formation of each vowel, consonant, and diphthong.

"You thought what?"

She was glad Ken couldn't see her standing there like a beached, gaping fish. She cleared her throat and spoke at normal volume—aloud and clearly, unhesitatingly, without any of the hitches and glitches that had halted her speech as long as she could remember.

"I mean," she said, fighting joyous laughter as a thrill coursed through her, "getting her to gossip about your having a 'girlfriend' with whom you're passionately involved?"

Ken smiled. "Yeah. That was the idea. Her—or somebody. Anybody." He shook his head. "Poor Ingrid. That's the second time I've used her for that very purpose. Or," he added, "used her name. She's a generous friend, though, and says she didn't mind my using her name. I wonder," he went on, rubbing his hand over his jaw and gazing—or appearing to gaze—across the room, "if she'd have minded that?"

Exultation at being able to speak to him without a stutter lilted in her voice. "She didn't. She didn't mind at all."

His gaze swung back toward her face. "Excuse me?"

"Ingrid didn't mind. I am Ingrid, Ken."

He slowly reached out a hand toward her. "Ingrid? Ingrid Bjornsen?"

"One and the same," she said, and felt and heard her words come out smoothly, articulately, exactly as they would have if she were speaking on the telephone or to the children she taught.

An unfamiliar sense of confidence mingled with brimming joy, mixed with caution, warred with fear, tangled with hope and disbelief. Emotions boiled and rolled within her, each one demanding the upper hand until she felt dizzy with confusion. She wanted to laugh. She wanted to cheer. She wanted to cry with sheer relief and back away in terror that it was just a fluke and her voice would fail her at any moment.

What was going on? What had caused this wonderful transformation? Could it be because she had, after long and serious thought, decided that it no longer mattered if Ken knew her for what she really was? If not caring that people knew, or not caring what they thought of her, was the answer, why hadn't she discovered it long ago?

Or—the thought struck with the speed and venom of a darting cobra—was it only because he was blind?

Could she function normally with him because he couldn't see her? Desperately she wanted it to be otherwise, wanted it to be because she had finally tackled a personal demon and won. It must be that! It must!

The world was not made up of blind people any more than it was made up of small, nonjudgmental children. *Oh, please, please*, she prayed silently. *Don't let it be just because he's blind.*

Because Ken Ransom was probably going to see again someday.

"Ingrid?" He took a few steps toward her and touched her shoulder. Turning his hand, he lifted it just enough to skim her cheek. "Ingrid. From Loving Voices. Can it really be you?"

"It's me," she said. "And that's *Living* Voices."

His smile lit the room. "Of course it's you. I can hear that angel voice now that you're not whispering. I can't believe this. You came to me. Why?"

"You asked me to."

"You broke a rule." He grinned. "Let's hear it for anarchy." Then, repeating that gentle touch on her cheek, he asked, "You did that for me?"

She swallowed the ache in her throat. "I did it for me," she said firmly, then released some of her burgeoning happiness in a laugh. "And the sky didn't fall in." On the contrary, she'd been rewarded more richly than she could have dreamed.

"I'm glad you came," he said, sliding his hand down her arm until their fingers entwined. "Come, sit down."

She shook her head before she remembered he couldn't see such a gesture. "No. I came to see if you'd like to go sailing. It's too good a day out there to miss. The breeze is up, the sun is warm, and the ocean is a deep, royal blue. You did tell me the other night you're an avid sailor."

Ken closed his eyes, seeing what she'd described, then dropped his hand and half turned from her.

"I don't think so."

"Oh." He heard disappointment in her tone, then a hint of nervousness as she asked, "Is there something else you'd rather do? I'm . . . free all day if you'd like some . . . company."

Yes, he wanted to say, *there's something else I'd rather do, all right.* He'd rather kiss her again. He'd rather take her to bed and explore that body of hers all over. He'd rather be able to look deep into her eyes and watch the way they changed—if they changed—as a result of his kisses. He was willing to bet they did. Oh, yes. They'd change, the way her nipples did, the way her breathing did, the way her heartbeat did . . . her entire, incredibly responsive body.

He clenched his teeth until he felt a stab of pain slice up into his scalp.

"What—what else would you have in mind?" he asked.

"I don't know," she said, sounding at a loss. "Sailing was the only thing I'd thought of. It doesn't matter, though. I just, well—" He suspected she'd shrugged. "I thought maybe you'd like to spend some time away from your apartment."

Underlying her light, offhand manner, he detected a note of withdrawal, as if she'd expected him to turn her down. While maybe disappointed that he had, she wasn't surprised, and was likely resigned.

"I'd like to spend time with you, Ingrid, anywhere. But I'm afraid I wouldn't be much of a crew, considering I can't see."

"*Molly Darlin'* doesn't need much of a crew. She's a little boat, only twenty-six feet, and I single-hand her all the time. I didn't come looking for crew, Ken. As you said a few days ago, this is the nineties, and women can do some of the asking."

"I believe I said 'courting,' " he said, taking her hand in his. She drew a quick, audible breath, and he wondered if her cheeks had turned pink, if her eyes now flashed with annoyance.

"I didn't come courting," she said, and he delighted in the crisp note his teasing had elicited. "I came looking for com-p-panionship." Her fingers fluttered within his clasp. "For a f-friend."

Her slight stutter charmed him, underlined her nervousness. Sure, maybe women in the nineties did have a lot of latitude, but he suspected she didn't often ask a man out.

Had she had to steel herself to do it, yet did it nonetheless? Tenderness threatened to swamp him. He tightened his grip and brought her hand up to his chest. He couldn't let her escape.

"Why?" he asked.

Ingrid fixed her gaze on his face, trying to lessen her awareness of the steady thudding of his heart under her palm. The question had been soft, but oddly weighted, and the green gaze that aimed itself with uncanny accuracy at hers shouldn't have looked so intense. But it did. It also demanded a reply as insistently as his lips on hers had demanded a response.

"Why what?"

"Why me? Surely you have lots of sighted friends who would crew for you—or merely provide company."

"No. Not ... many. Besides, I wanted you to come because I was ..." She hesitated, frowning, then shrugged. There was no reason not to tell him the truth. "Because I was lonely, and I thought you might be too."

He dropped her hand, almost brushing it off him. His square chin lifted an inch, and she saw his lips harden in rejection of her words. "I wasn't lonely," he said.

Of course. This was the man who knew no such thing as loneliness.

He continued. "I was about to—" He frowned as he broke off.

"I understand. You have other plans," she said. "That's fine. I should have called first." She put a smile on her face and hence into her voice. "Maybe another time?"

He caught her arm as she turned, his clasp firm. "I was about to go for a walk around the neighborhood," he said, waving a negligent hand in the direction of the door—and the white cane she now saw for the first time. "But if you want company rather than crew, then sure, I'll go for a sail."

She smiled. He'd do it. For her. But not for himself. Oh, no. Never.

She was glad suddenly that she didn't have to hide her grin. "Good," she said. "I'm glad. I promise not to dump you overboard."

He raised his brows. "Or let me fall overboard?"

"You look like a man who can look after himself."

He smiled. "Have a chair while I change into something . . . nautical," he said, releasing her and locating the doorknob behind him. His eyes straight ahead, not looking at her at all, he asked, "Can I pour you a drink while you wait?"

"No, le—" "Let me get it," she'd started to say, but remembered his irritation over neighbors who insisted on doing things for him when they dropped in, instead of letting him be the host. "At least . . . nothing alcoholic, thanks. I don't drink and drive—or boat."

"Now, there," he said, walking with sure, even strides across the room toward a set of louvered half doors, "is a rule I adhere to myself."

He came back carrying a glass of cola, and she spoke, commenting on the view, so that he'd know where she was. He didn't try to hand her the glass, but set it on a small table near where she stood.

She thanked him and watched him run his hand around the edge of the table, up the back of a love seat. Then he stepped away, turned ninety degrees, and walked confidently toward a partly opened door, through which she could see the end of a bed, a dark green chair, and the corner of a mirror with his reflection in it.

His face was set in concentration, his mouth taut, his eyebrows drawn inward. But she saw more than that, more than his having to focus all his attention as he counted his steps. She saw fear as well, fear she recognized and empathized with. He dreaded making a fool of himself in front of another person.

As his hand struck the edge of the door, relief flooded his features and a small, triumphant smile tilted his mouth. He'd made it.

"Won't be long," he said, then closed the door behind him.

Inexplicably, hot tears filled Ingrid's eyes, and she quickly took a large gulp of her drink as she blinked them away.

Ken Ransom would not thank her for pity. Therefore she would not dishonor him by feeling it.

But oh! how it made her heart ache to have seen that fear etched into his face.

She could only pray that his sight would return.

"This is great!" Ken lifted his face to the sun, letting the wind tug at his hair. The breeze was fresh even here in the small cove, where Ingrid kept her boat tied to a private dock. He felt the side dip as she jumped back aboard after casting off the bow line.

"You comfortable?" she asked as she dropped into the cockpit. "Feel secure? Know the positions of every-thing?"

He heard her clip the steel cable lifelines back in place. She'd removed them to ease getting aboard. "I feel perfectly secure." He'd explored the small, deep well of the cockpit with his hands, discovered the low-roofed cabin forward of where he now sat, learned the height of the boom, felt the neat coils of ropes. There was no clutter, no loose objects to trip the unwary, for which he was grateful.

Ingrid kept a tidy ship. Also, because she sailed mostly alone, she kept lifelines in place as a matter of course. He took a place on the starboard side, trying to keep out of the way as she readied the boat for sailing.

"Doesn't it smell good here?" she asked. "I always love the smell of the shore at low tide." He heard her open and close a locker. Something landed near his leg. "There's a Floater coat right beside you if you'd like to put it on. You might find the wind cool, with just that cotton shirt."

He felt the breeze flutter his shirt and shook his head. "Just warn me in advance if you plan to capsize."

She laughed, as he'd hoped she would, and he heard the stern line thud wetly onto the transom. She put the engine in gear to motor out of the cove.

"Here we go, then." She increased their speed.

A small thrill of excitement riffled Ken's blood as he felt the boat dance forward, as eager as a fresh horse to be off and running.

The breeze slid across his face, and he turned to it, shifting his legs and encountering hers as she stood with one hand on the tiller. His entire body jolted in galvanic response to the feel of her bare, silky skin against his own, and he jerked his legs away. He swallowed hard, wondering if she'd noticed. He knew she had when she replied breathlessly to his questions about the passing scene.

He wished he could see her as she stood amidships, steering the boat, gazing out over the cabin roof as she kept watch for hazards, navigating between other boats, around marina floats, and through the gap leading out of the small harbor.

"There!" she said presently, slowing the engine to just above stalling speed. "We're clear. I'll get the sails up now that we have some maneuvering room."

"Can I—" Ken broke off. Of course he couldn't help, dammit. He ground his molars together, listening to her move around, trying to guess what she was doing each time the boat rocked as she stepped from side to side, went up to the bow, returned, and left again without speaking to him.

He forced himself to relax. He'd known he'd be passenger only this trip. Useless cargo. What was wrong with him that he couldn't simply sit back and enjoy the feel of warm Gelcoat under his hand as it rested on the coaming, and the action of the lively little craft as Ingrid scrambled around?

Beside him she winched up the main. He felt the wind catch, hold, felt the boat respond, then Ingrid cut the motor.

"Keep your head down now," Ingrid ordered with a glance at Ken. The wind gusted up over the stern from the starboard quarter, smacked into the mainsail and heeled them over. With a shout of glad laughter, she leaned into the tiller, and the hull sliced through the waves. "Awaaay we go!"

They flew over the sea, spray stinging her face with a pleasant tingle. Wind tore through her hair, whistled in her ears. The boat heeled over, and Ken, grinning broadly, hooked his elbows over the cockpit side at his back and thrust his long, bare legs out for balance.

She was deeply glad she'd followed her instincts and asked him along. He toed off his sneakers, braced one foot on the opposite bench and crossed his ankles, and leaned his face up to the sun, closing his eyes.

"Enjoying?" she asked as she slid onto the seat beside him, hooking her left foot over the tiller.

He turned his face toward her and smiled. "You know I am. I think I'd forgotten how good speed feels."

"You like speed?" she said gleefully. "I'll give you speed! No tickets to avoid out here."

The angle of the hull increased along with their velocity. The low side must be almost awash, Ken thought as he gripped a lifeline and hitched himself onto the rail. He leaned back into the lines, feeling Ingrid perch beside him, hearing her laughter blend with his. Water gurgled along the hull, babbling louder and louder, slapping sharply. A sail boomed. Gulls screamed.

Ken threw his arms up and out to the wind and hollered, "Yah-*hoo!*"

FIVE

Ken still had his head back, mouth open, laughing, when a wave smashed into his face. He choked, spluttered, wiped his face in the crook of his elbow, and leaned out for more. On they sailed, spray soaking him, stinging his skin, the sun hot and strong against his face.

"Get down!" Ingrid shouted, hooking an arm through his. "We're coming about."

As one they slipped from the high side into the well, under the boom as she released it and swung the tiller hard to port. Then, hanging in the lifelines over the other side, they sped onward across the water. Her leg, hot from the sun, pressed against his momentarily as she changed positions. Her hand, reaching across to do something, brushed against his arm as he clasped a stanchion. At once he wanted to wrap that arm around her, pull her close with his hand on her hip.

Was her blouse as wet and clinging as his shirt? Did

her nipples show? His body responded to the thought. He hoped she wasn't looking.

Her hair, wet and salty, whipped across his mouth.

"Sorry," she said, and extricated the hair, her fingers light on his cheek. She might have been looking at him, but at least her focus had been on his face.

He leaned closer to her and felt her head graze his shoulder, felt her hair against his forearm, felt her draw in a deep breath and let it out slowly. Was it his imagination, or did it catch a little on exhalation? He shifted his leg, encountered hers again, wet and warm, and felt her quiver. But she didn't move away. He kept his face turned to the sun, trying to concentrate on its heat rather than hers, seeing the red glow of it behind his closed lids.

Suddenly a seal barked so close at hand that Ken and Ingrid both started. All four of their legs meshed in the well of the cockpit as they slid back inboard, dropping their feet to the deck.

Ingrid snatched hers out of the tangle, but she laughed.

"Dumb seal scared me half to death," she said, breathless and shaken, though not because of any seal. She eased off on the helm, bringing the speed down. "I thought he was a chunk of driftwood until he spoke."

"I didn't even suspect he was there." If he'd been able to see, Ken still didn't think he'd have noticed the seal. He'd been too wrapped up in a growing awareness of Ingrid.

Even now too many levels of his consciousness told him she was there, right beside him. Her forearm pressed lightly against his ribs as she hooked her elbow over the side of the boat. He remembered her fingers caressing his cheek as she removed her hair from his mouth, remembered her hand cradling his face as she sought his kiss. The memories, the sensations, got all tangled up in his mind, out of sequence. He remembered the sensation of her fingers combing through his hair. He recalled the way her shoulder had felt under his hand as he followed her to her boat, and the way her body had fit so perfectly against his back at the apartment. Was that the scent of her delicate perfume, mingling now with the tang of the salty wind, or was it just his imagination?

He felt her leave his side, stand, and sensed she was gazing out over the horizon. Again he yearned to see her.

If only he could simply open his eyes, blink, and know what she looked like. He had a mental picture of her as she must be now, the sun gilding her long hair, the spray beading it with diamonds. Her cheeks would be pink, her eyes, as blue as the sunlit ocean, filled with joy as she finessed the most out of the wind, keeping the sails full.

Slowly, carefully, so as not to startle her, he extended his legs again. One foot grazed her ankle. The other skimmed against the backs of her legs. She stood now between his bare feet, and it was as if he could see her on the tilted deck of the cockpit, hand on the tiller, eyes scanning the water, hair whipping back like a pale, shimmering streamer. Her slender legs bare, kissed by the sun, her arms, rounded and soft, her chin tilted up, her breasts thrust forward, her—

She moved, bumping his left foot with the toe of her shoe, and the image faded.

Frustration ground at his guts. No mental image could ever be enough. He needed to *see* her.

His fist clenched on a line. He got to his feet, gripping the boom where it angled out over the side, and used it as a guide until he stood behind her.

He wanted to haul her against him, to wrap his arms under her breasts, hold her with her shoulders against his chest while she kept her lookout. As he put his hand over hers on the tiller, he felt the push of the water against the rudder, felt the dip and sway of the boat. He longed to feel it echoed in her body, repeated in his, and he suppressed a groan of despair. He wanted a whole hell of a lot that he wasn't going to have.

Like seeing Ingrid Bjornsen for real.

And unless he could, until he did, there was no point in letting this insane attraction go one step farther. What woman would want a blind man? Backing off, he returned to sit quietly out of the way.

His good intentions lasted until a few minutes later, when Ingrid brought the boat onto a different heading, so that they were riding almost on an even keel. He felt the attitude of the hull change as she moved aft. He joined her, sliding around until they were seated side by side, the tiller jutting between them.

He rested his left arm on the transom and felt her fold the tiller bar to its shorter length. It formed an effective barrier between them. As he stretched his legs out toward the cabin, his thigh slid along hers. She jerked her leg away.

"Take it easy," he said. "That wasn't an attack." He let his hand rest on the center of her back. "You're right," he continued. "*Molly Darlin'* isn't very big."

He traced the shape of her shoulders from one side to the other with a fingertip, traced the dainty fineness of her shoulder blades. "And neither is Ingrid darlin'."

She laughed, and he thought she leaned a shade

closer to him, but maybe it was simply the tilt of the seat. At any rate, after a moment she relaxed, and the sun-warmed skin of her thigh came into sweet contact with his again. She let it remain.

Her hair, loose and beginning to dry, fluttered over his wrist, teasing it. He counted several vertebrae up her spine, then several down.

"Ingrid . . . what do you look like?"

She didn't answer. He asked her again. "I'm . . . kind of ordinary," she said, "and as you observed, not very big."

"Ordinary? I don't think so." He skimmed one thumb over the curve of an ear. His lips remembered the contours of it, the satiny texture. They remembered the peachy smoothness of her face, too, but not the shape. His hands had known too briefly the outline of her body. He wanted desperately to touch her again, to memorize that shape, imprint it on his mind.

She moved, restlessly, he thought, as if their closeness troubled her, but there was nowhere for her to go.

Her hair tickled the back of his hand as he folded his fingers around her shoulder, molding bones and firm flesh, feeling heat there too. He slid his hand down her arm, drawing her several inches closer. If not for that damned tiller under his arm, extending between him and Ingrid, he could have pulled her into a full embrace. He wondered when she'd put on the thick sweatshirt she now wore, and wished she hadn't. Still its thickness did nothing to block his memory of the way her skin had felt at his apartment when her upper arms had been bare and warm and silky.

She'd shoved the sleeves up. He trailed his fingers

around her wrist and felt goose bumps prickle on her thigh, a tremor course through her body.

"Are you cold?" he asked.

"No." He knew from the sound of her voice that she'd turned her face away from him. To watch for marine traffic? Or to put distance between herself and him?

"You shivered," he said.

She eased her leg away from his. "I didn't mean to."

"Describe yourself for me, Ingrid, please?"

Ingrid froze, then swung to face him. "I couldn't!"

He smiled and touched her cheek with two fingers, holding her face in position, as if he could see her. "Why not? You did a great job making me see those Canada geese, 'haughty and determined, heads up, chinstraps pulled tight' marching their babies across the road, oblivious of traffic. So let me see you."

"I . . . no. I'd feel foolish. I'm really a very shy person, Ken." A shy person who was not the blonde he thought her to be. It was foolish, but she liked his thinking she was the kind of woman he'd be attracted to. She'd said she was ordinary, and in many ways she was, but she knew without conceit that she had a good figure, and a nice, small nose in a pretty face. She'd been told many times that her large brown eyes were her best feature. Her hair, thick and straight, was a rich chocolatey shade. Men were normally attracted to her—until they heard her talk.

Ken's snort told her what he thought about her being "shy," and by his lights he was right not to believe her. Would a shy woman have gone into his arms as she had, responded so eagerly to his kisses? She wanted to tell him she'd forgotten her shyness in those moments. It shocked her to remember how swiftly she'd forgotten, how fast she'd been caught up in a vortex she couldn't control.

"Why are you shy, Ingrid?"

"What kind of question is that? You might as well ask why I have size-six feet. I suppose it's genetic."

"Are your parents shy?"

"Well, no, maybe not, but . . . It's just the way I am. I've never made friends easily."

"You made friends easily enough with me," Ken reminded her, touching her hair again. He couldn't get enough of its texture, its luxuriance. So thick, so alive.

"That's different. It was over the phone. You couldn't s— I mean you were just a voice. We were only voices to each other. We were never meant to be anything but phone friends."

Ken smiled. "Until you decided to break a rule. But if you hadn't, this is one phone friend who would have asked eventually what you looked like. Would you have told me if I had? On the phone?"

"I . . . don't know." Her laughter was tense and uncomfortable. "Could we change the subject?"

He frowned, still toying with the ends of her hair as he replayed her words. She'd come close to saying that she could be friends with him, over the phone, because he couldn't *see* her. She had also broken that rule regarding personal visits between Living Voices clients and volunteers. Why? Also because he couldn't see her? Did she have some kind of physical deformity that bothered her? A prominent birthmark perhaps?

"If you don't want to tell me, let me feel what you look like, then," he said softly, his fingertips under her jaw, waiting, not moving, not without permission.

It didn't come, but nor did she refuse. She sat very still, but he felt her erratic breathing, the curve of her breast rising and falling against his arm as he rested it on the tiller between them.

It all reminded him potently of those kisses they'd shared, and he sensed she, too, remembered. Was she, also like him, filled with a crazy kind of excitement, half hoping for that response, that powerful electric charge between them again, longing to feel it take over and carry them away?

"I guess that's sort of standard procedure for a person without sight?" she said, as if needing to be convinced.

She was right, if people were friends, but he chose not to make the decision for her. It was something she had to do on her own. This should have been a natural progression of their friendship, something that happened early on. While it might have been pleasant, it wouldn't have been fraught with sexual overtones as it was now—without the memory of those kisses between them.

But it was there, acute, as real as the bar of warm teakwood between them. And he still wanted to touch her face. Among other parts of her.

"Go ahead," she whispered, her voice all soft and trembly.

His fingers were, too, as he began his exploration.

Her chin had a hint of a cleft in it. He lingered there as long as he dared. Her cheeks, smooth below high, clearly defined bones, were sun-warmed; his mind conjured up a rosy pink tone for them—maybe some golden freckles? He smiled.

"What was that for?"

He knew she was watching him. "Pretty girls always make me smile."

"Do I feel pretty to you?" She didn't sound as if she were fishing for a compliment, but curious, and faintly wistful.

Her nose, small and narrow-bridged, tilted at the tip. He wanted to kiss it. "You feel beautiful to me." He felt her smile.

Her brows were thin and arched, a dainty shape, and he wondered if they bleached out in the sun until they were nearly invisible.

"I feel silly to me," she murmured.

He smiled again. Already he knew the delicacy of her jawbone, but traced it anyway, first the left side, then the right, fingers trailing around that sweet, pointed chin again. He brushed a thumb over her right eye, felt long, silky lashes quivering under his exploration, and prayed there were no other craft nearby now that her eyes had closed.

Yet he couldn't stop, not even to give her a moment to check the horizon. Besides, power gave way to sail, and he'd trust to other sailors to keep a better watch.

Her mouth . . . ah, that he knew intimately, but he still stroked his fingers over her lips, tracing their shape, feeling their sensuous fullness, and wanting them under his again.

Heat rose in her face, transmitting itself to his fingers. Her breath fluttered across his wrist, and he knew she, too, was responding to this examination with heightened senses, rising pulse, and growing need.

He flattened his hand on the side of her face, fingertips resting against her small ear while strands of her hair blew across his throat, tickled his mouth. He traced the line of her eyebrow again, then drew a finger down her nose and over her lips. The heat between them grew, radiated from her face into his fingers, up his arm, into his chest, settling deep inside him. He dragged the pad of his thumb over her lips. They were open, moist, trembling.

"Ingrid . . ." His voice grew rough. "Oh, hell!" He snatched his hands off her, locking them together around his updrawn knee as he fought for control.

"Look," he said, "just tell me what you look like before I do something too damned dangerous to contemplate."

"I told you. I'm just . . . me. My hair is long and straight. My eyes are brown."

He turned his face toward her. "Brown? Not blue?"

"Sorry."

"I'm very partial to brown eyes." He touched her face again. Something lurched deep inside him at the silky texture of her skin, and he quickly withdrew his hand. "I want to know all about you. Start with what you're wearing. Come on, this isn't some kind of kinky request like you'd get from a heavy breather over the phone. I want to know because I'm with you and I can't see you."

"Shorts," she said quickly. "And a sweatshirt."

He ran a hand up her arm to the side of her neck and under her chin and turned her face toward him again, unable to resist touching her. "That doesn't tell me a lot," he said. "What colors? Are they long shorts? Short shorts?"

When she didn't respond, he let her chin go and dropped his other hand to her bare knee. "I guess I have to find out for myself," he said with a grin, and started sliding his fingers upward one slow inch at a time.

Ingrid froze as she stared at his darkly tanned hand on the paler skin of her leg. "Green, quite short," she said with what she thought was admirable aplomb. "My sweatshirt is white and I'm . . . coming about . . . *now*."

She gave the tiller a shove, ramming it into his ribs.

"Oof!" He took his hand off her thigh.

"So sorry," she said, and he laughed at the innocent, overly solicitous tone. "Did I hurt you? I was so busy watching a passing ferry, I forgot you were there."

He laughed again, his face tilted to the wind as it crossed the cockpit at a different angle. "Really."

As Ken's laughter blended with hers, Ingrid felt a strong surge of happiness, like she hadn't known for a long time.

"Really," she said. "I am sorry if I hurt you. But . . ."

"All right," he conceded. "I deserved it."

"I agree."

"Well, at least we've established one thing." He got up carefully and, keeping a light touch on her right knee, then the long tiller, he sidled around her, ducking under the boom at a word of warning from her. He settled on her other side—out of reach of the tiller. "The lady knows how to look after herself too."

"Of course I know how to look—" she started, but just then the bow angled up and to port as they encountered the massive wash from the ferry. As the boat lurched and the boom crashed from side to side, she fought the tug of turbulence against the rudder. The boat's merry dance slid her along the seat toward Ken.

He caught her and held her close, their bare legs pressed together and generating more than double the heat. Ingrid kept a firm grip on the tiller—as well as on her emotions as she tried to forget the sensation of his large, warm hand creeping up her thigh. She could no more obliterate it from her memory than she could that feather-light touch of his fingertips on her face. Though the boat was on a steady course again, her heart beat so erratically, she felt dizzy.

"What's close off the port beam?" Ken asked, walking his fingers up her waist, then down again as if he were practicing his Braille on the weave of her sweatshirt. She felt each light touch to her marrow.

"Not much," she said. "A few boats a mile or more off. One under sail, three others, all big bullies of power cruisers, racing, I think, and throwing rooster tails to impress everyone."

"And what's to starboard?" he asked, clearly unimpressed.

She looked around, knowing he wanted more detailed descriptions, but finding her mind unequal to the task while she tried to adapt to the feel of their bodies so close together. "A naval vessel," she said jerkily. "The ferry, still on its way into Horseshoe Bay. Bowen Island. A bunch of boats fishing close to shore."

"And dead ahead?"

She stretched up, half rising to peer past the cabin, suddenly aware that she'd let herself curl into the curve of his shoulder. "Nothing much. Just a series of points of land, misty, growing hazy and purple into the distance."

Thank goodness.

She hadn't been keeping the best of watches these past few minutes. Too large a part of her attention had been focused on the sensations his fingers aroused as they tracked restlessly from her shoulder to her arm to her waist, where they now played little, sensual games against her skin, where her sweatshirt had hiked up.

"Good," he said, and slid his free hand under her chin. "Because I just remembered, I like to live dangerously."

"What?" She kept her gaze pinned to his, the conviction that he could see her growing at an alarming rate. Could a man look at a woman like that if he couldn't see? "Ken . . ."

He smiled. His mouth brushed across hers for just an instant. The tip of his tongue teased her lips, causing flutters in her belly and tingles across her skin before he lifted his head again, waiting. Ingrid knew she could stop what was about to happen with only another word, a hinted protest. None came to mind.

"This time," he said, "I want you to know I'm kissing you because you really are Ingrid."

"Oh."

"No pretense now," he murmured. "This time it's for real." His breath touched her face, and Ingrid realized she had closed her eyes in anticipation. Like a distant bell she heard a mental warning reminding her that if *she* didn't keep her eyes open, they'd be two blind sailors out on a windy sea.

She tried to force her lids up, but the sun made a heavy weight on them. Her heart set up a thunderous pounding in her chest. Her blood ran as fast as the water along the hull. The boat sailed on, steady on her course. The last time had been for real, too, at least for her.

His lips brushed hers again. This time his tongue added even more to the sensations and traced their shape, flicked at their soft parting.

She ached for that promised kiss, one truly meant for her, not one merely calculated to scare off the neighbors. "Ken . . ." She moaned his name. It was not a protest.

His breath fanned across her lips, and she forced her eyes open for one last glance around. Then his green eyes, so close to hers, filled her field of vision as if they could delve into her innermost thoughts, where even she dared not go.

She forgot to search the water for dangers, forgot everything but him. The dangers, more real and present than any others, were right there in the cockpit of her boat, but they were dangers she reached out for eagerly.

She slid her hand around his neck so he'd know she was ready and watched his thick lashes cover his eyes.

She squeezed her own eyes shut against the dazzle of the sun, then his mouth covered hers.

Yes, she said silently against the velvet touch of his lips. *Oh, yes . . .*

Had there been a fleet of battleships bearing down on them, whistles blasting a warning, she would have been powerless to steer clear—as powerless as she was to steer clear of this armada of feelings blowing up between her and Ken Ransom.

She made a small sound of assent as his tongue sought entrance, and she parted her lips for him. He probed deep, then retreated, inviting her to follow. She did, tasting salt on his lips, feeling it damp and sticky in his hair, smelling it on his sun-warmed skin. Her hand curved around his jaw, whispering against the faint rasp of midday whiskers.

Their not-quite-abrasive stroke sensitized her palm. Her heart rate increased. Her breathing grew labored. Her fingers curled against his chest, and she released a low moan of sorrow when he took his mouth from hers.

He teased her throat in a tantalizingly slow exploration of skin and pulse points, and she arched her neck. One of his hands trailed down her back and over her hip, then curved to mold the shape of her thigh. She shifted restlessly, filled with thrumming heat, with a need that grew and grew. She needed to be close . . . closer.

As if sensing that need, he lifted her legs and draped them over his. The rough, curled hair of his thighs tickled the soft skin at the backs of her knees, sending deep shafts of hunger through her. He was erect, hard against her hip, and she shuddered from the core out. His nails raked lightly from the edge of her shorts to the inside of her knee, then up again as her head fell back against his shoulder.

She opened her eyes and looked at his face, finding it filled with a taut, intent expression. She stroked his cheek with her fingers, his closed lids, his gold-tipped lashes, exploring every inch as if she were the blind one. "Ken . . ."

"Ingrid . . ." He said her name softly, on a note of wonder, and found her mouth again with his, probing deeply, thrusting again and again as she twisted to get closer. She filled her hand with his hair and clung to him, her other hand still holding the tiller, a small portion of her consciousness aware of the force of wind in the sail, the water against the rudder. But other forces swept her along, more powerful, more insistent, more irresistible.

She slid her free hand down, gliding it across his back, molding the shapes of his fluid muscles. His hand slid across her belly and up under her sweatshirt, separated from her skin by only the thin cotton of her blouse.

Her sensitive abdomen quivered under his touch, and he slipped in under the hem.

Her ragged moan blended with his at the delicious contact of his palm with her skin. Her shivers of pleasure urged him on, and he cupped her satin-clad breast.

"So firm, so responsive," he murmured against her throat as his mouth tracked downward, seeking her breasts. He released a frustrated growl as he met the neck of her sweatshirt. Gently he massaged her breast, then squeezed her nipple between finger and thumb, making her writhe and suck in a swift, tremulous breath. She wanted . . . she wanted . . . everything. Lips, tongue, teeth . . .

He raked a thumb across a nipple, and in response she parted her legs. With a moan of desire he dropped his hand to her belly again, downward, zeroing in on the warmth she'd instinctively exposed.

The boat lurched. The sail flapped loudly. The boom smashed back inboard, and a douche of cold sea water slopped over the rail into Ingrid's lap.

She gasped and swung her legs off Ken. Gaze darting wildly around the horizon, she grabbed the slack tiller, trying to head the boat back on its tack. The water, roiled by the wash of the three racing cruisers, now distant and still speeding north, chopped and battered at the hull while the wind twisted the sails, slatted the boom back and forth, and shook *Molly Darlin'* like a dust mop.

On her feet, Ingrid watched tensely as the wind found the mainsail, half filled it, then eased off and let it luff. It caught in the jib, dragging the bow around against the set of the flooding tide.

She set the tiller hard over, then grabbed Ken's hand and clamped it around the thick wooden bar. "Hold her steady," she said, and released the boom, then ducked under and reefed the main until it held taut. She kept an eye on it for a minute, then said, "Give me about another five degrees to starboard."

Ken swung the tiller a fraction to port, and felt the bow respond, felt the wind on his cheek. The angry flapping of the mainsail tapered off, and he heard the squeak of the winch again as the boat steadied up.

"Five more," she said, and he made the adjustment. "Looking good," she murmured. "Hold her there."

Ken held the tiller, reveling in the sensations of the spirited little craft answering to his demands. Through sound and touch he discovered he could keep her on the right heading. When the sea shifted, or the wind, he was able to sense it in the tiller, in the attitude of her lie, in the sound of the waves against the hull, and make the required modification to their course.

Ingrid spoke somewhere forward of him. "Bring her head a bit to port." Moments later, still from the same position, she said, "A bit more, oops, too much," she said as he felt and heard the sails begin to flap. He'd begun to make the adjustment even as she spoke. "There! Lookin' good."

"Where are you?" he asked minutes later when she failed to relieve him.

"Right here. I'm getting lunch ready. You okay?"

Lunch? Leaving him at the tiller? Ken frowned. "Don't you want the helm now?"

"Not especially. You seem to be doing fine. You're right. You are a good sailor. You have an inherent seat-of-the pants ability to marry wind and sail, keel and water, and create a perfect harmony."

"All I lack is the eyes to keep watch," he said, fine-tuning the angle of the tiller again, amazed to discover that she was right. He could still guide a boat through wind and waves.

"You don't lack anything." Her voice was quiet, just audible above the chortle of water as it tickled the hull. "I'll be your eyes this trip. There's nothing on a convergent bearing. If you're comfortable with that, why not carry on?"

He nodded, his throat too constricted to respond aloud.

She trusted him to sail her boat. All right, maybe it wasn't such a big deal; the Gulf of Georgia was wide at this point, and there was plenty of margin for error. Their luck in not getting into difficulties during those intense and very stirring moments they'd so recently shared had proved that.

But this . . . this was something almost as special that she'd given him.

Gently, tenderly, he stroked his hand along the tiller and let it speak to him in its own silent language. He angled his head, the better to feel the direction of the wind since he couldn't see the telltales, and the better to hear the waves as they quartered on the hull. The sorcery of scudding across the ocean filled him, happiness bubbling like the carbonation in the can of pop Ingrid put into his hand.

He threw back his head and smiled at the heat of the sun, saw it glow red behind his closed lids.

"Thank you," he said to Ingrid, then silently, *Oh, God, thank you for sending me Ingrid*!

Now he knew why she had an angel voice.

SIX

"How well do you know my sister?" Ken asked as Ingrid packed away the remains of their lunch of sandwiches and fruit. She'd offered him the option of eating as they sailed wing and wing, or finding a quiet anchorage.

Thinking of himself, Ingrid, and *Molly Darlin'* in a quiet anchorage and how combustible that combination might prove, he'd made a huge effort at being sensible and chosen to eat under sail.

Ingrid glanced up at Ken. "I know her pretty well," she said, and smiled at the almost proprietorial grip he kept on the tiller. He was so beamingly proud of himself for having handled the boat with only minimal assistance, that she was going to hate taking the helm from him when the time came. "Well enough to know that she adores you and that you likely feel the same way about her." She chuckled. "Despite the hard time you gave her over her thirtieth birthday."

"Hey, I gave her a huge party."

"And a hard time." She closed the ice chest.

"How come you weren't at that party?" he asked.

She laughed as she sat beside him again. "I suppose because you didn't invite me."

He found her hand and linked their fingers. She liked the feeling of having her hand engulfed. "I would have if I'd known about you, Ingrid."

She squeezed his hand. "Thanks."

"Would you have come?"

"Probably not. Janet and I share a birthday. My parents had a party for me the same evening." It hadn't been fun for her, but everyone else had seemed to enjoy it.

"Do you share a birth year as well?"

"Is that a subtle way of asking how old I am?"

He laughed. "You found something subtle in that?"

"I'm twenty-nine."

"Ah, a mere baby." He turned the appellation into a caress.

"Think so, grandfather? How old did that last uncelebrated birthday make you?"

"Thirty-eight. Old, old, old."

"Goodness! We'll have to buy you a cane."

"Thanks," he said. "I have one."

They both thought of the white cane he'd left in her car. "Sorry," Ingrid murmured. "I forgot you're blind."

He smacked his palm against his forehead. "My God!" he said. "Is *that* why you're letting me sail your boat?"

They shared a laugh, but then she took the tiller from him, saying it was time to head back in.

"How did you and Jan meet?" he asked after she'd changed their tack and they were beating almost into the wind. They shared the bench on the starboard side, Ingrid's toes hooked over the tiller.

"There's something called the Volunteer Recognition Banquet. I was in line for a minor award, and Janet was my presenter. She asked me to lunch the day before the awards so she could learn a bit about me, and we clicked." Ingrid hadn't wanted to go. She avoided luncheons, both one-on-one with strangers and even with people she knew well. But Janet, she'd learned that day, was hard to refuse.

"That's when she first began talking about her wonderful big brother. She's hardly quit since. I must confess, I was prepared to dislike you. I didn't think anybody could live up to being such a paragon and still be human."

He drew her closer. "And now?"

She shivered at the waft of warm breath over her ear. "I don't dislike you."

"Good," he said. "I don't dislike you, either, and I'm usually prepared to feel that way about Janet's friends. Lord! The women my romantic little sister persists in throwing across my path! If I had time for them all, I'd be some kind of superman." He paused. "I wonder why she never tried to push you at me until this Loving Voices opportunity arose."

Ingrid knew exactly why. "Janet likes living, and she knows I'd be tempted to bring her out here and deep-six her if she tried it."

"She did try it."

Ingrid hesitated before saying carefully, "I'm not so sure she did. I can't believe she ever really hoped I'd get— Never expected me to actually go to your place and meet you in person. Rules, you know."

Ken chuckled. "I won't tell her you broke one if you don't."

"She's told me how you gave up your youth by taking over and looking after her and your mother when your father left, making decisions, keeping everything together for them. That was a tough task for a fourteen-year-old to take on."

His mouth tightened, and he shifted uncomfortably. "I only did what had to be done."

"Most boys that age couldn't have done it."

He shrugged. "Jan was only a kid. My mom was devastated. Someone had to take charge and see that the old man didn't cheat her out of everything she had a right to. It was bad enough he'd cheated on her the other way. She'd have been willing to let him take it all, her home, her future security, everything, because she was so humiliated she only wanted him out of her life. But Mom pulled through, and Janet grew up. We all made it."

"But your strength is what kept it all together for your family," Ingrid said. "I admire you for that."

Then, because the moment seemed right, she asked quietly, "What happened, Ken? To your eyes, I mean? Jan only told me that you'd lost your sight in a construction accident, and that it was probably temporary."

He didn't respond immediately, and she thought she'd overstepped the bounds of their friendship, but then he shrugged. "I was inspecting a building under construction—one of my designs—and a scaffolding collapsed. I happened to be under it. It was worse for the two guys on it. They were killed, along with the building contractor. He was standing right beside me."

She sighed and stroked his hand. "I'm sorry."

"Me too." He lifted his chin. "I don't feel guilty, though, regardless of what Janet's told you."

"She didn't tell me that."

"I may have for a day or two," he went on as if she hadn't spoken, "but logic says that's crazy. I designed the building, not the scaffolding. I wasn't responsible for choosing the materials it was made from, or for erecting it. I'm blind because I suffered a blow to the head. It caused swelling in my brain."

"I see."

His jaw squared up. "Right."

Clearly unwilling to be the focus of discussion one moment longer, he asked, "Do you have brothers or sisters?"

"I had a brother who was two years older, but he and my father died in a car crash when I was five. I don't remember much about either of them."

He gave her a quick squeeze. "That's rough. Especially on your mother." He kept his arm around her.

Ingrid nodded. "She remarried a few years later, but she and my stepfather never had kids. I've always felt the lack of a sibling."

"It has its points, but there are disadvantages, too, believe me. Such as a lifetime of being fixed up with— please forgive the term—blind dates all the time." He grinned. "Dare I hope I'm your first blind date?"

She groaned and pulled a face at him, forgetting again that he couldn't see. "This isn't even a date," she said quickly, "blind or otherwise. It's just two friends getting together and spending the afternoon on the water."

He nuzzled her neck. "It feels like a date to me, every now and then." He touched her skin with his tongue. "It tastes like more too."

Her breath caught as she lifted his head in both hands and set him away from her.

"A lifetime of being fixed up?" she asked, determined to get him back on the subject they'd been discussing. "I thought it was only recently that Janet began worrying about your single state."

Or at least had begun to try to do something about it. While Janet might be a romantic, she was also a pragmatist—another reason to doubt that she'd really been trying to set up Ingrid and Ken. Jan knew what her brother needed and wanted and would be sure to offer him exactly that. She'd said on more than one occasion that since she loved her brother and liked spending time in his company, it was only smart to try to find him a wife who'd also be a sister-in-law she could like.

"Maybe not a lifetime," he said, "but a long time. The first was when she dolled up one of her pals, a leggy fourteen-year-old—I was twenty-two—and tried to pass her off as being eighteen."

"Did you buy it?"

"Almost," he said. "Until the girl made the mistake of opening her mouth and giving away her age simply by speaking. I was ticked off, thinking of how quickly I could have ended up in jail, the poor girl was humiliated, because she'd thought I wanted to take her out, and I figured at first Janet had learned a lesson." He grinned. "She hadn't."

"That's the one, single advantage I can see to this blindness thing, I guess. Jan spent all last fall and winter touting the charms of some senator's daughter she was desperate for me to meet."

Ingrid went cold as she stared at him. So much for thinking Janet knew better than to try it on her. Ken had a slightly mocking smile on his lips. She wondered exactly who the mockery was aimed at. Did he know she was that senator's daughter? Did he think she was party to Janet's devious game?

"Seems the woman's rich, gorgeous, and available," he went on.

Ingrid pulled herself together. "All being requirements you have in a woman?" she asked.

"All being requirements—and the only requirements—Janet is convinced I have."

"Did you meet her?" Janet might know any number of senator's daughters.

"No. I kept refusing, Janet kept bugging me, and then this happened. Since then Janet's backed off."

"A lucky escape for you, I'm sure," Ingrid said lightly. "Though I've always thought rich, gorgeous, and available were three prime criteria for any man."

His lips quirked. "Yeah, right, but I have one more requirement: The woman has to be blond. The only fly in the ointment that Janet could see with the senator's daughter, and one that she was sure my first meeting with the woman would overcome, is that she's a brunette."

Ingrid's mouth fell open before she shut it with a snap at this final confirmation of suspicions.

But . . . how had Janet guessed that she might leave the security of her "phone booth" and meet the man in person? Had she relied on her brother's charm, or on Ingrid's soft heart? Or on the two factors combined?

"Janet hates blondes," Ken continued, oblivious of her tumbling thoughts and agitation. "A holdover from childhood. Our father left us for one. She's never forgiven him. Or the blonde."

A much less disturbing subject. Ingrid clung to it. "That must have made for difficult visits with your father and stepmother."

"Difficult for Jan, yes. I was old enough to refuse to visit. Anyway, the first stepmother didn't last. She left the old man for someone with more money. He's been well punished for what he did to Mom." He paused, his head cocked, the wind ruffling his hair, his smile mocking again. "Three times. Now Jan thinks all blondes are lying, scheming cheats, whether they're beautiful or not."

"And you obviously do not. Like father, like son?" Ingrid kept her tone as offhand as she could. "You're saying that rich, beautiful, and available are not necessary, so long as the woman is blond? Shortsighted, my friend. After all, hair color can be changed according to whim."

"True, but I still like a natural blonde." He lifted a hank of her hair and let the wind tease it from his fingers. Ingrid watched the sun catch it, burnishing its inky darkness. She suppressed a sigh. With her name, people who met her over the phone nearly always assumed she was fair-haired and blue-eyed.

"Wealth and physical beauty I can do without," Ken said, "so long as the woman is intelligent, fun to be with, and knows her way around a dance floor."

"And is a blonde."

"Right."

"I wonder where Janet got the impression rich and beautiful are important to you," she said dryly.

Ken wished for the thousandth time that he could see her face. He certainly couldn't read her tone, but something in it suggested disapproval. "Maybe because for years she's seen me escorting women who admittedly do grace a dance floor or a dinner party and often have family connections to powerful men. But that's business."

He felt her nod, felt her body stiffen just before she stood.

"Especially if his business is selling his product to the movers and shakers," she said tersely.

"My product sold itself," he said, remembering what she'd said about her husband.

"How nice for you." She didn't sniff, but it was there. "A man in a million."

She started the engine. It ticked over quietly, still out of gear. He heard sounds that suggested she was bringing in the sails. The boat wallowed in the choppy sea.

She put the engine in gear, revving it up. It seemed louder than it had on the way out. He let its rumble fill the void where conversation should have been.

What seemed like hours later, but was likely only thirty minutes, Ingrid spoke again. "Hold on now, we may bump a bit."

They bumped against the dock, and Ken clenched his jaw when she said, "Sit tight. I'll get the boat secured."

"I'll—" He broke off and balled his fists as he heard her, felt her, leave the boat and take care of the mooring lines. He'd what? Do the job for her? Help? Get in the way? Step off the edge of the float into a couple of fathoms of water and have to be rescued?

Pain and fury churned up until he managed to put a lid on it.

He'd had a hell of a lot better day than he'd expected to have. A hell of a lot better day than he'd had in a long time.

Ingrid finished stowing the lifejackets and turned to zip a sail cover. Ken still sat in the stern, his face calm and patient, the sun slanting across it, setting his hair aflame.

As if sensing her regard, he smiled slowly. "Did I remember to say thank you for this wonderful day?" he asked.

Her heart turned over. "I think so," she murmured, and touched his hand, indicating it was time to go. "Keep low under the boom."

He wrapped his fingers around hers, and together they climbed onto the dock. Still holding her close to his side, he breathed deeply. "Wild roses?" he asked.

"All along the shore."

"It's a very quiet marina," he said as they stepped down onto the oyster-shell path. "No other boats, no other voices."

"This isn't the marina. That's out in the main bay. This is just a little bight in the southeast corner of it, not big enough for much more than *Molly Darlin'*."

Ken sensed space around them, no other houses nearby, no sounds of traffic, things he'd failed to miss when they were heading out in the boat. "Private dock," he said. "Large, waterfront estate. Are you very, very rich, Ingrid Bjornsen?"

She laughed. "You make it sound like an affliction!"

He stopped, pulled her around to face him, and kept his hands on her shoulders. His intense gaze fixed on hers in a way that made her feel, not for the first time, that he could see into her soul—that she could see into his. What she saw now was frustration, even anger, and sadness. "Not an affliction," he said gruffly. "But if you are, it changes things. For me. I'm not rich. Not by a long shot. What I am is an unemployed, unemployable man on a disability pension." Plus the returns on some pretty good investments, but he didn't think he'd ever be filthy rich.

"I'm not rich," Ingrid said.

"You live here."

"It's my stepfather's home. And my mother's of course. But it's been in his family for three generations."

His eyes widened. "You live with your parents?"

"I live in a self-contained suite at the end of one wing of the main house. They had it built for me after my divorce. They spend little time here and wanted someone on the premises. Would you . . . would you like to take a walk around the grounds?" She assured him there were no dogs, kids, or bicycles. She didn't tell him of her dream the night before.

With another of those smiles she was coming to love, he agreed.

An hour later he sighed and said it was time for him to go. If his mother called and got his answering machine too often in one day, she'd fly into a panic and possibly even fly across the country thinking he'd fallen down the elevator shaft and needed to be rescued.

Ingrid laughed as she led the way to her car. "Don't make fun of your mother."

"I'm not. She has a serious fear of my doing just that. I've told her and told her, the doors won't open unless the elevator is there, but she won't be convinced. I just wish she wasn't so paranoid on my behalf."

"She's your mother, Ken. She loves you."

"I'm thirty-eight years old! I've been looking after myself for a long, long time. But despite that, she'd have forty fits if she knew I'd spent the day on a sailboat . . . and even sailed it."

Ingrid opened the passenger door of her Miata for him, and he slid in. "Then don't tell her," she suggested.

"Do you keep things from your mother?" he asked as they shot up the steep, winding driveway. The wind blowing through the open car nearly whipped his words away, but Ingrid caught them and laughed.

"Of course!"

"Such as this date with me?" he asked. "I noticed you didn't introduce me to her or your stepfather."

"Mainly because they aren't here," she said easily, but felt just a tad guilty. If they had been in residence, she wouldn't have invited Ken to her home at all. The thought of her mother's effusive welcome, her eager friendliness toward any man who showed an interest in Ingrid, would have stopped her.

"Besides," she added. "As I've already pointed out, this wasn't exactly a date."

He took her hand and held it as she drove, releasing it only when she had to change gears, then gathering it into his again. "It was a date, Ingrid. Our first. I don't want it to be our last."

She said nothing. She didn't want it to be their last, either, but did she dare continue seeing him? It would last, she knew, only until he could actually see her. Then, for certain, it would all fall apart.

At the entrance to Ken's building she pulled the car to a halt. "You're home," she said.

He turned to face her. "Thanks, Ingrid. Thanks for . . . everything."

She smiled. "You're welcome. I enjoyed it too."

"Will you come up for a few minutes?" he asked, lifting her hand in his as he brushed his knuckles under her chin. "I don't want our day to end yet."

Something in his tone, in the expression on his face, sent a surge of excitement through her. "I want to finish it like the date you say it wasn't."

"How?" she whispered.

"We could sit on the terrace, talk for a while, maybe have a cold drink. Anything you want."

She thought of things she might want, being in his apartment, with the door closed, alone with him. She thought of the kisses they'd already shared that day. If she went up with him, there'd be more. She knew that as surely as she knew she'd take another breath. While she might try not to breathe, it would be impossible. As impossible as it would be not to melt if he touched her again.

If he raked his thumbnails over her nipples, she'd want his mouth, his teeth, on her the way she had wanted that on the boat. And in his apartment there'd be no shipping-lane dangers to keep her good sense anywhere close to the surface. If he slipped his thigh between hers, she'd open for him. And this time they wouldn't be in the hallway. No angry neighbor would startle them apart by dropping a tray.

They might be on his couch. They might sink down until his weight was on her, her thighs cradling him and . . . And they might end up in his bed.

Merely thinking of it made her ache with a yearning so deep, she knew she was likely already beyond redemption. Was she falling in love with him? Did she dare to fall in love with him?

"No," she said. "I'd better not." Her tone was low with regret.

He slid his fingers up and around the back of her neck under her hair. She squeezed her eyes shut. "Why not?" he whispered.

She felt his other hand join the first, on the other side of her neck, one thumb pressing gently against the rapid pulse in her throat. She swallowed. "Because I . . ." She firmed her voice and opened her eyes. "We don't know each other, Ken. Not really."

He lifted his brows. "We've talked for hours every night for nearly a week. We spent the whole day together. We—" He broke off. His grin was crooked. "You know as well as I do what else we've done. And how well we did it."

"Yes . . ." She breathed the word out. "But if I came upstairs with you, we'd end up doing it again."

"And you're not ready for that."

Though it had been a statement, not a question, Ken felt her shake her head. He smiled again. "Okay. You're right. If you count this one, and I do, we've only had one date."

She nodded this time. "Would you . . . would you like to have dinner with me on Thursday?" she asked.

Ken let loose a long breath. He should have been the one to ask that. Only . . . how could he? Dining in a restaurant was out of the question until he knew more about what he was doing. As for inviting her to his place . . . It was all he could do to successfully heat up a frozen entree for himself. Entertaining was out of the question.

"Dinner?" he said.

"At my place. We'll barbecue."

He slipped his hands from around her neck and fastened them over the top of his cane. "You mean *you'll* barbecue. You may trust me to sail your boat in the middle of the gulf, but I'm sure you won't trust me around an open flame."

"Of course you can cook your own dinner if you want to," she said. "Mine, too, for that matter. There's nothing wrong with your nose, is there? Burning meat has a distinctive odor that even a blind man should be able to identify. And burning fingers are self-evident."

All of a sudden he had to laugh. He loved her voice when it went all crisp like that. He also loved the way she refused to let him feel sorry for himself. "Thanks," he said. "I needed that. Feel free to knock the chip off my shoulder anytime."

She brushed a hand over his shoulder. "I'm glad to. It doesn't become you."

He caught her hand and pressed it to his cheek, needing her touch. Leaning closer until he felt her breath fanning over his cheek, he tilted her face up with easy pressure under her chin.

Ingrid went all mushy inside, but he didn't kiss her.

She ached for it. She moistened her lips with her tongue. Naturally he couldn't see that, couldn't know how great her yearning had grown. Naturally—and fortunately. No, dammit, *un*fortunately. She wanted him to kiss her. So, what was to stop her from kissing him? She hesitated while her heavy eyelids fluttered down again.

"I dare you," he said.

Her eyes popped open to take in his grin. Dammit, how had he known? "I don't take dares," she informed him primly.

"You don't take dares and you play by the rules," he said, shaking his head. "What am I going to do about you, Ingrid?"

"Nothing. It's far too late to change me." Even Clairol couldn't help.

"Is it? I have a feeling that if a guy could come up with the right dare, you'd take it."

"No one ever has," she murmured.

"Someone will," Ken said, touched by the wistfulness in her tone. "Consider yourself warned."

He opened the car door and got out, then leaned back in over the door.

" 'Bye, Ingrid," he said. "Call me tonight, okay? I can't wait to talk to you."

"But we've talked all d—"

He shut the door firmly and aligned his back with the side of her car. Cane swinging in short arcs before him, he took his first real steps toward independence since those he'd taken at the age of eleven months.

Don't say anything, he begged her silently, knowing she sat watching from the car. *Don't offer to help.*

"Ken!"

He stopped, shoulders rigid, but didn't turn.

"I'm a brunette," she said—almost desperately, he thought.

He threw back his head and laughed at the blatant lie. Sure she was. Ingrid Bjornsen, Norse princess in disguise, was no more brunette than he was bald.

Swinging his cane before him, he strode forth, aiming himself in what he fervently hoped was the right direction to reach the flight of stairs leading up to the entrance of his building. His aim was true. He felt the first concrete obstacle in the path, measured its height, his closeness to it, then stepped up. The steps carried him to the wide entry patio, which he crossed unerringly.

As he found his key in his pocket and slid it into the lock, he heard Ingrid start her car. He turned before opening the door and waved. Seconds later he heard her car drive away.

He was so brave, Ingrid thought, watching Ken walk up the steps. She forced herself to remain where she was, not to go after him and offer to see him to his door. He had to do it on his own. He wanted to do it on his own.

She wondered if his face was as tense as it had been earlier when he'd strode, with every outward appearance of confidence, across his living room to his bedroom. She wondered if that same, stark fear drew his mouth taut, created a white line around his nose. If it did, no one would guess it from watching him walk away.

He faced his blindness with gutsy determination not to let it ruin his life, despite the odd moment of forgivable and understandable self-pity, a self-pity that bordered on self-disgust, for he perceived it as a weakness.

Would a man with his brand of courage accept her lack of it?

She would have to tell him the truth about herself sometime, preferably before he found out accidentally. Only . . . she wasn't quite ready to do that yet. She didn't know him well enough, didn't yet trust him not to think less of her for her inability to speak fluently in most situations.

Yet she felt she knew him so well, felt almost a part of him. It was those kisses, the way they aroused her to a point of mindless surrender. How, she kept asking herself, could she respond so readily, so totally, to a man unless she knew him well?

The fact was she didn't know him well, and therefore her response was wrong. Wrong? No. But it was . . . unwise.

For five out of six nights they had talked, maybe a total of less than ten hours in all. Yet they had been intense hours, hours they had filled with each other, no distractions, no interruptions, no other people to have to deal with. She knew what authors he liked, the books he reread and considered old friends. She knew his favorite movies and shared many of both preferences with him. They even agreed politically. They'd been raised in the same religion, though neither practiced it much. They found the same things funny, the same activities fun.

They both liked sailing, skiing, and swimming, and both played tennis only when pushed. Ingrid had a fear of any ball that came at her fast; he simply found it a waste of time. They had argued about who was likely to beat whom at Scrabble and made a date for "whenever."

If was the word Ken had used. She had insisted on *when*, though at the time of that conversation, she'd still been adamantly refusing to meet him in person. Somewhere deep down she must have known she wouldn't be able to resist forever.

She knew his secret fear of driving across bridges; he knew she had hated boarding school, the place where she'd learned to obey rules so rigorously. She knew his all-but-forgotten boyhood dream of creating the ultimate computer game, the one that would make him a millionaire. She knew, as well, his longing to design a real home for himself someday. And for his family? He had never said, but what he'd described had sounded like a family home. It had also sounded like a house she could live in.

Oh, yes, they'd talked, they'd shared, but did any of that mean they really *knew* each other?

No. At least he didn't know her. If he did, he wouldn't admire her at all.

As she watched, Ken got to the front door, took out a key, and fit it into the lock. She was glad for him that he managed it without fumbling. She started her car. He turned, and as if he could see her, waved.

She lifted her hand and, as if he could see her, waved back. She thought he smiled, though at this distance it was hard to be sure, and went inside, letting the door close between them.

She drove away.

Ingrid, Ken thought, leaning back against the elevator wall. *Ingrid*. Now more than merely her voice would haunt him.

There was her mouth. He could almost taste it. There was the shape, the weight, the resilience of her breasts. His hand curved over the top of his cane. There was the delicacy of her facial bones, those flyaway eyebrows and long, silky lashes and her hair blowing in the wind.

For the past week her voice in all its nuances, and his own fantasies of her, had filled his dreams. Now there was more; there were all the sweet realities. The scent of her! The husky angel voice tenfold richer than what he'd known over the telephone. The feel of her body against his, her erect nipples, her erratic breathing, the heat of her mouth, the silk of her skin.

She filled his senses when they were together. She filled his mind when they were not.

He had a sneaking hunch that she was the woman, at last, who was destined to fill his heart.

"Why now?" he asked when, safe inside his apartment without mishap or embarrassment, he slumped into an easy chair. Why had he found her now, when he had nothing at all to offer?

SEVEN

"Did you have a long list this evening?" Ken asked when Ingrid called him Monday night. "You sound tired."

He didn't, she thought. He sounded eager, as if he'd been waiting for her call.

"No longer than normal," she said. "But the day was."

"What made it long? Tell me about it."

The warmth of his caring cloaked her, and she pulled her arms in close to her sides to hold it there, almost losing the phone in the thick down of her pillow.

What should she say? It was long because she'd known from the moment she woke up that what she needed most in the world was to hear his voice? Why not? It was true. "I . . ." She hesitated, then said, "All day I've needed to call you."

"Why?" His tone was sharp. She could see him sitting erect, alert, watchful. "What's wrong?"

"Nothing. I just . . . wanted to call you."

His relief showed in his laughter. "I thought you were going to say you needed to call me to tell me you couldn't call me anymore."

"Why would I do that?"

He didn't respond at once. She waited. "I guess," he said ruefully, "because I know I'm a fraud. I'm taking up your time, taking your calls, and I'm not truly a shut-in. I'm just . . . selfish." His voice dropped. "Your calls are very important to me."

She shivered with the pleasure his low tone gave her. "They're important to me too. I'll call you every day. I thought that was clear. I promise."

She knew he smiled. "Not every day. Every night."

She sighed. "Every night." Yes, and then every night she'd go to sleep with the fresh memory of his voice in her ear and dream of him.

"I'll hold you to that," he murmured. "Now, why did you need to call me earlier?"

Because she missed him? "I don't know. Just . . . because."

"So why didn't you?"

"Time kept getting away from me. I thought I'd do it on my lunch break, but I ended up taking one of the kids to emergency to get a split lip stitched up. I wanted to do it before dinner, but there wasn't time. Then I planned to do it during my dinner break, but somehow dinner never happened today."

"You haven't had dinner yet? It's after eleven!" he scolded. "Get off the phone! Go and eat."

"You sound like my mother," she said with a laugh. "I had a sandwich at my desk about nine. I'm okay."

"Why did you miss your dinner?"

She yawned. "Things snowballed on me."

"You sound like you need sleep more than conversation."

"Not yet. Tell me about your day first."

Ken was glad she didn't want to sleep yet. "Janet was here. She spent the afternoon with me." He chuckled. "It was all I could do not to tell her that you'd called, that we close each day by talking together."

"Why didn't you?"

"Hah! If I'd admitted I'd even heard of you, even if I'd so much as hinted to her that you'd been in touch, her head would have swelled intolerably. She loves to be right. If I'd told her how much your calls mean to me, how much I enjoyed our day together yesterday, she'd have been unbearable with her smug I-told-you-so attitude. Therefore I didn't mention your name, so naturally neither could she. But she sure tiptoed around the subject a lot. She thought she was being subtle."

"Too bad you forgot to tell me it was supposed to be a secret from Janet," Ingrid said, grinning. "She came to see me today, too, to bring me a 'reward' for being 'kind' to her big brother."

"You sold me out for some paltry reward! How could you?"

Ingrid giggled. "I didn't sell you out. She asked if I'd called you and I admitted it, but she knew already. She only wanted confirmation from me. She'd guessed you were punishing her by not mentioning it."

"She would. There's no mold on her, is there?"

"Not a speck. She credits me with your not being an evil-tempered grouch, and she rewarded me with four adorable little mice."

"Mice?" he hooted, obviously choosing to ignore the

remark about his former frame of mind. "I always knew she had lousy taste."

He lowered his voice. "Believe me, if you give me a chance, I'll find something a whole lot better than four squirmy rodents to show my appreciation." He lowered it still more. "In fact I'll show you the best way I can without knocking over a jewelry store the very next time we're together."

She went warm all over. Just thinking of his "showing his appreciation" made her quiver. She knew what his methods would be.

"The only thanks I want are shown quite adequately at the Volunteers' Banquet every August," she said quickly, mainly to distract herself from those errant thoughts.

"Why did Janet bring you mice?"

"I collect them. China mice, wooden mice, blown-glass mice. You name them, I've got them. People have been giving me mice since I was about nine years old." She paused and added, "It was after I earned the nickname 'Mousie' in boarding school."

"Your tone tells me you hated that."

She hadn't realized she was so obvious. "I did. I used to cry myself to sleep over it. I wanted a cute nickname, one bestowed as a result of popularity, not spite. I got that one because I was timid and geeky and a crybaby. It was always used derogatorily, as in 'Don't choose Mousie! You want us to lose?' And 'Oh, look, Mousie's crying again. What a sissy.' "

"Damn them!" Ken said fiercely. "And damn my stupid little sister for bringing you mice as a 'reward.' Why don't you tell her you hate them? And who started it, anyway, giving you mice?"

"My mother, and I don't hate them now. What I

hated was that the other kids despised me. I love my mouse collection, though. I got over those childhood hurts long ago." And she had, mostly, but it still felt good that he had championed her again.

They talked on until he said, "Did I hear you trying to stifle a yawn? I'm sorry, honey. Why don't you tell me to shut up when I go on too long?"

"Because I'm interested in what you have to say."

"Ah, I bet you tell that to all the guys."

"Nope. Believe me, it's a change not hearing about how some poor soul walked nineteen miles across the bald prairie through seventy-below temperatures in order to light the woodstove in the one-room school before the teacher and the other first-graders arrived."

Ken laughed. "That bad, is it?"

"No, not really, and some of my old duffers have some truly great stories. Like you do."

"Are you calling me an old duffer?"

"Well . . ."

"Hah! I get it. That was an attempt at distraction. Nevertheless I know I heard you yawn. Get off the phone right now, Ingrid, and go to bed. You're tired, and tomorrow is another day with your savages."

"I am in bed."

Silence hummed in her ear. "Are you still there?" she asked.

"In bed . . ." he echoed. "That's a crummy thing to tell a man who's spent an entire day thinking about you, fantasizing, remembering the way you feel, the way you taste, the way you smell." He did that thing with his voice again as he added, "The way you respond to my touch."

"Oh." It came out as a long, soft breath.

She thought she heard a low groan. "Ingrid, get over here. Now."

She giggled like a giddy teenager. "What's with all these orders? Ingrid, get off the phone. Ingrid, go eat. Ingrid, go to bed. Ingrid, get over here. How could I be in bed and over there at the same time?"

"Oh, baby. Let me tell you . . ."

"I don't think I want to know."

"Wanna bet? You'd love to . . . know."

Ken heard her draw a tremulous breath. "Good night, Ken. Sleep well."

She set the phone down gently, and he did the same. He'd sleep a hell of a lot better if he had her beside him.

Frustration ground into him. It still lived within when he arose the next morning. It gave a bad flavor to his coffee, soured the milk on his cereal, and made him short with a neighbor who came to remind him about the barbecue on the back patio that evening.

The only barbecue he wanted to think about was the one at Ingrid's place on Thursday. Just him and her . . . and time together. Sunset, followed by twilight, followed by starlight. Not that he'd be able to see any of it, but what the hell? There'd be good conversation, Ingrid's sweet scent, her angel voice and velvet skin to enjoy with his other senses. There'd be summery breezes, food, laughter and—a bottle of wine? Yeah.

Wine. And he would provide it, as a good guest should. He was also going to go out and get it himself.

If he was going to spend the rest of his life as a damned blind man, then he'd better start working a lot harder at making it a life he could ask a woman to share.

A life he could ask Ingrid to share.

It was time to get started now. Right that minute.

Determination set his jaw as he showered, shaved, and smoothed his hair. It made his neck stiff as he picked up his cane and opened his door. It kept his shoulders square as he strode the eleven paces across the lobby to the front doors and kept fear at bay when he turned right on the sidewalk at the bottom of the stairs.

The liquor store was three blocks away.

The rest of his life lay beyond that.

"Hot damn! I made it!" Ken couldn't wipe the grin off his face as he stood outside the liquor store clutching a bottle of wine in a bag under his arm and talking to himself. Maybe people were staring. He didn't know, and this time he didn't care. He couldn't expunge the triumph from his soul. He had walked three blocks by himself, crossed three intersections, found the liquor store, and made a purchase. He wanted to jump in the air and bang his heels together. He wanted, like a little kid who had finally mastered his two-wheeler, to keep on performing his miraculous trick.

He felt as if he could walk for miles. He wanted to stuff his hands in his pockets, throw back his head, and whistle while he strode to draw attention to himself. People would look and say, "Hey, now there's a blind man who knows where he's going, knows what he's doing. Everybody look at the blind man in charge of his own life!"

He wanted to swing his white cane with jaunty insouciance, wanted everyone to know just how damn good he really was. He wanted to tell the world.

No. A thought brought him up short. He didn't want

to tell the world. He wanted to tell Ingrid. And that he wanted to do right then too.

Well, why not? He started at the sound of a voice from within. It was clear and challenging, and he tried to shove it away.

Don't be an ass, he retorted. *Three blocks is one thing. But Ingrid's clear across town in a neighborhood you know even less than you know this one, which isn't, you have to admit, very damned well at all. Setting out for a blind trek of that distance would take more guts than stepping into that open elevator shaft your mother worries about.*

The multitude of streets between him and Ingrid had more than a few potential twelve-story drops. They had semis, and buses, and hot-rodding teenagers, and careful moms distracted by station wagons full of kids. They had darting skateboarders, zooming motorcycles, silent bicycles, and pushy blade runners, intersections and train crossings and—

"Taxi, mister?"

"And taxis! Yeah!" He beamed, wheeling in the direction of the voice. "Right! A taxi's exactly what I need." He felt for and found the door, settling into the backseat. "Why in hell didn't I think of this myself?"

"Beats me, buddy. Where to?"

Where to? Ken laughed aloud. Why, to find Ingrid, of course!

"Here you go, buddy. Saint Justine's. That's what you said, right?" The cabby sounded unsure. "This ain't the best of neighborhoods, you know. You don't exactly look like you belong."

Through the open window Ken breathed in the stale,

ancient smell of broken brick, coal smoke, and decay. He shrugged. "It can't be all that bad. A friend of mine runs a day care here for preschoolers."

"Okay, suit yourself. Want me to wait?"

"No, thanks. What's the damage?" The man told him, and Ken hauled out his wallet. The bills were folded, each denomination in its special manner, and he sorted through them. He handed over the money, hoping he was right.

He must have been bang on. "Two-fifty-five change," the guy said.

"Keep it." Ken grinned with elation as he opened the door and stepped onto the curb, then he hesitated. Where was he supposed to go? How did he get inside the church?

He squared his shoulders and put his cane into position. He'd gotten this far, he could go the rest of the way. All the way . . . to get to Ingrid.

All the way . . . with Ingrid.

He tucked the thought behind a door. This, like life, had to be taken one step at a time. He was blind. He couldn't go leaping off into space.

He grinned. But, by God, he wanted to!

"There's a gate in the fence about three feet ahead on the right," the cabby said, and Ken realized the man had been watching. "Sign says the office is around back."

He was glad of the help, and equally glad that he hadn't set forth yet and tripped over anything. "Just keep on that path," the cabby added, "around the building to the right, and you should be okay."

The cab pulled away, and except for the cooing of pigeons, a thick silence descended. It beat in Ken's ears, kept pace with his footsteps, slowing as he did, making his way along the cracked sidewalk.

When he halted, though, it continued, a heavy thud, thud, thud that he realized was the beating of his own heart.

With the cab driver's leaving, the world had just become enormous—empty, lonely, and very, very dark.

Sweat broke out on his forehead, ran down his chest under his shirt. Suddenly this wasn't as much fun as it had been. His sense of adventure slithered under a rock and stayed there.

Gritting his teeth, he moved on, fumbled with a wrought-iron gate, opened it, and walked through.

Moments later he stepped off the path onto dry, lumpy grass. The sidewalk had taken a sharp turn to the left. Back on track again, he tripped on what sounded like an empty bottle as it rolled away and then fell silent.

He frowned as the walk took another turn and the smell of stale urine assailed his nostrils.

Why would anybody run a day care in a place like this? It smelled like someplace rummies hung out. Was he even still at the church? Had he overshot? He prodded the air to the left with his cane, struck a solid wall. The scraping and clicking sounded like brick or perhaps cracked concrete. Lowering the cane, swinging it, he took several more steps, hoping to encounter a flight of stairs, even just a step or two. Those usually led up to a door. Beyond a door there'd be people.

He felt nothing with his cane. Just more sidewalk. He followed it, more slowly now, with less certainty.

It was too quiet, even for a church. There were no voices, no phones ringing, no footsteps around him. Maybe he'd found the cemetery?

He stopped again, listening, trying to sort out and place the sounds he did hear. A recognizable tune—a commercial jingle on a radio. Where? In the church office? He could pin no direction on it, but it wasn't close at hand. The swish of traffic on streets seemed to come from ahead of him and from the right. The continuous cooing of pigeons surrounded him. Something fell onto his shoulder. Grimacing he brushed it off. Only a leaf.

Children played somewhere, shrieking with laughter. A dog barked.

Children. Ingrid's group? Courage stirred.

Hoping his ears would lead him to the sound, he took three more steps, swinging his cane before him to detect obstacles. If he encountered Ingrid, he wanted to be striding along, confident, sure of himself, head up. He lifted his chin, pasted a smile on his face, . . . and stepped off the edge of the world.

It was a very distinctive sound, a bottle rolling down the stairs and banging into the door. Ingrid's head jerked up at the first clatter. The thud of a large, solid body hitting the door was distinctive too. It was also distressingly familiar.

"Not again!" She groaned as she leaped up and collared two small boys, both of whom had headed gleefully for the door. "Bruce, Ivan, sit down and stay put."

Three times in the past few months drunks had fallen down the stairs. If only Father Ralph could find the money to have the railing repaired. She'd offered, but he'd refused. "You do enough, my dear," he'd said. "God will provide." Maybe now both God and Father Ralph would see it her way.

Only the week before a man had tumbled down the stairs, impressing both Bruce and Ivan with the amount of blood issuing from his nose and from a cut on his arm. He'd landed on the bottle that had likely been the reason he was at the foot of the stairs. Harsh-smelling red wine had soaked him, and another man, equally drunk, had cursed foully at the spillage. The second man had stood teetering at the top of the flight, as if he, too, might come tumbling down and fetch up inside her classroom door. Mercifully he'd staggered off after realizing the wine was irrecoverable.

She didn't want the kids exposed to that any more often than she could help. Some of them enjoyed it far too much.

"Sit down, you two," she said sternly. "Stay there. Wait."

With another admonitory wave to keep the eleven children inside, she eased open the stairwell door. Feeling weight against it, she stepped back as an intact wine bottle wrapped in a brown paper bag rolled into the room. This was closely followed by a man who slithered along with the opening door, one arm over his face, one leg extending up the doorframe, the other tangled around a walking stick.

She stared as he sorted out arms, legs, and cane and got to his hands and knees, shaking his head like a bull about to charge. He clasped the doorframe in both hands, pawing his way upright. His cane—his *white* cane—lay abandoned on the floor.

Ingrid's jaw dropped. Her eyes opened wider. She shook her head in disbelief. "Ken? What? I don't—I can't bel—" She grabbed his arms. "Are you all right? Did you hurt yourself? What in the *world* are you doing here?"

He let go of the doorframe, pulled his sleeves down,

and gave her the biggest, happiest grin she'd seen this side of Christmas. He caught her in a bearhug, lifting her off her feet. "I made it!" he crowed. "I did it, Ingrid! I found you."

"I didn't know I was lost," she said as he set her down. "How did you get here?"

She took another step back, kicked the wine bottle, and turned to gape at it. Bruce, unable to contain himself another second, bounced off the edge of his chair, where he'd been seesawing between obedience and desire, waiting for just such an excuse. He ran over and picked up the bottle. He held it out to Ken, who of course didn't see it.

"It's not broken, mister," Bruce said. "The last guy broke his. He bled." Ken had obviously fallen far short of Bruce's expectations. "Do we get to call an amblance again, Inky?" he asked, turning big, eager eyes toward her.

"No," she said. She took the wine bottle from him and shooed him back to the table. To her relief Jennifer, her assistant, must have heard the commotion. She came out of the rest room to investigate, assessed the situation at a glance, and restored order, distracting the children with a new game that involved a lot of hand clapping and marching.

Jenny knew the ropes.

"What are you doing here?" Ingrid asked Ken again, her voice a sharp whisper.

He grinned. "I was in the neighborhood. I thought I'd . . . drop in."

She retrieved his cane and put it in his hand, then brushed away a smear of dust from his shoulder. "Are you sure you're not hurt?"

"I'm fine," he said, making a supreme and successful effort not to wince at the pain her sweeping hand caused him. In truth he'd wrenched that shoulder and he was fairly sure there was no skin left on his right knee, but yes, he was fine. He was more than fine. He was there! He had done it. He had found Ingrid!

"Why did you come?" she asked.

Why, he wondered, was she whispering? Those kids were making so much racket with their singing and foot stomping and clapping, they couldn't possibly overhear. He'd thought her group consisted of eleven children. She must have invited a local rock band for the morning. Nevertheless he whispered back, "Because I couldn't wait until Thursday to see you again."

"Ken . . ." She puffed out a gusty breath as if blowing her bangs off her forehead. He didn't think she wore bangs. He touched her hair. No bangs. It felt tight, pulled back from her face. She jerked her head away. "That's no answer."

"All right. The truth. Because I went out to buy a bottle of wine for Thursday so I could contribute to dinner. It was my first solo off my own block." He grinned. "I was so damn proud of the accomplishment, that I"— he shrugged—"I wanted to brag. I needed to tell you what I'd done."

Ingrid couldn't help herself. She touched his cheek. He felt freshly shaven. He smelled freshly showered. She wanted to touch him a whole lot more. He'd only stressed the pronoun *you* a tad, but she'd picked up on it.

"Me?" she said softly.

Ken shifted uneasily. "Yeah. I . . . uh, yeah."

Oh, hell, he was standing there shuffling his feet like

a twelve-year-old! He felt as gawky as that kid from the "Anne of Green Gables" miniseries, the one who got the girl in the end. The last thought heartened him. He felt her fingertips leave his cheek.

He touched hers, needing that contact. She leaned into the caress, releasing a rocket in his belly. "Now that I'm here, may I stay? It's almost lunchtime, isn't it? If I could take you out for lunch, we could count that as another date and be that much closer to the time when we can—"

He broke off, bit his lower lip, and heard her giggle. "You're a crazy man!" she said.

"Crazy about you. Getting crazier every minute. Please, Ingrid?"

"Okay."

He sighed, sliding his hand around the back of her head. Her hair was in some kind of intricate braid. He wished it were loose and free, but even pulled back it felt so good to touch, he wanted to spend the rest of the day doing that. Undoing it. And a few other things, all of which involved having his hands on Ingrid Bjornsen. He ran the backs of his fingers down the side of her face.

"Thanks, honey. I promise I'll leave right after lunch. All you'll have to do is call me a taxi and—"

"A taxi?"

"That's how I got here." He laughed and waggled his cane. "Good Lord! Did you think I'd walked?"

In truth she hadn't given it much thought. She'd asked, he hadn't answered, and she'd let the question go. It was enough that he'd gotten there. But by taxi?

"My God!" She forgot to whisper. "You *are* crazy! Your clothes, your bearing. Everything about you looks affluent! You're out of your mind, getting into a car with a stranger! You could have been robbed."

"He was a cabby," Ken protested, laughing. "I've taken quite a few cabs in my life."

"But you're blind now, Ken! He could—" She was shouting, and broke off as Jennifer took a step toward them. The other woman stopped, but watched them, alert for trouble. "He c-could have been an unsc-sc-sc-scrupulous c-c-c-cabby!"

Ingrid lowered her voice, turning away from Jennifer. "You could have been taken for a ride!" She wanted to hit him. She wanted to shake him. She wanted to cuss him out, but there were the children to consider. She contented herself with a heartfelt, "Idiot! You could have been driven down to the dockyards and rolled. You—" She broke off as Ken laughed again and gave her a small shake.

"Hey! Curb your vivid imagination. Obviously none of that happened. Talk about sounding like somebody's mother!"

Ingrid subsided like a popped balloon and cast another glance across the room at Jennifer and the children, all of whom were staring at her and Ken now.

She bit her lip and fixed her gaze on his face as he said, "Besides, aren't cab drivers bonded or something?"

"I, uh, yes. I g-guess so."

"I guess so too. Come on, when was the last time you heard of a cabby harming a fare?"

Ingrid sighed. "Never." Dammit, she'd had a fit of paranoia on his behalf. He was right, she had sounded like his mother, as if she thought he couldn't look after himself. And he hated that, didn't he? Right. So she'd call him a taxi and send him on his damned, stupid, independent way! She'd—

"I'll drive you home," she said. "Later. You can spend the afternoon here."

His eyes widened. "But—"

"Are you in some kind of a hurry?" she challenged him, hands on hips. "You have a hot date?" Now that she'd decided to keep him here, he wanted to go? No way! Not a chance!

His lips quirked with humor he tried to conceal, but it got beyond him. He grinned broadly, but there was an underlying tenderness that said her concern pleased him. "No hurry and no hot date—unless you'd care to skip class this afternoon and sneak out with me?"

Dammit, she couldn't even stay properly mad at him for laughing at her, not when he smiled like that.

"Then stay and spend the afternoon with us." She touched his hand again. He turned his and caught hers. "You said you'd like to sometime," she reminded him. "So why not now? And maybe you can teach the kids something."

He snorted. "Like what? How to take a header down the stairs and survive?"

"Like how to go after something you really want, despite the odds."

He grinned and curled his fingers more securely around hers. Swinging her arm to the small of her back, he pulled her closer until the tips of her breasts brushed his chest. "I don't think you want me to teach them that, Ingrid," he whispered. "But if you'll wait till later, after you take me home, I'll teach you."

"Inky." Jennifer spoke from right beside her. Ingrid jerked her hand free and whirled to meet Jennifer's amused and curious gaze. "Carol's here. Are you going to take your lunch break now?" Carol, one of the mothers, provided lunchtime relief so that either Ingrid or Jennifer could get out for a few minutes.

"Y-y-yes," she said. "If you've fi-fi-fin-finished yours?"

"I am." Jenny gave Ken the once-over—twice. She looked impressed, then grinned, tilting her head to one side. "Got a date for lunch?"

"I . . . uh—" She leaped at the idea. "Y-yes. J-Jennifer, meet K-K-Ken."

The two exchanged polite greetings, then Ingrid grabbed Ken's hand. "Be b-back soon."

"No sweat. Take your time." Jennifer's calm underlined Ingrid's own agitation. "See you."

"Okay." With that, Ingrid dragged Ken out into the stairwell and closed the door behind her.

She felt sick. Now he knows, she thought. Now he'll comment. Now he'll shake his head in pity. Now he'll take his white cane and walk away from the geeky girl with the bad stammer. She held her breath.

He chuckled. "I love the way you get all flustered and stutter and stammer when I tease you like that."

She released her pent-up breath in a whoosh, hauled in another to tell him the truth, and gagged.

Yucch! Why hadn't she remembered? Shallow breathing or, as the kids insisted, no breathing at all until you were well clear of the stairway. Its depth, walls, and wide overhang made it a good nighttime shelter for the homeless, and no amount of bleachy scrub water or careful sweeping could ever eradicate the odor.

Ken gagged too. "Why in hell do you have to have your day care here?" he demanded, holding her arm as they ascended the noisome staircase. "Even the taxi driver was reluctant to let me out because the area's such a slum."

"The rent's right," she said.

"How come you need low rent? I've heard friends bellyache about the high cost of day care. Doesn't that cover rent?"

"None of the parents of my kids is well off, but their children all need treatment they can't get through other sources for a variety of reasons, the prime one being that they aren't quite poor *enough*. This way I can provide it at a rate they can afford."

Ken pulled her to stop on the sidewalk. His eyes burned into hers in that uncanny way. "Treatment? I thought you ran a day care."

"It's a day care, yes, but it's also a treatment center for preschool kids with behavioral problems."

"What does that mean, 'behavioral'? No discipline?"

"Not always. It means their behavior—both good and bad—is so far from the norm that it causes problems for them or others. Some of them act out, yes, but others withdraw. One can be as damaging as the other. A child who won't, as my grandmother used to put it, 'say boo to a goose' can be at great risk. All kids need to be street-proofed, assertive enough to tell a stranger to get lost. I have one little girl who simply loves everyone to death. Mi-Jung would walk up to anybody, I mean anybody and if he said 'Come with me,' she'd go, willingly. We're working on that problem.

"And then there are kids who are overly aggressive and need to be toned down. If they aren't helped now, they may grow into troubled teens."

And criminal adults, she added silently.

Ken felt Ingrid's body angle away from him. Hand linked to her elbow, he turned the corner with her. "But why? What causes something like that to happen to a little kid?"

"Who knows for sure?" She opened the gate, and they stepped through. Traffic whished by with metronomelike regularity. Ken tightened his grip on her arm, pulled her a little closer to his side. Ingrid smiled. It made her feel protected, despite her being the one who provided the eyes for their walk along the street.

"I don't try to work out the reasons—that's someone else's department," she went on, after pressing the walk button. "My task is to try to alleviate some of the results of the problems."

"I'm sure you're too polite to say it, but you do mean abuse and neglect, don't you? Damn, but I hate people who hurt their kids! If anybody should be jailed, it's a guy—or woman—who abuses a little child."

Ingrid was touched by his ferocity on behalf of her kids. "Most of the time it has nothing to do with either, at least not purposeful mishandling of the child. It's usually the parents who've sought help, often on the advice of a physician."

The light changed. The cuckoo bird spoke, and Ken and Ingrid stepped off the curb as one. "Each of my kids has someone who cares deeply about them, or they wouldn't have been referred."

Ken liked the way she called them "my kids." They certainly did have someone who cared deeply about them. Her. That love and caring rang out in her voice.

He wondered if she'd wanted children with her husband, and why they'd had none. He wondered if she still wanted children, or did the kids in her day care compensate?

He wondered why he was wondering, given his present circumstances.

Hell, one minute he was so full of himself, he thought he could take on the world and win, and the next he was tumbling headlong down a flight of stairs into foul reality. That reality was that he couldn't see. He couldn't do his job. He couldn't earn a decent living.

What kind of catch did that make him? And what reason did he have even to assume Ingrid was fishing? Except for those delicious, wanton kisses of hers . . .

"What can you do with a child who's withdrawn?" he asked quickly, before his mind could take him off on a tangent best left unexplored for now. "Or one who, as you put it, 'acts out.' Is that what used to be called acting up?"

She laughed. "Yes." She went on to tell him of the many different ways they had of achieving their goals for the children in the day care.

After a couple of blocks she drew him to a halt outside a building from which emanated tantalizing aromas.

"There's a little coffee shop here," she said. "It serves the best old-fashioned English-style fish and chips on the coast. We can eat inside, or order to go and take it about half a block to sit in a park. If you don't want fish and chips, there are other things." She started to read him the menu off the wall by the door, but he stopped her after only a few items.

"Fish and chips sounds good to me, and so does the park." If he avoided ketchup, fish and chips would leave his clothing socially acceptable after eating. And in a park any bits he dropped could be seen as a favor for the ants.

He pulled out his wallet, extracted a twenty, and added, "But only if you let me buy. I invited you. I'll wait out here."

"Thanks," Ingrid said, readily taking his money, making him feel ten feet tall, making him feel like some kind of stud, taking his girl out for lunch. Making him feel in charge of his life, like a man who could accomplish anything.

Such as discovering where those hot kisses they had already shared were going to lead. It was a discovery he planned to make very, very soon. A guy didn't need sight for that.

EIGHT

Ken brushed the crumbs of crisp batter off his chest, wrapped his arms around Ingrid, and drew her back between his legs. He leaned on a tree, resting his chin on the top of her head.

"The sun feels good," he said, though they were in the shade. "And this"—he squeezed her lightly—"feels better."

"Mmm," she said. They both fell silent, each feeling the other breathe, both happy simply to sit in the shade and be together.

"What are you thinking?" she asked presently.

"That this is the best second date I've ever had." His breath tickled her ear. "What were you thinking?"

"Much the same kind of thoughts." She hesitated for a moment, then added, "And that I wish I didn't have to leave."

"But you do."

"Not right away." She lifted her head and a languid arm and glanced at her watch. "Twenty minutes."

"Then for twenty minutes don't think about it. Just rest and let me worry about the time. Haven't you ever heard of my famous time sense?"

She hadn't, but leaned back at his urging, resting her head on his shoulder. He cradled her face for a moment, then his hand slipped from her cheek to the side of her neck, over a shoulder half bared by her peasant blouse. She quivered.

"Shhh, relax," he said. "You're much too tense. Feel the peace." He stroked her hair back from her ear. "Listen to the soft, gentle cooing of the doves."

"I hate to break your bubble, but those are pigeons."

"Who's doing this, you or me? Pigeons won't relax you. Doves will."

She curled her legs up, tucking her feet under her full cotton skirt. "Not if they peck my toes."

"I won't let them peck your toes. Haven't you ever heard of my famous pecking-pigeon sensor either? I must say, you're woefully ill informed. I'll have to make sure you read the manual. But in the meantime lean back, relax, close your eyes, and drift. Absorb the warmth." He smoothed the hem of her skirt back several inches above her left knee, his palm hot on her already warm skin. She jumped.

"Relax. . . ."

She pushed his hand away and tugged her skirt down. "Then stop that," she hissed. "There are a hundred other people in this park."

There were maybe twenty, tops, and none were looking, but still. . . .

He laughed softly, close to her ear. "Sorry. I forgot about the shyness factor. Okay. Now, let's get serious about this relaxation thing." He stroked her throat. "That's it, lean your head back." He massaged her upper arms. "Let your shoulders go loose, your arms, your hands, all your muscles." He worked his way out to her fingertips. "Loose, soft, relaxed. . . ."

Ingrid tried. Bees buzzed around the daisies on the grass. Pigeons pecked and cooed. Other people chatted, strolled by, sat on benches in groups or alone, enjoying the small park. The soporific warmth, Ken's quiet voice, the steady, slow caresses of his hands as they roved over her arms, her shoulders, her hair; brushed against her waist then over her stomach, just under her breasts, should have seduced Ingrid into rest, if not sleep. But they did not.

If only he hadn't wrapped his big hand over her thigh like that, so hot and hard and . . . She gulped. If only he hadn't commented that this was the best "second date" he'd ever had. She couldn't get the touch, or the words, out of her mind. The words *second date* had reminded her forcibly of their first one, and the excesses she'd indulged in. His words had put the idea of third and subsequent dates right up front, and she couldn't stop thinking about how it would be, what would happen, when it would happen, where.

Her heart rate increased as she thought about it, wanting it, wanting him. She felt the heat of his palms on her arms and "absorbed the warmth." She tried to hear the "gentle cooing of the doves" and heard instead his heartbeat. She tried to "feel the peace," but what she felt was a growing restlessness within. Want. Desire. Need.

She tingled. She ached with yearning. She wished they were alone. She wished his hands were on her skin . . . all over her skin. She wanted to turn within the circle of his arms and legs, unbutton his shirt, and press her breasts to his chest, to ease the piercing need of her nipples to be caressed. This was terrible. He was trying to help her relax, and she was lusting after him!

She sighed, changed positions, and came up hard against solid proof that she wasn't the only one suffering from lust. She jerked away.

Ken chuckled and moved her back where she'd been. "What's the matter? Don't you like the things you do to me? I like them, Ingrid."

"I didn't do anything," she protested. "I was almost asleep."

He laughed again, and she knew he didn't believe her lie. "What were you feeling, Ingrid?"

"I . . ." She tried to lift her head, but he pressed it back down.

"Tell me," he said. "You know I'm aroused. Aren't you? Even a little bit?"

She was glad he couldn't see her. It made it easier to say, "Yes. A . . . lot."

"Does it feel bad?" he asked, his fingers fluttering across her shoulder, then slipping under the elastic of her blouse. "Or good?"

She released a tremulous breath and caught his hand, stilling it. "It feels good. Even though I know it's not going anywhere, it feels good."

"It feels good to me too."

He bent one leg, half turned her, nestled her more closely to him. Ingrid murmured a worried lament about fairness to him, about women—never men—having the name of "tease."

"Don't worry about it," he said, and to her amazement, as he touched her again, stroking all the way from her earlobe to her fingertips, she didn't.

If she could enjoy the sensuous pleasures of being slowly, inexorably aroused, though she knew there'd be no outlet for that arousal, couldn't he? He could, it seemed. And did.

He stroked her hair, the side of her face. She sighed again, her cheek against his shirtsleeve. It smelled fresh and masculine. She heard the steady *lub-dub*, *lub-dub*, *lub-dub* of his heart. She felt wonderful, with her right hand curled over his knee, her back tucked up inside his bent leg, her head on his chest, and his arm around her.

She felt aroused, yes, but she felt . . . cherished too. He was the only man who had ever made her feel both at the same time, the only man who had ever made her feel cherished at any time.

She opened her eyes, and the world looked golden. The air seemed effervescent, sparkling with newness. Heaven help her, she was falling in love with him. Or had she already fallen in love and was only just now recognizing what had happened?

Suddenly her throat was tight with tears. The backs of her eyes stung as she squeezed them shut again. She wished this could go on forever, but knew that it couldn't. In the end there would be . . . the end.

She sat erect and, using his knee as a lever, pushed herself away. She rose to her feet, looking down at him.

He held out a hand. "Hey, come back." His sexy smile belied the laziness of his position.

She didn't look at her watch. "Your time sense must be off. I have to get back to work now."

He grinned and tucked his hands behind his head as

he stretched out his legs. "My time sense is fine, and I think we still have at least another ten minutes."

She checked. "Seven," she said, then wished she hadn't confirmed his guess that their time wasn't up.

He laughed. "So call me a liar for three minutes."

She poked his ankle with her toe. "Just for that I should leave you here."

"Go ahead." He slumped a few inches farther down the tree, still grinning. He looked as if he should have a straw hat tilted over his brow and a piece of grass in the corner of his mouth. "I wouldn't be the first man to spend the afternoon napping in a park with a bottle of wine in my elbow."

She laughed. "Especially not this park, but sadly I left your bottle of wine back at the church." She reached down and took one of his hands, dragging it from behind his head. "Come on, you can have a nap with my five little ones, but now I have to get back. Jennifer and Carol need to leave in fifteen minutes to take the other six to kindergarten."

Ken rose reluctantly. Ingrid handed him his cane. "How long does it take them to do that?" he asked. How much time would he and Ingrid have alone, with the younger children nicely bedded down?

"I'm not sure. They don't come back afterward," Ingrid said as they struck out across the grass behind Ken's red-tipped swinging cane. "Carol's a lunch-mom volunteer, and Jenny works part-time unless we have more than the five tinies staying late. I can handle the five alone until their parents pick them up."

"Ah, but can you handle me along with them?"

His devilish smile caught at the edges of her heart. "Certainly." She kept her tone brisk. "I have a perfectly adequate bad-boy chair. If you're not careful, you'll spend the entire afternoon in it."

She loved the sound of his laughter, loved the way his hand wrapped more tightly around her upper arm, the backs of his fingers pressing into the side of her breast. She loved, too, the way his hair curled over his ears, the way his mouth quirked up at both corners when he smiled down at her, as if sensing that her gaze was on him.

Oh, Lord, how she loved him! The intensity of it made her feel almost sick. Where had it come from, this vast well of love for a man she hardly knew?

Except . . . she felt she knew him as intimately as if they'd been together for twenty years.

It must be something in the Ransom genes. She'd had this same kind of instant rapport with his sister.

But what she felt for Janet had nothing on the emotions she had tied up in Ken. She stumbled over a broken slab of sidewalk, and he caught her. He held her until she was steady, then wrapped his arm around her as if he would steer her around obstacles in their path.

She took his arm and tucked his hand back around her elbow. It was safer for him that they walk thus.

And it would be safer for both of them if she suppressed all these wild emotions, never let him know the degree of her heart's involvement, because there were moments when she suspected he was beginning to share it, the emotion, not merely the lust.

Was a love destined to die soon worth pursuing? For either of them?

But what about its being better to have loved and lost than never to have loved?

She shook her head. No. She'd loved. And she'd

lost. The pain had been terrible. The pain of losing Ken would be unbearable if she ever had him in all the ways the term *to have* implied.

Yet questions nagged at her. Had she ever felt quite this way about Ron? No. This was different, deeper. Wouldn't giving this kind of feeling free rein, filling herself with it, allowing it to overflow until it flooded her entire world, give her something precious to remember in the days when it was gone?

Oh, God, but she wanted it. She sighed without meaning to as she pushed open the gate in the church fence. Naturally he noticed.

"Tired?" he asked.

It was as good an excuse as any. "A bit."

He drew her closer to his side and said in his deepest, sexiest voice, the one that never failed to pop goose bumps up all over her, "That's because you let me keep you awake too late talking on the phone. Why don't we both take a nap while your students sleep?"

They turned the corner and were in the quiet of the churchyard. She tried a sultry voice of her own. "With or without the bottle of wine?"

He laughed, and she nearly got lost again in looking at his face, in hearing the sound of his laughter rise toward the blue sky.

No! Stop it, Ingrid. Sternly she said, "During naptime, I do paperwork. You can sit in a corner and think about what you want to teach the children this afternoon."

"Yes, ma'am," he said, his devilish grin at odds with his meek tone. "Or, who knows, maybe they'll teach me something instead."

He pulled her to a halt and let go of her arm. Putting his hands on her hips, he brought her tightly to him, their thighs aligned, her breasts against his chest, his lips light and seeking at the corner of her mouth. "Or maybe you will, hmm?"

Ingrid sighed and turned into his kiss.

It was, after all, exactly what she wanted.

"Come up for a while?" Ken asked as Ingrid stopped in front of his building.

She hesitated. "I . . . no, Ken. I should get home."

It wasn't what she wanted to say. It wasn't what she wanted to do, but how much self-indulgence could she permit herself in one day? She'd had lunch with him. They'd indulged in secret foreplay in front of a passing audience in the park. He'd kissed her weak and witless in the churchyard, where anyone—even Father Ralph— could have come along and seen them.

She'd kept him with her all afternoon and reveled in the different nuances of his tones, in the rapidly changing expressions on his mobile face, his silliness with the kids, and the warm, intimate smiles he saved especially for her.

But enough was enough. She had to be sensible, ration out the pleasure, not take it all in one gulp, all in one day.

He touched her wrist where it lay draped over the wheel and used it as a guide to find his way up to her shoulder. He slid his hand around her nape, under her braid.

"No pressures, Inky," he said. "Not even any kisses, if you want it that way. I just don't want our day to be over yet."

Neither did she, but she still shook her head. She loved that he'd picked up on the kids' nickname for her and started calling her Inky. She'd have loved, too, to spend the rest of the evening hearing him call her that. Or anything else. And taking all the kisses he wanted to share with her, feeling them get out of hand, *letting* them get out of hand.

But . . . "I'll call you later, okay?"

Reluctantly he slid his hand out from under her braid, down her arm, and off her fingertips. "Okay. If that's the way it has to—"

"Ken!" They both jerked around at the sound of the eager voice. "And . . . Ingrid, isn't it?"

Maddie didn't sound so eager about that.

Ingrid nodded and murmured a polite hello.

"Nice car," Maddie said, running her fingers along the bright red paint until they came to rest against Ken's shoulder. "Is it yours, Ken?"

"Mine?" He laughed. "It's Ingrid's."

"Oh. It doesn't look like an Ingrid kind of car." She smiled at him, ignoring Ingrid. "It looks like a Ken kind of car. I thought you'd just . . . let her drive it, you know, for now."

It was obvious to Ingrid that Maddie knew Ken's blindness might be only temporary. Just as obviously she could see herself sitting behind the wheel of the Miata a lot better than Ingrid did.

She flicked Ingrid a lukewarm smile. "I saw you dropping Ken off on Sunday too. I was surprised to see you made him find his own way inside."

A spurt of anger at the implication of neglect allowed Ingrid to say, "Ken's quite competent."

Maddie patted his shoulder. "Of course. I know that."

Ingrid's hand curled into claws. Her eyes felt as if they were bugging out when Maddie rested her hand on the back of Ken's neck and said, with a husky little laugh, "I got the wrong impression the other day, that you two lived together."

"N-no," Ingrid said before Ken could speak. "I live in W-West V-v-v—" She broke off, her mouth working as she tried desperately to finish the word "Vancouver." She never got a chance.

"How nice," Maddie said with a dismissive smile as she opened the passenger door, taking Ken's elbow in her hand. "Let me help you, Ken," she said tenderly, as if he were an invalid and she his loving nurse. "I'll see you get inside safely. We wouldn't want to keep Ingrid hanging around in the no-parking zone too long. I'm told the cops tow cars left here. Especially if a tenant complains."

Her smile told Ingrid that if she stopped there again, for sure one tenant would complain.

"Besides," Maddie went on as Ken fumbled with his cane, with the wine bottle he'd carried all the way from the church, "with the distance she has to travel, it'll take her forever to get home through rush-hour traffic." She tried to take the wine bottle. He tucked it under his left arm, out of her reach.

"Are you all ready for the barbecue this evening?" she went on. "The grapevine has it that Jake Smythe caught a twenty-three-pound spring salmon and has invited everyone in the building to share it."

She slid another glance over Ingrid and made a little moue of fake regret. "Sorry, tenants only. No guests this time."

Ingrid clenched her teeth, glared at the statuesque blonde, then leaned over and linked her right arm around Ken's neck. She pulled him back around to face her and planted a kiss square on his mouth. She felt his splutter of surprise—or maybe of laughter—against her lips, but then he responded to her kiss with all-out enthusiasm. In seconds he'd made it his kiss, their kiss, breaking away only when she pushed her hands against his chest. They both were breathing hard.

She gazed into his blind eyes, amazed to see that they looked as dazed as she was sure hers did. She stroked his cheek and spoke, keeping her gaze focused on him, willing her stubborn tongue to forget Maddie's presence. "I'll be back just as soon as I can, honey, with the French bread."

She picked up the bottle of wine that had, during their kiss, rolled to between her feet. "Leave the wine with me, though. I'll bring it in when I come back. S-see you upstairs. Get that casserole warmed up, okay?"

"You betcha," he said. Holding her face between her hands, he rubbed the tip of his nose against the tip of hers. "Don't be long, sweet." He grinned at her. "And the casserole isn't all that'll be warmed up."

She sighed and kissed him again before reluctantly letting him go. Then, over his shoulder, she smiled sweetly at Maddie.

"You won't be coming to the barbecue, then?" Maddie asked as Ken got out of the car.

"No," he said. He turned toward Ingrid with another grin that settled right into her heart and made it swell. "Inky and I have other fish to fry."

As she knocked on Ken's door, Ingrid was still gloating over the way Maddie had stomped off earlier, leaving Ken to find his own way into the building.

He jerked the door open as if he'd been standing right beside it, waiting, and swung his hand until he caught her arm. He pulled her inside and shut the door, leaned back on it, and dragged her into his arms.

He kissed her until her head spun. He kissed her until she dropped the bottle of wine. He kissed her until she was limp against him, clinging to his neck with one arm, and making soft, mewling sounds deep in her throat.

He kissed her face, nuzzled the soft skin under her ears, and nibbled at the tendons in her throat. He slid the shoulder of her peasant blouse aside, along with a bra strap, and kissed every inch of her right shoulder before doing the same to the left. He undid the ribbon that held the end of her braid and slid his fingers through the twists of hair until it hung loose and wild around her head, then he kissed her mouth again, deeply, sweetly, loving her with his tongue.

"Stop, stop," she gasped finally. "Let me go. Let me breathe. You're squishing the bread."

He laughed as he let her have about six inches of breathing room, but did not let her go. "Bread? I thought those were your breasts."

"Hah! I should be so lucky. I never felt inadequate in that department until I met Maddie."

Ken squeezed the bread with both hands and looked shocked. "You mean you're *not* Maddie? Oh, excuse me, miss. I've made a terrible mistake. I'm blind, you see."

Ingrid laughed. "For that I should leave right this minute and stop by her apartment to tell her I'm gone." She dropped the ruined bread to the floor beside the wine.

He caught her before she could leave him, and held her with a tenderness that made her eyes burn. Pressing her cheek to his chest, he rested the side of his face on the top of her head. "Ingrid . . . I seem to be saying it all the time, but thanks, honey." He chuckled. "I love it when you rescue me."

She leaned her head back and smiled at him. "What a fake you are. You needed no rescuing."

"No?" he asked, amused. "Then why did you do it?"

Ingrid moved out of his arms. She wished he hadn't asked the question. She wished she didn't know the answer. She hadn't been rescuing so much as protecting what was her own. Maddie had been trying to move in. All she'd done was indicate there was no room.

To her relief he let it go. In the kitchen the microwave oven beeped.

"I did as you suggested," he said. "I started to thaw a casserole. I don't know what it is, I don't know how long it'll take, and I don't know if you came back because you wanted to or because you thought you should—in case Maddie was watching. But whatever is in the oven, and whatever your reasons for being here, I'm happy to share it with you, and I'm glad you came."

Ingrid bent and scooped up the wine and bread, then touched him on her way by into the kitchen. He followed her.

"I can probably figure out what you're cooking," she said over her shoulder, "if you really want to know."

She set the bread on the counter, put the wine in the refrigerator, and looked at the wrappings he'd taken off the casserole dish. "It says 'Broccoli and beef with steam-fried noodles.' "

He leaned on the counter, crossing his arms over his chest. He looked not at her, but at a spot on the floor between her and the stove.

"What do you think?" he said. "Will you like it?"

"Probably," she replied, moving closer to him. "But that's not the point." She stroked his crossed arms with both her hands, bringing them apart.

They folded around her when she stepped in close. "What is the point?" he asked.

"The point is, I came back, not for your casserole but because this is where I want to be. With you."

He closed his eyes and rocked her from side to side.

"Ingrid." His voice sounded strained. "I don't want broccoli-beef casserole. I want to make love with you. Now."

She waited a beat until her throat permitted her to speak, then said softly, "Yes. I want you, too, Ken. Now."

Kisses took the place of oxygen. Murmured words, heady sensations, mutual need seemed to waft them toward his bedroom.

Standing beside the bed, Ingrid slid his shirt off, then kissed his chest, his hardened nipples. He lifted her head and tugged her peasant blouse down over her shoulders to her waist, pinning her arms until she worked them free. His teeth raked her collarbone, then he bent lower, nudging aside her bra. She reached between her breasts, opened its front closure, and shrugged out of it, then drew his hands up to cup her.

With a moan of pleasure he kissed her throat, he kissed the undersides of her breasts, he kissed her nipples, making her sigh with wanting more. He slid her skirt, slip, and blouse down over her hips. She stepped out of them as she unfastened his belt. After sliding his zipper down, she eased his jeans over his hips, underwear along with them, then stepped back.

"What are you doing?" His voice was rough.

"Looking at you."

He kicked out of his jeans and underwear, then stripped off his shoes and socks. Then he stood there for her, a sliver of light slicing in through a crack in the drapes, gilding one side of his face, his shoulder, arm, and hip. She wanted to throw open the curtains on the corner windows, flood the room with light, but stood mesmerized by his body, which seemed cast in bronze shadows and golden light.

"You like what you see?" he asked hoarsely.

"Yes." The word was inadequate. He was spectacular. Fully aroused, his face dark with desire, his eyes glittering green through half-shuttered lids, he was beautiful. His hair, rough and untidy from her hands, looked almost black in the dim room. His shoulders dropped squarely into powerful arms, arms whose muscles flexed as he stepped to her, lifted her, and laid her on his bed, then knelt astride her.

He bent forward, kissed her mouth, then each of her breasts. "I wish I could see you."

She took his hands and placed them on her face. "Then look at me," she whispered.

His hands shook as slowly, tenderly, he "looked."

He touched her face as he had that day on the boat. He stroked her throat, trailed his fingers over her shoulders and down her breasts. His hands spread as they spanned her waist.

"Your skin is so smooth," he said, lovingly discovering the flare of her hips, the curve of her thighs as he drew her bikini panties down and off. He pressed his face between her breasts, inhaling. "You smell like a flower garden."

Ingrid quivered as he gently parted her legs, his fingers sliding through her pubic hair. A jolt of pleasure sent a spasm through her. He smiled and stopped the caress. She made a soft sound of protest, but he murmured an assurance that he'd never forget she liked that. He simply wanted to know all the other things she liked.

He lifted her left leg, bending it at the knee, and traced its length from thigh to ankle, then back up. Placing her foot on his leg, he stroked each of her toes, then laid her leg flat again. He drew the other one up and learned its textures and contours, each of the sensitive areas where his touches made her shudder, elicited soft sounds of delight.

He sank back on his haunches between her legs, caressing her from her knees to her hips. He stroked both hands up over her waist, her breasts, her shoulders, and down her arms, learning her body in intimate detail. Lifting her hands, he leaned forward and kissed each palm, stroked between each finger with his tongue.

"You're so silent," he said. He cupped her breasts, thumbs pressing nipples. "Do you like what I'm doing?"

"Yes . . ." She could scarcely manage the whisper.

"Just that?" He rolled her nipples between thumbs and forefingers. "Or everything?"

"Ken . . ." She groaned as he tugged gently. "I like . . . I want . . . everything you do. Just hurry and finish 'looking' at me. Please."

He chuckled. "I can't hurry this. I like what I see too much to want to rush."

She ran her gaze lovingly over his body, his shoulders, his chest, his strong, brown legs between hers, and

the evidence of his desire. A small pearly bead moistened the tip of his erection. She touched it, but he
jerked away.

"Not yet," he said roughly, dropping down to cover
her with his body. He held her wrists in the manacles of
his fingers, his breathing as erratic as her own until he
regained control of himself.

"I like what I see too," she said, raking her nails across
his back the second he let her hands go free. "I want to
touch."

He rose up again and took her mouth in a deep,
thrilling kiss. "If you touch me there, sweet, I won't be
able to look my fill. And I want that. So much."

"Then look," she said, cradling his face in her hands.
"Look all you like."

He continued. Ingrid suppressed her sighs, suppressed
her moans of pleasure. She could not suppress, however,
the involuntary shudders that shook her at each new
discovery he made.

She writhed. She quivered. It was too much. She
couldn't stand it. But, like the different, gentle arousal
they had shared in the park, this also felt too good
to stop.

She clenched her fists, curled her toes, and sighed as
she gave Ken this time to learn with his hands what his
eyes could not tell him.

He discovered every small curve, every warm depression of her body with the same thoroughness he'd
learned about her and her life during their nighttime
telephone talks.

He concentrated long on her breasts, molding their
twin shapes, memorizing them, teasing their tips to
almost agonizing hardness with fingers and thumbs.

She ached for his lips, for his tongue, but he denied them both that pleasure. He picked up her legs again, bent them, and slid them with slow, sensuous movements in between his again, then he turned her onto her stomach.

Her sensitized breasts pressed against the cool satin of his blue bedspread. He stroked her back with the flat of his hands from shoulder to waist. Her skin burned in the wake of his caresses as he followed the indent of her waist, the curve of her hips, and the mounds of her backside.

"Beautiful," he murmured, and stroked down her thighs to the sensitive areas behind her knees. She sighed as he lingered there, then moaned as his touch ascended, one finger taking a short side trip between her legs. Her hips bucked, and she gasped.

"I didn't forget and I'll be back." The promise in the murmured words sent new spasms through her.

He measured the width of her shoulders, spent long minutes counting her vertebrae, brushed her hair aside and kissed the nape of her neck, then the points of her shoulders, then her elbows. Her breath came faster and faster, her body quivering at each new feeling.

Sensation tumbled over sensation. Need grew, doubled and redoubled. Again he made that slow, tantalizing pass between her legs and she tried to roll over, needing him. He held her in position, bent and nibbled at the backs of her knees, nipped the soles of her feet, then the cheeks of her bottom.

Her hips bucked again, and he took the opportunity to slide a hand under her, touching her, teasing her, caressing in just the right way as she squirmed and parted her legs for him.

She thought she'd go mad before he turned her to her back again. He slid his palms down over her breasts, her abdomen, her thighs. He took her feet and placed them on his own thighs, palms pressing until her legs fell apart.

Her head came up. "Ken . . ."

"Shhh. Let me," he whispered.

Her legs quivered as his thumbs parted her hair. She sucked in a harsh breath as he delicately separated the moist, hot folds of her flesh, probing with one finger, holding her open with the others. His face was intent, his head slightly back, his unfocused gaze on the wall over the headboard.

Though she knew he couldn't see her with her legs spread in abandon, never had Ingrid felt more exposed. And never had she felt more adored. Had he been able to see and asked this of her, she knew she could not have refused.

He stopped only when her breath started to come in short, labored spurts.

"Hurry," she gasped, writhing against the stilling hand he cupped over her sex. "Ken . . . Ken, I need you now!"

"Oh, yes," he said, his mouth halfway between her breasts and her navel, that one finger moving again, in a slow, sensual rhythm that made her sob aloud. He withdrew, inserted two fingers, mimicking the act she craved with greater and greater intensity.

"So hot, my sweet. So wet. So ready for me."

"Yes!" she said raggedly, her hips heaving. If he didn't stop, it was . . . going . . . to . . . be . . . too . . . late!

"You can be more ready," he said, but Ingrid had had enough of his teasing.

She snapped her legs closed, pinning his hand as he laughed in delight.

She surprised him then by squirming out of his grasp. In trying to catch her he tilted sideways and lost his balance. He shook his head, not sure what had happened or where she was, and got back to his knees on the unsteady surface of the bed.

Her sexy laugh, the brush of her fingertips over his lower belly, tempted him to find her as she escaped.

NINE

"Torture me, will you!" Ingrid said, this time raking her nails down his back. He spun awkwardly, still on his knees, but she was gone.

"Ingrid . . ."

She laughed, a hot, breathless sound that he couldn't pinpoint, then she was upon him, her arms around his waist. She pinned his own arms to his sides, then her mouth was hot and wet on one nipple. He went rigid as she sucked on him. She bit him, and he groaned, trying to break free without hurting her. She let him go and disappeared so unexpectedly, he was unprepared.

"Come back here," he said, sweeping an arm across the wide expanse of the bed.

"Why?" she said. "Are you ready too?" She laughed breathlessly again as she challenged, "Come and find me, then, lover."

"Hey, you're not playing fair," he said, feeling her roll away.

"And you were?"

He knew she was off the bed, but where? He got unsteadily to his feet, turning in the direction he thought she'd run. He groped for her.

Suddenly she knocked him flat right back on the bed. With a crow of triumph she straddled him, planting her warm, firm fanny on his most sensitive area, and began to dole out a kind of agony—and delight—he'd never experienced before.

She wriggled on him. She lay forward and kissed him, her tongue bold and aggressive, her thighs quivering as she held them rigid against his attempts to lift her. She tucked her toes under his legs and continued to kiss him until he brought his arms up around her back, one hand cradling her head, fingers sliding through her thick hair.

He nearly got control of the kiss, nearly managed to roll her to her back, but she broke her mouth away and tightened her legs around him, rendering him helpless again. She pinned his arms to the bed, as he had hers, and slithered down a few inches, her weight and heat adding to his torment. Her hard nipples teased the flesh of his stomach until he groaned and begged for mercy.

"Oh, no," she said, lifting her head. "Remember? It's my turn. I'm going to pretend I'm blind. I'm looking at you."

"No fair," he protested. "I looked with my hands, not my mouth, my tongue. . . . Oh, God, Ingrid! *This* is *shy*? Baby, baby, stop!"

"Never." She sucked on his earlobes, nipped his throat, raked her teeth over his shoulder, then bit him so hard, he stung, but loved it. "You used more than your hands," she said.

"Mostly . . . mostly I just used hands."

"Too bad. You look your way, I'll look mine," she murmured, and continued to "look."

He wrapped his hands around the backs of her thighs and tried again to lift her, to position her over him for his thrust, which must come soon, but she wasn't done.

"Sweetheart, Ingrid . . ." His hips rose and fell quickly under her. "Come to me. Ingrid. Please, love. I need you!"

"Good." Her voice was low, husky, breathless. "Need me more."

Her thighs locked around his hips. Her strength grew as his diminished and she continued to torture him. Her hair got in his mouth, in his lashes, in his ears. He caught her head in both hands and pushed her hair back from her face, feeling her cheeks work as she sucked on his nipples.

He gave up. Why fight it? He loved what she was doing. He loved her weight on him. He loved the little growling sounds she made as she slid farther down his body. Her breasts, sweet and firm, straddled his erection as she lay over him, her waist between his legs.

He groaned as he thrust upward between the warm, soft mounds. She pressed her arms in close to her sides, squeezing her breasts together, squeezing him between them, and he thought he would black out from the effort of not coming right then. He ached. Sweat poured from him, slicking his skin, slicking hers.

She kissed his belly, kissed his hipbone, causing a spasmodic flexing of his knees.

She slipped deeper between them, flicked the hot, wet tip of her tongue into his navel, but when her seeking mouth grew too close to his surging erection, he grasped her shoulders, turned her onto her back, and wrested control from her.

Ingrid relinquished it eagerly. She cried out as Ken, one hand planted square on her middle, slid away from her. But as she heard him open a drawer, heard it thud to the floor, and felt him leave her entirely, she knew what he was doing.

He growled in frustration as he swept his hand over the carpet, and she leaned over, located what he needed, and gave it to him. He ripped the package open with his teeth, and then together, somehow, they managed to sheathe him.

He flipped her to her back again and entered her, deep, right to the hilt all in one smooth motion.

They both went very still, locked together, feeling waves of pleasure wash over them. She heard his in the guttural growl that ground out of him, felt it in the strained trembling of his body, and knew he must feel hers in the deep quivers of her interior muscles as they clasped him, held him, loved him. Her arms held him. Her legs. Her body. Their mouths locked together, his hands tangled in her hair, their ragged breaths mingled.

Then he slowly pulled back, to the point where she gasped and tightened her legs around him to hold him. He thrust into her as she lifted to receive him. His eyes were open, appearing to be staring into hers, and she saw a smile stretch his mouth as a high, pleasured sound broke from her.

"Yes!" he said, his body rigid. "Yes!"

He pulled back again, then drove into her as she clenched her hands in the taut flesh of his buttocks. Her legs rose high around his waist as together they found a rhythm that grew faster and faster, until all the world was a blur.

I love you. I love you. I love you. The words in her heart kept pace with the lifting and twisting of her body, the pounding of his powerful hips. She tried to tell him, but there was no sound beyond the roaring in her ears. There was nothing but Ken, and his weight, his scent overwhelming her, his deep, splendid penetration of her body and the way her flesh quivered and squeezed in response. She cried out as wave after wave of pure energy grew and crested, until she was immersed in fire. Then, with a roar, it released her, leaving her with soaring, singing blood and shudders of completion.

"Honey . . ." Ken nuzzled her shoulder. "Ingrid."

"Mmm."

"Are you awake?"

"Sort of." She wrapped an arm around his waist, her leg over his, and turned her face to the heat still rising from his chest.

"Are you okay?"

"I think so."

"Did I hurt you?"

"No." She hugged him with all her strength. "Oh, no."

He wiped a hand over her face. "You're crying."

She was surprised to feel the wetness of tears as he spread his damp hand on her shoulder. "Not from pain. Not from sadness either. From . . . the beauty of what we made together."

He said nothing, only kissed her.

When Ken returned from the bathroom moments

later, he found her under the covers, waiting for him. He slid into bed with her, held her, and they basked in a lovely silence interspersed with whispers, kisses, strokes of hands over glowing skin.

Presently they slept.

Ken awoke first and lay listening to Ingrid's steady, quiet breathing. Her head lay pillowed on his arm, while one of her arms was draped over his chest. Their legs meshed together like pieces of a puzzle correctly assembled.

He didn't want to move, but he was starving. His stomach rumbled. Because he'd missed dinner? Or because he'd missed dinner and breakfast? He eased his arm out from under her, replacing it with a pillow as he cradled her face on his palm. Her breathing never lost its sleep rhythm, but she turned to kiss his hand.

Stealthily he disentangled their legs and edged away from her warmth. He hitched himself onto an elbow and fumbled across his bedside table. The lamp rocked and rattled and he swiftly steadied it lest its sound waken her. Finally he located his watch.

The pocket watch Janet had given him flipped open as he pressed the button at the bottom of the case, and he gently touched its hands. Ten-fifteen or thereabouts. But . . . morning or night?

He sat up quickly. Was Ingrid late for work on account of him?

But if it was still night, he wanted to let her sleep. He smiled. He'd worn her out. He stretched, feeling good. She'd worn him out, too, but he was recovering fast. If it was night, he probably wasn't going to let her sleep through all of it.

Edging to the side of the bed, being very careful, very quiet, he sat, swung his legs out, and stood.

All at once he was fighting for balance, flailing, arms windmilling, as his left foot got stuck in a corner of the drawer he'd forgotten was on the floor. He took a hopping step with his right, landed on a pen, which rolled, and sent him flopping onto the bed, his back across Ingrid's legs.

She hitched herself up until his head and shoulders were on her lap, patted his chest, and said, "Who is that?" Her hand moved lower, caressed, encircled. "Oh, it's *you*. Dropping in again?"

He laughed into the hot kiss she pressed to his mouth. "It's fifteen minutes past ten," he said. "I don't know if it's morning or night."

She twiddled her finger in his navel. "There's not much light coming through the drapes, so I guess it's night." She slid her fingers through his chest hair. "What are you doing awake?"

He nibbled up under her breasts. "I'm hungry. We missed dinner. I was trying to be quiet."

She laughed. "I'd hate to hear you if you were trying to make a racket."

He covered her hand with his, wrapping it more tightly, moving it over his hardening flesh. "Since we're both awake anyway . . ."

"*I* wasn't," she said, "until you woke me with your thrashing around. You may, you realize, live to regret it."

Her hand moved of her volition. This time he held it still. "Oh, yeah?"

Her strength surprised him, weakened him again. He let her move her hand as she said, "Oh, yeah . . ."

He turned his head and pressed a kiss to the soft,

scented skin of her belly. "I'll have you know I wasn't thrashing around. I was being very considerate, very stealthy, very quiet so that I wouldn't disturb you until—and unless—I had to. At least till I tripped over the drawer."

She laughed. "And that you did with your usual grace and charm. It was all really quite funny."

He sat erect and knelt over her, his legs astride hers, pinning her lower half under the covers. "You were awake? You were watching me? And you didn't warn me about the drawer?"

She linked her arms around his neck. "Warn you? Are you crazy? I knew *exactly* what would happen! I counted on it. You're back in bed with me, aren't you?"

He tipped backward, slowly, pulling her with him until he lay on his back with her on his front, between his legs. Somehow she'd managed to leave the covers behind. "Is that what you wanted?"

She wriggled against him. "Let's talk about what you want."

"Let's not talk," he murmured against her mouth, and the way she kissed him was all the answer he required.

A long time later, Ken realized he wasn't hungry after all.

This time Ken knocked on the door leading to the day care, instead of crashing against it.

Ingrid opened it. He knew it was she because her light, sweet scent wafted out toward him. All was quiet within.

"What are you doing here?" she whispered.

"Are the kids napping?" he whispered back. She said that they were, and to be quiet, better yet, go away, because she had work to do, but even as she was saying the words, she was pulling him inside the room and shutting the door and backing him up against it, pressing herself tightly to him.

Ken wrapped his arms around her, loving the way she came into his embrace so smoothly, as if she'd spent her whole life doing it, and initiated a kiss guaranteed to boil blood.

"God, but I love this shyness of yours," he muttered before going back for a second helping of the same.

He loved the way she fit so neatly into the hollows of his body, the way her hollows welcomed him. He loved the way her breasts squashed against him, the way her nipples hardened so that he could feel them, the way her breath caught as she hugged him tightly.

"I missed you," he said, straining her closer.

She'd been gone when he awoke that morning, and of course she hadn't been able to leave him a note. She had left him freshly brewed coffee, though, making him feel cared for.

"That's no excuse for interrupting my work," she said, her strong arms wrapped around his neck as she pulled his head down to kiss him again. "I'll have to punish you."

He let her have her way and grinned when she broke free, breathless. "You punish a guy good, teacher."

"I hope you feel properly chastened."

"Well, maybe not yet. Perhaps I should sit in the bad-boy chair—with you on my lap?"

She "punished" him again until he begged for mercy.

"Hey, come on. I risked life and limb and unscrupulous taxi drivers to come and tell you I missed you." He tilted his head to one side. "Is it all right to do it now?"

He heard her smile. "I think you just did."

"I think so, too, but what I had in mind was more along the lines of showing you."

"You just did that as well," she whispered.

"Not me. That was you, showing me."

She sighed and slipped out of his arms. "It was, wasn't it? But anything else will have to wait, because I see Mi-Jung lying there on her pallet looking at us with big, puzzled eyes. I think she's wondering why I'm hugging you and not her."

"Hmmph! Seems to me it was my hugs she wanted yesterday more than yours."

"Come on over to the couch," Ingrid said. "You can make her a lap and tell her a story while I get the juice poured. The others will be awake in moments."

Ken didn't care. He'd gotten what he came for: a fix-up dose of Ingrid's angel voice and devil kisses—in the middle of the day.

The rest of the afternoon grew progressively lively, starting with three-year-old Mikey "acting out" a scene from a book Ingrid had just read. The book had shocked Ken; Mikey's actions more than shocked—they soaked. With Story Time done and Outdoor Activities about to start, Ingrid made the mistake of turning her back as she went to the other side of the room to get the bubble-stuff ready.

That was when Mikey struck. Children shrieked with

laughter, yelling at Mikey that he wasn't a pig, that Mr. Ken wasn't the principal, and Ken realized what the warm, wet stuff streaming across his feet was. Mikey was peeing on him.

Ingrid shouted at Mikey as she saw Ken snatch his feet out of range and realized what was going on. Ken leaped off the couch, and Ingrid swooped toward Mikey, but in doing so, she managed to send a long, snaking stream of bubble soap across the tiles. As Ken started away from Mikey's continued assault, his shoes hit the slime. He skated for ten feet, then sat down hard.

Again the children howled with laughter, as if he were a clown hired for their entertainment. As Ingrid tried to pick him up, her feet went out from under her, and the two of them lay there, winded, children skating around them.

Ken heard Ingrid gasp, felt her try to sit up as she said, "Joanne, no! Don't dump the rest of it ou— Oh, *no!*"

"She dumped it?" Ken asked.

Ingrid sounded resigned. "She dumped it."

The sounds of merriment increased. "Inky, look! It's really, really slippery! Hey, look at me go!"

Ingrid groaned again. "All right, everybody! Take off your shoes and socks."

"I think day care's fun," Ken murmured against her ear as she struggled again to rise. The soapy tiles prevented it. Ken's arms around her waist didn't help much either. His weight pulled her back down. He rolled her to her back, one hand under her French braid, one leg pressing on her. Cool bubble soap soaked the back of her jeans, penetrated her T-shirt.

It scarcely mattered.

Around them five children skated and shrieked. That scarcely mattered either.

"I think having a blind man in to teach the kids is a hell of a good idea," Ken said. "What do you suppose they're learning from this?"

"Why, how to make lemonade of course," Ingrid replied solemnly.

As happened every few minutes when he was with her, either on the phone or in person, Ken found a satisfying laugh climbing up his chest and escaping. "You mean, because life delivered lemons in the form of spilled bubble soap?"

"Yes."

He kissed her, quickly but hard and with a great deal of meaning.

"Is that what you're doing?" she asked in a tight whisper.

"Honey . . ."

Ingrid looked up into his face. It wore an intent expression. His voice was quiet, deep and husky and intimate, as intimate as the erection pressing into her belly. "You're no lemon," he said, easing back from her. "You're a ripe, luscious peach and you taste . . ." He ran his lips over her cheek to her earlobe, nibbled. "Yucch! Like *soap*." He wrinkled his nose in disgust.

Ingrid laughed shakily and slithered out from under him, leaving him to get to his feet on his own. He made his way back to the side of the room through five thousand fast-moving, invisible obstacles.

Feeling like a winner, having gotten there unscathed, he sat down, slipped off his shoes and socks, and joined Ingrid and the children as they skated in the soap.

He thought he could learn to like the taste of soap if it were combined with the taste of Ingrid. He also thought he could learn to make day care with Ingrid a habit, even if kids like Mikey did "act out."

He had a few scenes he intended to act out himself in the very near future.

Half an hour later he sat back, all damp and squishy, and listened as Ingrid and the kids cleaned up, with the promise of snacktime egging them on.

It was good, he mused, just realizing that maybe he did have a future worthy of thought.

A future. And Ingrid?

Ingrid slipped outside with the children just before six o'clock, explaining to Ken that she'd wait for the parents out there while the kids got some fresh air. He thought they'd had plenty of that, after spending most of the afternoon out in the churchyard blowing bubbles, drying off in the sun, and playing horsey, but who was he to say how much fresh air kids needed?

"I'll come with you," he said, but she pushed him back down onto the lumpy sofa where he'd collapsed after returning inside. He'd been the horsey.

"No. You rest. You're not used to this. I'll bring your socks back in when I come."

"My socks are outside?"

"I washed them and hung them on the fence."

He sat erect. "You washed my socks?"

"Of course. None of those in the emergency box looked like they'd fit you. You didn't want to spend the rest of the day in piddly socks, did you?"

He sat back, listening to her chivy the kids along,

matching lunch boxes with owners, pairing off shoes and putting them on small feet. Velcro skritched for what seemed like a solid five minutes. Then, with loud exhortations to one another not to breathe, Ingrid and the kids went up the stairs, leaving Ken with silence.

Silence and peace and sweet, burgeoning joy.

He propped his heels on a Munchkin chair and wiggled his bare toes. Ingrid had washed his socks!

No one had done that for him since he'd left home. Even Ellen, the woman he'd lived with for nearly four years, had never done his laundry. Of course he'd never done hers, either, though he had changed the oil in her car.

But *Ingrid* had washed his socks so he wouldn't have to spend the rest of the day piddly.

He closed his eyes and leaned his head back, feeling his smile grow wider and wider as he contemplated the rest of the day. With Ingrid.

"Now, you look like a contented man," said a male voice.

Ken nodded. "Yeah. Ingrid washed my socks."

"Ahh." There was a chuckle in the voice. "Yes. I can see how her doing that would make a fellow smile in just that way."

Ken jerked upright, snatching his feet off the little chair and slapping them onto the cool tiles. Dammit, he'd been almost asleep. It wasn't fair of the guy, sneaking up on him, startling him so that he blurted out inanities.

"Our Inky's a very special lady," the man went on. "We're all in love with her."

Ken clenched his fists and thrust out his chin in the direction of that voice. "Oh, yeah?"

The man laughed. "I'm Father Ralph," he said. "And you are . . . ? Besides being a friend of Ingrid's, I mean."

Ken relaxed marginally. "Ken Ransom. I'm waiting for her. She's going to drive me home as soon as the children have all been picked up. She's outside if you want to see her now."

In other words, get your business over with and leave, Father. He felt momentary guilt, but not deeply.

Father Ralph's reply was complacent. "It can wait." A spring in the couch squeaked and the far end of the old unit sagged as the priest sat. "Nice to meet you, Mr. Ransom. I came to give Inky a message. One of her volunteers called this afternoon to say that she can't do her session this evening. I know Inky will step into the breach—she always does—so I came to invite her for dinner. She's very fond of seafood, and my housekeeper left a large shrimp salad in the refrigerator. But if she has plans for the evening, I won't tell her that Mrs. Mortowski can't oblige. I'll improvise."

He patted Ken's knee with what felt like a ham-sized hand. "That is, if she has plans?"

It was a do-*you*-know? kind of question.

Ken honestly didn't know if she did or not. But it didn't matter. *He* had plans, and every one of them depended on Ingrid's not stepping into any breaches except the Ingrid-sized one in his life, and not dining on shrimp salad with any priest.

His plans would likely shock a priest right out of his cassock. They depended on Ingrid's driving him home, coming up to his apartment with him, melting into his arms, and letting passion soar.

"Is Mrs. Mortowski a Loving Voices volunteer?" Ken asked, knowing he had to say something. It was rude to sit there mute, contemplating something the priest was forbidden even to consider.

"Loving . . . ? Oh! Er, that's—"

"*Living* Voices. Yeah, I know. Sorry."

"You wouldn't be a volunteer yourself, by chance, would you, Mr. Ransom?" the priest asked hopefully.

Didn't this man know his own volunteer staff? "No." Ken tapped his white cane on the floor and stated what to him was obvious. "I'm blind, Father."

"I see." That the priest clearly did not see what Ken was getting at was evident in his tone. "I believe one or two of the others are as well."

"Are they?" Ken felt an uncharacteristic need to justify himself. "I don't see how they can be. I mean, I couldn't make Lov—Living Voices phone calls. How could I read the files?"

"Files?" The man sounded perplexed.

"The ones you keep on the clients so the various callers have some details about the people they're calling. Ingrid explained to me how it works."

"Oh! Yes. I see. Then you know how important Living Voices is to her. Dear Inky. If she could, she'd adopt every lame duck in the world. As her friend, you'd be willing to help, I'm sure."

"Of course if I could, Father, but . . ." Ken shrugged. "I'm not much good for anything just now. I'm still learning how to be blind." Maybe the other blind volunteers had managed to master Braille, he thought. But would church records be translated? Hell, most good modern fiction wasn't!

"Ahh . . ." The sympathetic sound cut into Ken's thoughts. "Did you lose your sight recently, Mr. Ransom?"

"A few months ago." Defensively he added, "But it could come back any day."

"The waiting can't be easy. May I ask how it happened?"

Ken wasn't sure why he responded. Maybe because the man was a priest, and who could tell a man of God to mind his own business and take a hike? He explained about the collapsed scaffolding.

"How sad. I'm so sorry. Are you a construction worker, Mr. Ransom?"

"No, I'm an—" He felt the familiar tightness constrict his throat, but swallowed it and went on. "I was an architect."

"Was? And what are you now? I mean, what do you do?"

Ken clenched his teeth. "Nothing of course. What can I do?"

"My dear Mr. Ransom, there are any number of things you could do. Become a volunteer, for one. Why, that's exactly what you should do. Think what a help it would be to Ingrid. She has a waiting list of people wanting to have their loved ones on the Living Voices roster, and not nearly enough volunteers.

"That's why she works three nights a week, trying to fit in as many as she can. That girl understands the agony of loneliness. Though you may not be able to see, someone—I, for instance—could tape a series of numbers for you, along with the names of the clients. You can use a touch-tone telephone, can't you?"

"Of course, but—"

The priest clapped his hands before Ken could finish. "Yes! What a fine solution to this evening's problem as well! It would be such a big help to Inky, you know. A chore shared is a chore halved. Then if she does have plans, she can get to them that much faster. I hate to tell her, but I know I must. Living Voices is her baby, and no one should interfere, though as I said, she really does too much. It's hard to get her to take a break. We all rely on her so. And dinner? You'll join us of course."

"I . . . well—"

"Good!" Ken felt the couch shift as the priest heaved himself to his feet. "You'll pass on the message to Inky, won't you please? Meantime I'll go and prepare that tape for you."

Ken thought about it. Sure, why not? As he considered it, he saw some distinct possibilities taking shape— Monday, Wednesday, and Friday evenings as assured hours with Ingrid.

He nodded. "If there are two separate phone lines into the church, yes, of course I could take on part of the list." He smiled. "But I'd have to be on duty at the same time as Ingrid." He tapped the floor with his cane as a reminder of his handicap. "She'd have to pick me up and bring me here. And take me home." He liked that part especially well.

"Oh, I don't think that would work," the priest said worriedly. "She rarely leaves the church between the day care closing and her phone sessions. That's when she does our church office filing, to help out the secretary. But you could do as most of the volunteers, Mr. Ransom, and make your calls from your home."

Ken frowned. "From home? But I thought that wasn't allowed."

"Of course it's allowed. Come, now. These people are volunteers. They can do the job any way they want. Who would dictate to them? Certainly not Inky. She's much too kind for that, and grateful for their help. Indeed most of the volunteers are shut-ins themselves, rarely getting out."

He made a tsk! sound. "I wish we could change that. Though Inky does her best with the get-togethers she organizes four times a year.

"The summer one's coming up in two weeks, Mr. Ransom." His tone was encouraging. "As a volunteer you'd be most welcome to attend, meet some of your Living Voices contacts face-to-face."

"Really?" Ken sat forward, angling his head toward the priest. He could almost hear again Ingrid's refusal when he had first asked to meet her face-to-face. Policy, she had said. Rules. The same had gone for handing out her phone number.

"At these parties I guess, volunteers and clients could even exchange addresses, phone numbers?" he asked the priest.

"Of course, if they haven't already. And they often have. That was Ingrid's sole aim in creating Living Voices—getting lonely people together with other lonely people. Some solid friendships have been cemented at our parties, held in this very room. There's even been one wedding, a seventy-year-old widow and a sixty-eight-year-old widower, both in wheelchairs."

"I see," Ken said, but he didn't.

Hell, he saw nothing. How could he? He was blind. Blind in more ways than one.

"Ingrid started Living Voices?" Ingrid was the one who made all the rules, set what policy existed?

"Yes." Father Ralph went on, "She's made an amazing success of the venture, from its conception, through its execution and its continuation. I often bless the day she came to me with the idea, offering to trade her time and effort in organizing it, coordinating the volunteers, for free rent of this room for her day care."

The rent's right, she'd said. "Ingrid did all that?"

"Oh, all of that and more. She's an amazing young woman, Mr. Ransom, even when one doesn't consider the obstacles she's had to overcome. But as her friend, I'm sure you know that, and know how hard she works. So . . . will you join us?"

Ken hesitated, then put a smile on his face. It felt stiff. "Yes, Father. I'd like to join you. As a volunteer, and for dinner if Ingrid wants to stay."

"Fine, fine." There came the sound of hands rubbing together. "Well, I'll be off to make that tape."

Ingrid opened the outer door at that moment. She blinked at the dimness inside in contrast to the brightness outside. "I'm back, Ken," she said. "Are you ready?"

"Inky, my dear." Father Ralph stepped forward. "I just introduced myself to your friend. We've had a nice chat. I invited you both for dinner. Have you plans for this evening?"

Dismay flooded her. Oh, yes, she had plans. Her "plans" for the evening sat over there on the couch, looking in her direction, his face more grim than welcoming. He got to his feet and strode confidently toward her as if he could see. He seemed to be looking right into her eyes, and his eyes seemed to be filled with questions, with . . . was it anger? Yes. Why? What kind of "chat" had he and Father Ralph had?

"It's shrimp salad, Ingrid," Ken said. He slipped an arm around her, holding her tightly. "Father Ralph says you like seafood. So do I."

Sickeningly aware of Father Ralph's indulgent smile

as he watched the two of them together, Ingrid said, "Y-you do?"

"Oh, yes. Very much. What do you say? I explained that since you're my ride home, I have to be governed by your wants."

The steel of his hand around her shoulder left her feeling that she was governed by him. She wished she could read his enigmatic face. "You w-want to st-st-stay?"

Say no, she begged him silently. *Say that I have to drive you home because you have an important meeting or something, just get me out of this.*

He smiled at her again, a smile that should have been reassuring but wasn't. "Yes, I'd like to stay." His tone lacked all the warmth it usually held. "If you would." Keeping his arm around her as if to prevent her escaping, he steered her, as if she were the blind one, back toward the priest.

As if she were the blind one, Ingrid let him. Her head spun, her heart felt as if it were about to trip her. "Father has a message for you from one of your volunteers," Ken said.

"That can wait," said Father Ralph. "Dinner in half an hour, my dears. Will that give you enough time to finish up down here, Inky?"

She nodded, unwilling—no, unable—to utter a sound. Dinner with Father Ralph and Ken? She couldn't spend the entire dinner in silence, could she? What was she going to do? What was responsible for Ken's odd attitude? What had Father Ralph told him?

"And I have something to tell you too," Ken said. She swung her gaze back to his face. "I'm your newest Loving Voices volunteer."

"Loving Voices," Father Ralph said musingly into Ingrid's stunned silence. "You know, I think maybe I like that better. Hmm, yes, indeed. Loving Voices. It has a certain ring to it."

TEN

Father Ralph's voice faded away. A door closed. Ken let Ingrid go. She watched as he sat down on the sofa and crossed one ankle over his knee. He leaned back, his eyes fixed on her.

"What—what do you mean, *my* newest volunteer?" she said, sinking down onto the little chair nearest the sofa.

"Loving Voices is yours, isn't it? You conceived it, put it to work, made it pay, so to speak, according to Father Ralph. So the volunteers are yours. As are the rules, Ingrid. And the policies. Right?"

"Ken . . ."

"You don't break rules," he said. "You adhere very closely to policies. You don't break promises either. But you do, it seems, tell lies."

She got up, feeling like a penitent child perched on that little chair under his steely, if blind, gaze. It didn't look blind. It looked furious. She stumbled to the other end of the couch. "Lies?" She slumped down, wedging herself into the corner. She pulled a hard plastic horse from behind her and clutched it in her hands.

"Policy," he reminded her. "Rules. You couldn't give me your phone number. You couldn't come and meet me in person. Against the rules. Against policy."

"What difference does it make who made the rules, who set the policy? So I made them. That doesn't make them less valid."

"It does when they apply only to me. As a Loving Voices client, was I going to get an invitation to the summer party, Ingrid? Would I have met you face-to-face then?"

She drew in a deep breath. "You did meet me face-to-face. Or we wouldn't be having this conversation."

"So the lies about rules and policy were to make me feel special when you eventually 'broke' them?"

"No. No," she moaned. "It wasn't like that."

He leaned toward her. "What was it like, Ingrid? Explain it to me. Please."

"I called you as a favor to Janet," she whispered. "I didn't want to, but she has a way of getting what she wants and— Well, I agreed to do it, but I didn't want to meet you in person. So I made up the rules and policy thing so your feelings wouldn't be hurt."

"Ah, yes. You didn't want to meet me. You were prepared to dislike me."

"You were pre—" She broke off. He didn't know he'd been prepared to dislike *her*, to dislike the senator's daughter Janet had wanted him to meet. He didn't know she was that woman. "Yes," she said. "But . . ."

"But?"

She thought his eyes had softened a fraction. It made

it easier to say, "But after we'd talked a few times, I knew I didn't dislike you. But I was . . . still afraid . . ." Her voice trailed away to almost nothing. "Afraid you wouldn't . . . like me once we met."

Ken remembered her telling him about her childhood, being the shy little girl with braces, last to be picked for teams, last to be picked to dance. The little girl who had grown up into a woman whose husband had left her because she didn't meet his standards as an escort at social gatherings.

He couldn't see her, but he could read her misery in her silence, in her strained, shallow breathing. He reached out until he found her. She flinched away from his seeking hand, but he followed, feeling her bent head, the arms she wrapped around herself, knees drawn up as she huddled in the corner of the couch.

Mousie, he thought, stroking her hair. The timid child from a boarding school, sure of nothing in life but rejection. Her husband had rejected her. Had other men? If so, why? Because of that shyness? Had she expected the same thing from him? Because he wasn't a senior citizen, nor really a shut-in, and possibly had only a temporary disability, had she been afraid to meet him for fear that he would walk away from her when—if—things changed?

If those had been her reasons for lying, her reasons for fear, he had to admire her because she had overcome that timidity. She'd reached out to him because his sister had persuaded her he was lonely.

He recalled her saying that the day she came to invite him to go sailing. He of course had denied it. He'd done his share of self-protective lying too.

She had broken her own rule, set aside a self-made

policy, both of which she'd created to protect herself, and come to him because a warm spring Sunday should be shared.

"Ingrid . . . honey, come here."

He gathered her in to him, stilling her attempts to break free. Something poked him in the chest. He took a toy horse from her and dropped it over the arm of the couch.

"I met you, Ingrid," he said, cupping her face in his hands. "I met you and I liked you. I liked you before we ever met in person, and I liked you even more after we did."

He felt tears on her cheeks and kissed them away. "I more than liked you. Baby, I love you."

He heard a gasp of protest, felt her stiffen. "Ken—"

"Be quiet." He placed his fingers over her warm lips. "It's my turn," he said. "When I'm done, you can talk."

She relaxed a trifle and nodded. He moved his fingers, slid them down over her throat and spread them across her shoulder. "Before you came to my house that day, I'd fallen in love with your voice. As soon as I kissed you, I wanted you in every way a man can want a woman—before I even suspected that you were the woman with the angel voice. That the woman in the hallway turned out to be my Ingrid, the real manifestation of a dream I hardly knew I had, stunned me. And before the day was over, I knew I'd fallen in love with you.

"Love wasn't something I was looking for, not something I even welcomed, because I have nothing to offer you, Ingrid. Not even any real hope that things will change." He looped his arms around her loosely so that she could go if she wanted to, and leaned his head back against the couch.

"It will, Ken! Surely it will. Janet said—"

"Janet said what we all hope, what the doctors say should happen. Only . . . it should have happened months ago if it was going to happen at all. That it hasn't is my fault. I don't know how, and I don't know why, but I'm what's preventing my sight from returning."

"No. No. The swelling. When it goes down . . ."

"No." He shook his head. "I know I told you that, but what I didn't tell you is that there was no detectable permanent trauma to my optic nerves. The concussion may have caused temporary swelling in my brain that blocked them for a few days, but then, as near as the doctors can figure, it went down, and I should have been able to see again. Only I didn't.

"They sent me to psychiatrists, who concluded that I can't see because I'm too damned scared I'll never see again."

"That doesn't make any sense."

"It doesn't make any sense because I'm doing it to myself. I have to stop worrying about it. I have to learn to relax, not try so hard to see, but I can't figure out how. I'm an architect. I can't work without sight. I can't be what I've always been. I'm a head case, Ingrid. I'm—"

He broke off. "I don't even know why I'm telling you this, except I want you to know I may never be any better than I am right now. I mean it when I say I have nothing to offer. Except my love."

Ingrid stayed very still for several minutes, then stirred. He let his arms fall away, let her go.

His body felt cold where she had been resting. She rose. He longed to be able to see her, to try to guess from the expression on her face, in her eyes, what she was thinking. Where was she? Why didn't she say something? Had she left him there? Abandoned him?

He started at the touch of her cool fingers on his bare foot.

He sat erect. "What are you doing?"

"You can't go to Father Ralph's for dinner barefoot," she said chidingly, as if he were one of her children. She put a sock over the toes of his right foot and rolled it up to his heel, smoothed it onto his leg, straightened it, and patted the sole of his foot. "Other one, please."

Exasperation made his voice sharp. "Ingrid!"

She clasped his left ankle, put his foot on her thighs, and tugged his other sock on. Then she wiggled his shoe over his toes. He slipped his foot down into it and let her position the other one for him. Sensing she was still crouched before him, he reached down and found her arms. He clamped his hands around them and drew her up as he stood.

"Aren't you going to say anything?" he asked. "About what I told you?"

"I can't believe Father Ralph actually recruited you as a volunteer," she said, her voice high and tense. "But if that's what you want, Ken, I'm all for it. As I'm sure you realize, there is no policy that says calls must be made from the church off—"

He shook her. "Ingrid, I told you I'm in love with you. I also told you the truth about my condition. Either statement deserves a response. What kind I can't dictate. But I want something from you in return. Do you care about me? Do you despise me now that you know the truth? I may not know what the hell's going on in my own head, but I'm damned sure about my heart. And I'd like to know about yours. I'd also like to know what you're thinking. Whatever it is, let me in on it so that we can deal with it together."

He felt a shudder course through her, then she wrapped her arms around his torso and clung to him, her face tucked against his throat. She trembled so hard, he thought she'd fall apart. He held her close, trying to help her keep it together.

"I love you," she moaned. "I love you, Ken, so much! But I'm scared. Oh, God, I'm so damned scared!"

"Because I'm blind?"

"Yes!" She lifted her head, shaking it violently. "I mean, no! Oh, I don't know. Your blindness is part of it, but it might be even worse if you could s— Please, let me go! I can't talk about it. I can't deal with it now!"

She didn't want him to let her go. He knew that because she burrowed closer, her hands splayed on his back, fingers digging in as if she could penetrate his skin, climb inside him, hide from whatever demons pursued her.

He held her, stroking her back, her hair, her cheeks, until he felt her relax, grow calmer.

Lifting her face, he kissed her, not the way he wanted to kiss her, not the way a man should kiss a woman who has just answered his declaration of love with one of her own. He kissed her gently, as if she were a frightened child. He kissed her softly, as if she might break. But he kissed her with all the love growing within him, and felt a responding quiver in her lips.

Breaking free from him, she gave him his cane and pulled his hand under her elbow.

"Father Ralph will be waiting," she said huskily. "Shall we go up to dinner?"

He wondered why she sounded as though they were going to the gallows.

Ken came back to life—minimal life—with Ingrid spread over his body, her hair across his face, her breath fanning his neck. It still shuddered in and out of her in gusty puffs.

He half lifted her until they were no longer so intimately joined, and rolled to one side, carrying her with him. He brushed her hair back from her brow. "I blew it, baby."

Slowly Ingrid lifted her head from his shoulder. She hadn't been ready for conversation yet. "Blew what?" She managed to open her eyes. His were open, too, and his face was etched with concern.

"I forgot to use a condom."

In the fifteen days since they had made love for the first time, he had been scrupulously careful, often to her frustration. Lord, but he got her hot! So hot it was almost impossible to wait.

She smiled and dropped her head back down. "I'm not fertile this week."

He groaned. "You know what they call women who say that, don't you?" Before she could reply, he did it for her. "Mothers, Ingrid. Mothers."

"I have heard that," she said, and hitched herself up, edging away from him. For reasons she couldn't fathom, she dragged up a corner of the tangled spread and tucked it around her breasts, smoothed it over her thighs. "Don't worry. I'd never saddle a man with an unwanted child."

How odd, she mused. In the past two weeks this was

the first time she'd so much as thought of motherhood, even in passing.

It had been enough, loving Ken, knowing he loved her, living for the day—the night.

Somehow he knew exactly where her hands were. He caught them both, pulling them down from where she clasped the spread between her breasts. He tumbled her across his chest and held her there with one hand in the middle of her back. Her hair fell forward over his face. He puffed it away from his mouth, clubbed it behind her neck with his free hand, and kept her face in front of him.

His jaw was square. His eyes held a steely glint. His lips were tight.

"I would not," he said, "repeat, *not* feel 'saddled' with a child if I got you pregnant. If you were to have my baby, I would feel lots of things. Proud, delighted, honored, to name a few. And humbled if you chose to bear my child and be my wife too. But I have nothing to offer a woman, no way to make a living for a family, keep it safe and secure financially. And until I have that—if I ever have that—I choose not to make you pregnant."

Ingrid felt humbled by his words, and ashamed of hers. She drew in an unsteady breath. "Okay," she said.

He rolled her flat on her back and kissed her. When he was done, she felt the rise of his desire against her legs.

"If you ever have the things you think are necessary," she said, "and if you offer to make me pregnant, then . . . I will choose you as the father of my child."

His chest heaved as he pulled in a long breath. "Children," he said. "Plural."

She nodded, and buried her face against his shoulder.

They held each other, lost in their own thoughts, for a long time until Ken spoke again.

"Did we just sort of propose marriage to each other?"

Ingrid whispered, "I think so."

He laughed into her hair. "I wish you didn't sound so scared, honey."

I am scared, she wanted to say, but didn't. If he loved her even half as much as she loved him, wouldn't it be all right, even when he realized the truth about her?

She could scarcely believe that he didn't. Even after that disastrous dinner they'd shared with Father Ralph, he still seemed not to have noticed her stutter. He hadn't found the dinner traumatic at all.

She clenched her teeth hard, recalling it. He and Father Ralph had talked, finding several common interests. Both had tried repeatedly to draw her into the conversation, but she'd been hardly able to force out more than a syllable or two. Finally they'd taken pity on her and allowed her her uncomfortable silence.

"She's tired," Father Ralph had said, excusing her quiet mood. She'd denied it and smiled, but something in Ken's face had chilled her heart. She'd known he was wondering, that he suspected something more was bothering her.

"Maybe she's afraid that you'll tell me all her darkest secrets," he'd said.

"T-terrified," she'd managed to say, and smile, and smile and smile.

But all the rest of that evening, until they were in bed together, she'd held herself rigid, waiting for Ken to accuse her of subterfuge at the very least, and at worst gross misrepresentation of herself. He hadn't, though, and she'd felt even more guilty for not telling him the truth when he had kissed her gently, stroked her hair, and held her close.

"Poor, tired baby," he'd whispered. "I won't keep you awake tonight. Go to sleep. Just let me hold you."

Remembering, she held him tightly, almost desperately.

He lifted himself up and lay full-length on her body. "I love you, Ingrid Bjornsen. I love you more than I have words to tell you."

"So show me," she said, sliding her legs apart and letting his body slip in between.

With a groan of compliance, he proceeded to do so, in fine and exquisite detail.

Ken awoke on a Wednesday morning, knowing even as he did that Ingrid was gone. More and more he hated Mondays, Wednesdays, and Fridays as much as he hated waking to an empty bed. Those days, he knew Ingrid wouldn't be home—home with him, home in his arms—until after nine in the evening. Though he filled those empty hours making the calls Father Ralph had arranged for him to make, he still lived for the nights, and Ingrid.

Actually he filled most of his hours apart from Ingrid making Living Voices calls. When he wasn't doing that, he was busy gaining new volunteers for the organization. The school for the blind had provided twelve; two senior-citizen clubs he'd approached had garnered another sixteen, and out of five clubs for immigrants he'd gotten seven foreign languages represented, with more in the works.

That was something that had been badly needed for

a long time. Often, as people aged, their facility in an adult-learned language diminished, making calls in their mother tongue doubly welcome.

He smiled as he folded his hands behind his head. He'd enjoyed organizing things for Ingrid, getting more callers who could make themselves available in the daytime. The waiting list no longer existed, but as word got around, he was sure it wouldn't take long for more names to be added to it. He was determined that no one would ever have to wait again, or suffer loneliness for want of a friendly voice over the phone.

It might be a challenge, finding and keeping volunteers, but he had the time for it, as well as the energy, and he didn't have a day care to run five days a week, twelve hours a day.

Ingrid said she wished she'd had him five years ago.

He wished he'd had her ten years ago. He wished he had her right that minute.

He lay there with his eyes shut, reliving the night before, anticipating the night to come. He smelled the coffee she had made for him, and breathed deeply, stretching luxuriously. In a minute he'd get up, pour himself a cup of that coffee, and get to work. One thing about his new job, his commute was short. From the bed to the shower to the kitchen for coffee, then to the living room or terrace with the phone and the tapes Father Ralph continued to make for him.

Life was looking up.

A shaft of sunlight spilled across his chest, warm as it came through the drapes Ingrid half opened every morning. The drapes blew in the breeze, sliding the patch of sun up over his face. It burned red against his eyelids.

His eyes stung suddenly. He covered them, and the

burning stopped. He took his hand away and felt the heat of the sun on his lids. He saw—*saw*—that red glow again, felt the burning, felt tears sting.

He lay frozen, hardly daring to hope, then shakily he sat up, turning his face fully to the light. The stinging returned, the red glow intensifying.

He tried to open his eyes, but his lids seemed sealed shut. Tears streamed from between them.

An ache rose between his brows to accompany the sharp pain behind his lids. He groaned, flung a crooked elbow over his eyes, and turned from the light. The pain eased. He breathed again, becoming aware that he hadn't been doing so for very long.

Cautiously he removed his elbow. The pain resumed, the red glow, the tears. He groaned and rolled to the side of the bed, away from the light, then stood and staggered into the bathroom, attacked by vertigo.

There he wiped his streaming eyes with a cold cloth, managed to open them, and saw . . . nothing. He sank to the edge of the tub, burying his face in his hands.

The doorbell rang. Shave-and-a-hair-cut-six-bits. Janet. He grabbed a bath sheet from the rail by the tub, dragged it around him sarong-style, and richocheted off the doorframe as he tried to run. He tripped and reeled, dizziness assailing him at every step. He bounced off every piece of furniture in the room before he got to the door.

He ripped it open, stood swaying as he clung to it. "Jan!"

She grasped his elbows. "Kenny! What's wrong?" She backed him inside, closed the door, and forced him into a chair. "You're so white, you look green. Are you sick?"

"I think . . . I think my sight is coming back. I think you'd better get me to the doctor."

"Oh, Kenny!" she shrieked, and burst into tears as she hugged his neck.

"Hospital?" Ken turned his face toward where the doctor stood beside the examining table. "What the hell for?" He tried to sit up, but the doctor pressed a hand against his shoulder. "I'm not sick, dammit! I'm getting better!"

"Maybe you are. Maybe you're not. You say that several weeks ago you saw that red glow behind your lids when the sun was on your face. I wish you had reported it at once, along with the pain you've experienced at other times. Didn't the doctors back east tell you that?"

"The doctors back east told me I was a nutcase."

"Hmm." The sound was noncommittal. It always was. They stuck together, those physicians.

"Besides," Ken added, "everyone gets headaches and everyone sees red if they face the sun with their eyes closed."

"I know, I know. It's such a commonplace thing, you didn't recognize its significance at the moment."

Ken hadn't. The first time it had happened, he'd been so wrapped up in his awareness of Ingrid as they sailed aboard *Molly Darlin'*, he hadn't given the glow any attention at all. He'd seen the same thing through closed lids a million times before in his life when he lay on a beach. It was only this morning, when the glow became intolerable, that he remembered—and recalled that it hadn't hurt him then.

"You saw it then, but since that time, until this morning, nothing more?" the doctor recapped. He lifted Ken's lid for another look. The clicking sound suggested he'd turned on his ophthalmoscope again. Ken saw nothing.

"The vertigo and eye pain this morning concern me, though," the doctor said, "even more than the ache between your brows. They indicate a greatly increased light sensitivity. Your pupils don't appear to be responding to light at the moment, but clearly they did an hour ago when you awoke. That suggests they will again, and likely in the same painful manner. I want your recovery, if that is what we're getting here, to occur under controlled conditions. So, the hospital it is."

He let Ken sit up slowly, keeping a hand on his back as if afraid the dizziness might return. It didn't. He put a pair of glasses in Ken's hand. "You'll have to wear these, indoors as long as you're in a lighted room, and outdoors at all times until your sight is normal again. They're nearly black and will block out most of the light."

Ken wanted to tell him he wanted the light, wanted it even if he had to suffer pain to see it, but maybe the doctor was right. Controlled conditions might mean a safer, more complete recovery.

"I'll just step out and ask my receptionist to make arrangements to have you admitted. Put the glasses on now, please, so that I can turn on the lights."

Ken put the glasses on, feeling the solid side flaps, the curved extensions on the rims that fit close to his face all the way around like safety goggles.

Recovery! It was a concept he'd hardly dared believe in for over four months. Getting back to work. Having a life again. A life to share. Ingrid! He had to call her, tell her. He couldn't wait.

"It's all arranged," the doctor said, returning. He

checked the fit of the glasses. "Your sister will take you to the ophthalmology department at University Hospital and then go and get whatever you want from your home. I want you out in the sunlight as little as possible, despite the dark glasses. Either you agree to that or I send you by ambulance."

Ken grinned happily. "At this point I'm feeling pretty damned agreeable, Doctor. Jan can get what I need. I won't want much."

"Good. You won't have space for much. Your room will be little more than a windowless cubicle for a while."

"All I'll need is a phone in my room and a place to plug in a tape recorder. I have a big list of calls to take care of today. In the excitement, I nearly forgot."

It would be exciting, too, to share this news with the people on his list. It was amazing how he rejoiced with them, over their happy events, people who, until three or four weeks ago, had been strangers. He had no doubt that each of them would be delighted for him.

"There's no telling how long you'll need to stay," the doctor warned as he ushered Ken out of the office and into the waiting room. "Come prepared for a long haul, though you may be fine in a matter of days, even hours. There's simply no way to predict."

He gave Ken an encouraging pat on the back, and Janet handed him his cane.

"Um, you know that Loving Voices volunteer," he said as Janet drove across town. "The one you asked to call me?"

"Ingrid, yes."

"Could you, uh, give me her number, maybe? I'd like to call and tell her I won't be home for a day or so."

It occurred to him then that at any time in the past month, Ingrid could have given him her number. She never had. It hadn't been necessary. She left his bed every morning and returned to him every evening. Their night talks had been made with their heads on the same pillow.

"I'll let her know for you," Janet said.

Ken clenched his teeth, wanting to insist that he be allowed to tell Ingrid. Because of a tacit agreement the two of them had come to, though, not to admit anyone else into their magic circle, he had to pretend that that was all right.

Ingrid would find out which hospital he was in. Ingrid would come to him. Ingrid would be there when his sight returned, and for the first time his eyes would drink in the beauty his hands and body knew so well and loved.

He rested his head back and smiled, thinking of it, anticipating her joy.

"Inky! How's my favorite miracle worker?"

Janet Ransom bounced into the church office and perched on Ingrid's desk. It was Wednesday afternoon, and Ingrid was about to begin her Living Voices calls. She suppressed a groan at Janet's appearance. She wanted to hurry through her calls and get home to Ken, but knew she owed each of her clients the time they expected, the concentration they were accustomed to her giving.

Though she adored her, she didn't want Janet wasting her time. Nevertheless she smiled as she set down the phone she had just picked up to dial.

"J-Jan," she said. "Wh-wh-what are you d-doing here? I th-th-thought you had a f-f-f—" She broke off.

As Janet waited patiently, her smile never faltering, her wide, affectionate green gaze never sliding away from Ingrid in embarrassment, Ingrid swallowed the tension, relaxed her lips, and substituted *trip* for *flight*. Ken had told her that Janet was flying out that evening, and Janet had also left a message to that effect on Ingrid's machine.

"I did," Janet said, beaming, "but I had to cancel. I dropped in to see my brother on my way out this morning, and ended up taking him to the hospital. He's—"

"Hos—" A wet black cloth seemed to drape in front of Ingrid's eyes. "Hospital?" She heard her voice from afar. "Wh-wh-wha-wha—"

"Ingrid!" Janet's voice echoed strangely. She shook Ingrid, and Ingrid thought her teeth rattled in her slack jaw. She opened her eyes. Janet's eyes were filled with concern. "Are you okay? He's all right, you know. In fact there's a strong possibility his sight's coming back. Sheesh! You shouldn't get so wrapped up in your clients, though since Kenny's my brother, I'm happy to know you care enough to be concerned for him."

"His . . . s-s-sight?" Ingrid felt tears flood her eyes, blinding her. "He can suh-suh-suh—?"

The room spun. *No. No. No.* She wasn't ready for this. It was too soon. She hadn't had enough of all the good things they made together. It couldn't happen. It couldn't be over. He couldn't see her. But . . . his sight. Oh, God, what it meant to him! His sight, his career, his *life* . . .

She buried her face in her arms on the desk and wept.

"Inky . . . Oh, hey, come on." Janet rubbed her back. "Please don't do this. What in the world is there to cry for? I mean, I hate to see you upsetting yourself like this. Come on. . . ." She was beginning to sound desperate. "You'll have to get the award this year for the most 'involved' volunteer."

Ingrid struggled to bring herself under control. "That's just it. I am inv-v-v-volved. W-with Ken." The last was a wail of despair, and she dropped her head down again.

"Involved? What do you mean?"

Ingrid wept harder. Janet dragged her erect, jammed a wad of tissues into her hand. "Now, you cut out that bawling right this minute. Wipe your face and talk to me! What exactly do you mean, 'involved'?"

"I l-love him."

Janet's eyes grew wide. Her mouth made a round O of dawning hope. "What, exactly, do you mean, 'love'?"

Ingrid could only look at her, but her expression must have said it all. Janet let out a wild whoop and hugged her, pressing Ingrid's face into her bosom and pounding her on the back. "When?" she demanded. "How did this happen? Where was I? Why didn't he tell me? Good grief! Are *you* the reason why he hasn't been answering my special knock so many mornings of late?"

She laughed in delight and thumped Ingrid again. "I *knew* he had a woman in there, but I figured it had to be a blonde. I never imagined you two would have progressed so far, so fast!"

Ingrid finally managed to break free of the smothering hold and pull her head off Janet's chest. Her friend's exuberant greeting of the news had stemmed her tears. Lack of oxygen had helped too.

"He d-doesn't know I'm n-n-not a blonde."

Janet giggled. "Good for you!"

"I d-didn't l-lie, Jan. I told him. He didn't b-believe me."

Janet only laughed harder. "I'm not sure I do, either! You and Ken? You're actually getting it— are really, well, lovers? No wonder he wanted your phone number. I said I'd take care of letting you know. And I thought he was simply being polite to a Living Voices volunteer."

"Oh, my Lord, this is crazy," Ingrid said, more to herself than to Janet. "He's the man I love. I've spent every night over the last month in his bed and he doesn't even know my phone—"

She broke off as Janet burst out laughing again. "You have? The last *month*? And I never even suspected!"

She hugged Ingrid again, her voice softening. "This is the best news ever, you and Kenny in love and— He does feel the same way about you, doesn't he?"

Ingrid gazed at her friend as several different ramifications of this entire situation popped up like moving targets in a shooting gallery. Ruthlessly she pushed them all down, concentrating on her reply. "He suh-suh-suh-says he does." She drew a deep breath. "Yes," she said with more conviction. "Y-yes. He d-does."

"Have you talked about . . . Well, I know it's none of my business, but dammit, he's my brother and I've been trying to find him exactly the right wife for years and years, and I want to know. Marriage. Is there any chance? Oh, please say yes! It's what I've been hoping for ever since you and I became friends, only I couldn't get him to agree to meet you. I knew once he did, he'd love you like I do."

That wet black cloth threatened Ingrid again. "Babies," she said, gazing from a past moment into a future that she couldn't see. "We-we-we t-talked about babies. But he said he c-c-couldn't sup-sup-support them, and—-"

"Hoo-boy!" Janet jumped to her feet and whirled across the office, her eyes shining, the gold braid on her uniform sleeves glittering in the light of the sun as it angled through the window behind Ingrid. "He loves you. And he wants to make babies with you. And he still thinks you're a blonde! Ain't he going to be one surprised puppy when he first lays eyes on your beautiful chocolatey hair and your big brown eyes!"

The world sank away from Ingrid, leaving her alone and adrift, with nothing to cling to as she realized the truth she had been trying to push back into a little room in her subconscious. It grew and grew, forcing out the walls, bulging through the door she wanted to slam, to lock, to weld shut.

"He-he-he c-can't know," she whispered. "Oh, J-Jan, he can't! He can't s-s-see me. I c-can't l-let him. *He doesn't know I st-st-st-stutter either!*"

Janet walked back slowly, sat on the front edge of the spare chair, and looked at Ingrid long and curiously. "How in the world can he not know you stutter if the two of you are having a relationship? Unless I've completely misinterpreted what you're saying."

"I d-don't know why, but I n-nev-never stutter when I'm w-with him. I can t-talk like a normal p-p-person, and I think it's be-be-because he c-can't suh-suh—" Her eyes flooded, and she couldn't make her mouth form the word. "I'm su-su-such a crip-cripple, J-Jan!" she wailed. "I can only t-talk to bl-blind men and little k-k-k-kids!"

"Ah, sweetie, no, no." Janet hugged her, sitting on the arm of the old oak swivel chair, making it squeak and dip so that Ingrid flopped against her. "You're no cripple, hon. And even if you do stutter when he can see you, it won't matter to Ken. He's not like that. I promise you, he's not. Inky, you've made such a difference in him, in his whole life. It's no wonder he loves you. Why, you, and your love, might just be responsible for his sight's returning. Think of that! If you refuse to see him after he can see you, he might lose it again."

Ingrid lifted her head from Janet's shoulder and composed herself.

"I w-won't see him," she said. "I won't. L-l-let him re-muh-muh-member m-me as a whole puh-puh-puh-person until he for-for-forgets me." Her mouth trembled. "L-let him remember me as a b-blonde."

She looked at Janet for a long moment, then picked up the phone again and dialed her first call. "Hello, Martha. How are you this evening? Are your grandsons still with you? This morning? I bet you miss them already. . . ."

"Kenny, she refuses." Janet sounded as if she wanted to rip her hair out in frustration. "I've been back to the church three times. I've gone to her house. What can I do, knock her out and drag her over here?"

"You can give me her home phone number! I'll call her until she listens."

"I can't. She made me promise not to."

Ken wanted to howl into the darkness that had come back over him like a cloud. It was more than the blackness cloaking his vision. This involved his soul. His euphoria of four days ago had evaporated, wiped out by Ingrid's refusal to come to him. For the first time, Ken truly felt like a blind man. Inside and out, he felt blind.

And afraid. He wanted his sight back. He wanted that very, very much. But he wanted Ingrid more.

Father Ralph's words kept returning to haunt Ken: "Ingrid collects every lame duck." Oh, God, was that why she refused to come to him? Because if his sight returned, he wouldn't be a "lame duck" anymore?

He couldn't buy it, not really, though the thought recurred with depressing regularity no matter how hard he crushed it down.

"Why, Jan? Dammit to hell! Why? She loves me. I know she does, so why is she doing this?"

"I . . . don't exactly know, Ken. I only know she says she can't come to the hospital, can't see you again."

He glared in her direction. Dammit, she did know but for some obscure, female reason, she'd taken Ingrid's side in this whole damned mess! Women! They stuck together even worse than doctors. Where was Janet's loyalty to him, her only brother? Where was Ingrid's professed love for him?

Where was Ingrid?

He wanted to shout that he'd been counting on her to come, counting on her to be with him that evening, every evening that he had to be in the hospital, to spend all her free moments with him and be there when he opened his eyes and finally saw again.

He'd been counting on so much.

He rolled to his side, away from his sister. "You'd better get out of here," he said, but he was grateful that she sat beside him, her hand against his back, warm, comforting. It was nice having her there.

But it was Ingrid he wanted with every fiber of his being.

ELEVEN

When it happened, it was almost anticlimactic. Ken simply woke on Sunday morning—he believed it was Sunday morning—opened his eyes in the dim, windowless room, and saw shapes. He lay there looking at them, identifying them in the minimal glow cast by a tiny light near the floor. The light was to give the nursing staff enough illumination to move around, he guessed.

There was a television rack on an extendible arm, above and to the right of his bed. No TV on it. He saw a high table somewhere between his feet and the wall. Likely the one his meals had been placed on. He noted idly that his depth perception wasn't great.

A rectangle of a slightly paler shade of gray suggested a picture on the wall. He stared at it, trying to bring it into focus, but his eyes burned and he closed them again, blinking a few times. When he opened them, the rectangle on the wall had resolved itself into a framed painting of—a bowl of fruit? Maybe flowers? He wiggled his feet back and forth like semaphores under the covers and watched them move. He held his hand up in front of his face and counted his fingers.

When he sat up cautiously, there was no sudden ache between his eyebrows, no tear-inducing pain in his eyeballs. He swung his legs to the side of the bed and sat, expecting the dizziness that had accompanied his last spell of vision, but he was steady.

Empty, but steady. Lord, it was quiet. Maybe it wasn't morning after all. In the hallway beyond the closed door he heard rubber-soled shoes squeaking on polished tile. Should he ring for a nurse? Should he put on his dark glasses and block out the faint glow of the night-light? He drew in a deep breath and rejected the idea.

No damn way! He could see, and it felt good. He refused to let them take that away from him.

He stood and went into the bathroom, rubbing his hands up and down the wall on both sides of the door, looking for a light switch. There was none of course. It would be outside his room, inaccessible to a patient who was supposed to remain in subdued lighting. He wondered if the door to the hall was locked. What would happen if he opened it?

The thought of there being a painfully, brightly lit corridor beyond killed that idea. He finished in the bathroom and went back to bed.

What difference did it make, being able to see? The one thing in the world he wanted to see wasn't there. It never would be. Ingrid's face. Her smile. Her hair, her eyes, her shape. Why?

Lame duck . . . lame duck . . . lame duck . . .

"I need to get away," Ingrid said to Janet, who had telephoned and caught her on her way out the door with a duffel bag over her shoulder. "I'm taking some vacation time, going sailing in the Gulf Islands. I may even sail up to Desolation Sound."

Yes. That sounded right, she thought. Desolation Sound. Why not? It was certainly appropriate, given her mood.

"Dammit, Inky, you're hurting. Kenny's hurting. You can't do this to him. His vision is back to normal. They released him from the hospital a week ago Friday."

Ingrid knew that. He'd called her at the church the evening of his release. She'd said she was glad for him, then she'd hung up. She'd told Father Ralph she felt ill, and he'd taken over her Friday calls. She'd fled, lest Ken come to the church.

He wouldn't be able to find her at home. He didn't know where she lived. She was glad that all the time she'd known him, she'd never given him her phone number, and she could only pray that Janet wouldn't. She'd spent the weekend arranging for vacation time, arranging to have the day care fully staffed, knowing she didn't dare show her face there, for fear he'd find her.

Then she'd spent the following week holed up at home, seeing no one. The emptiness had echoed too loudly, and she knew she had to leave.

"He doesn't deserve what you're doing to him," Janet said, breaking in on her thoughts. "At least phone him. Tell him it's over, if that's what it is. He needs to get on with his life."

"Was—was his bid accepted?"

The minute he could see again, Ken had put in his bid on a huge government contract, Janet had told her.

Before the accident he'd been working on the proposal. Because he worked alone, not as part of a team, his blindness had brought his work to a dead halt. In the meantime other architects, mostly with prestigious firms, had been going full steam ahead with their schemes. Luckily the gears of government turned slowly, so his four lost months might not cost him the job.

"Not yet," Janet replied, "but it's been short-listed. And now he has to go back east and start talking it up, putting the good word in the right ears, making sure the people who count know he's the right man for the job, that his design works, is what's needed, that the price is right. It may be taxpayers' money spent on the job, but with an election coming up, even government functionaries are being cagey when it comes to laying out cold, hard cash.

"I know it, everyone else knows it, but he simply won't admit it. He needs to be in the right places at the right times, with the right people, and he would be there but for you. Where you're concerned, he's as blind as anytime since the accident."

Ingrid closed her eyes, shaking her head. "Has he said so?"

"No." Janet's tone was one of total disgust. "You know him well enough to know that's not his way. He simply insists that he prefers to stay here for now, but *I* know he's waiting for you.

"Dammit, I can't make him see that he's missed too much time already. He's going to let one of the most lucrative contracts of his career, to say nothing of a building of great prestige, one that could give him a place in history books, slip right through his fingers. Since I can't get through to him, I'm hoping I can make you see the truth. Ken needs you."

"Like he needs a forty-pound anchor around his neck. Janet, don't you see? You've just made my point for me. He has to go east and sell his proposal. That means doing all the things I can't do, meeting with politicians and bureaucrats in social situations where most of these kinds of decisions are made. Believe me, I know. After all, my mother's a senator. She's been in politics for twenty-five years. I know the way it works, and for Ken, with me as an escort, it would *not* work."

"Then tell him that, for God's sake. Over the phone, if you absolutely must. At least that way you won't have to worry about stuttering. But believe me, I see your concerns about that as taking a pretty low second to Ken's concerns—what should be his concerns—about losing that contract."

Ingrid thought she probably would stutter, not that it would matter now. Janet had likely told Ken everything. But worse than stuttering, she knew she'd cry. That was why she'd had to hang up so abruptly that Friday night. If she cried, then how could she make Ken believe her when she said it was over? It would be that much worse for both of them because she'd have to say cruel, untrue things to convince him.

"It's over," she said to Janet. "You tell him for me if you think he hasn't figured it out."

"Oh, he's figured it out, all right," Janet said angrily. "He believes it's over just as strongly as you seem to. Only he thinks it's because you collect lame ducks, and now that he's not one, you have no more use for him. I can almost hate you for what you're doing to him, Inky."

Ingrid set her duffel bag on the floor and sat on it, clutching the phone, choking on her tears. "I don't want him to hurt, Jan," she managed to say. "I never wanted that. That's why I'm doing this. Because not to stop it right here would hurt him worse in the end. Tell him," she pleaded. "Tell him . . . good-bye for me."

"Oh, I'll tell him all right! I'll tell him he was wrong, tell him I was wrong, that the woman I hand-picked as a sister-in-law is a coward! He'd do better to take up with Maddie McKee. She may be a blond ditz, but at least she's got the guts to go after what she wants. And she wants Ken.

"But you, Ingrid? You want him, too, but not badly enough to fight. Hell, I always thought you were brave."

"No, I'm not! I've never been brave. I'm Mousie!"

"Balls! You faced up to your stutter before and you could do it now if you wanted to. At last year's Volunteer bash, didn't you force yourself to stand up and address a thousand strangers to gather Living Voices volunteers?"

"That was dif—"

"It was not. And it was also the moment I decided I wanted you for Ken. You talk to parents, to medical personnel, church elders, on behalf of your kids, you talk to everyone you can collar about Living Voices, and stutter your way to success, but where's your courage when it counts? What will you do for the man you love? Zip, that's what! Because you're too scared to trust him, too gutless to trust his love. Well, forget you!

"I don't want a coward for a sister-in-law, and I'll tell Ken that he can do better than a wimp for a wi—"

Ingrid set the phone down gently and rushed to her boat. She started the engine, cast off, and motored out of the cove, not stopping even to put up the sails until she was well out into the Strait of Georgia, beyond the reach of any human voice. Right now about the most she could cope with was seals. Seals, and the echo of a voice that kept berating her, even as she sailed.

Coward . . . coward . . . coward.

She and *Molly Darlin'* beat northward toward Desolation Sound, fighting wind, tide, and need for every tenth of a degree gained in latitude. Running, running, running. To hide.

Up there she'd be beyond all but the most powerful radio signal, isolated, alone, safe.

Isolated. Alone. Safe.

And lonely.

After Ingrid had been anchored in Roscoe Bay for three days, the loneliness was like a living, breathing entity sitting astride her shoulders. She thrust it away time and again, but it returned.

During those three days she watched a pair of bald eagles fishing, swooping into the water and rising, talons full. They fished together sometimes, other times apart, but however they worked, they always soared off over the trees in the same direction. Feeding their young, she surmised.

Supporting their babies.

Sometimes she cried at night.

Had he gotten the message yet? Had he left for the east and that lucrative government contract? He'd need it to get his career back on track. A four-month absence could make a difference to a rising star.

His presence aboard her boat was often too strong to bear. She could see him sitting on the starboard seat, his big, bare feet braced on the opposite side, his face tilted up to the sun. She could hear his laughter, see the glow of self-satisfaction that had emanated from him when she had left him in charge of the helm. Even more, she could still feel his arms around her, his lips on hers, and his fingers stroking her face as he "saw" her for the first time. The memories drove her to dive over the side and swim hard from one side of the bay to the other. Sometimes she was forced to escape him by hiking the short trail inland to the warm freshwater lake where everyone anchored in the bay took their baths.

She hadn't stuttered in days, simply because she'd spoken to no one.

Suddenly she wanted to. She wanted to call Janet and ask if Ken had gone, ask if it was safe to go back to the day care. She missed the children. She'd never taken this much time away. Would it ever be safe to go back, or would the memories there kill her slowly too?

She cried again that night.

She cried the next morning when she awoke at dawn and couldn't get back to sleep for hearing Janet call her a coward. She cried when she saw the eagle pair fishing together, and her loneliness increased. It was insane to stay in Roscoe Bay, moping. What she needed to do was go home, call everyone on her Living Voices list, make contact with her friends, talk to people, work out their problems with them and put her own to rest.

The tide was dropping fast. If she didn't up anchor and sail out over the sandbar, she'd be stuck in Roscoe for another twenty-four hours. The evening tide was a small one. It wouldn't put enough water in the pass for her to navigate into the outer bay and hence into Desolation Sound.

Still, she sat and watched the tide run out. It was easier to let nature make her decision for her. A duck drifted by with the falling tide. She stared at it so hard, it flew away, its wings whistling as it fled. It had, she saw, only one leg, poor thing. No wonder it was nervous, poor little lame duck.

No! Suddenly she recalled with perfect clarity Janet saying that Ken believed she had no use for him now that he was whole again, that he wasn't a "lame duck."

With a choking cry she raced to the bow, hauled up the anchor hand over hand, water flying, mixing with tears. She had never thought that of Ken. Never. Not for an instant! She had to tell him, make him understand that it was nothing like that keeping them apart. It was her and her alone. Her defect . . . and her cowardice.

The engine cranked over at her first attempt, and she made it out over the bar. *Molly Darlin'* hesitated, heeled a few degrees as her keel scraped through the muck, but then she was free and away.

Out in the sheltered channel she motored until she picked up a fresh breeze, then she gave *Molly Darlin'* every square inch of available sail. They flew over the water before a favorable westerly. It whisked them homeward, and Ingrid prayed as she had never prayed in her life.

A single word, that prayer. *Please, please, please.* God would know what she meant.

His name remained on the mailbox. He hadn't left. As she'd sailed and motored home, never had a journey seemed longer, slower. But now the elevator seemed to take just as long.

Yes, Ken still needed to leave. Yes, he still needed to get on with his career without her. But he also had to know that she had never thought of him as anything but a complete human being. She couldn't bear to think of his leaving until she'd told him that.

She stood outside his door at last and lifted her hand, noticing in a strangely detached way that it shook, that her knuckles were white. She rang the bell. Shave-and-a-hair-cut-six-bits, stealing Janet's code. She tried not to think of the times they had lain in bed together giggling like fools, waiting for Janet to go away.

She used Jan's ring so he wouldn't look through the peephole, see a stranger, and refuse to open the door to another "helpful" neighbor.

It was the first time she'd ever thought of Ken looking through the peephole, the first time she'd actually realized that when he saw her, he'd be seeing a stranger.

She shook all over, thinking of him looking at her, thinking of having to attempt even such a mundane word as *hello* with his gaze on her face.

She squared her shoulders. She would not be a coward any longer. Stutter, stammer, it didn't matter. She would face him and tell him in person that she had never thought he was a lame duck and certainly didn't prefer him to be blind.

He opened the door before she had finished steeling herself to face him. He looked at her. She tried to speak, and not so much as a squeak emerged.

He said nothing, merely snatched her hands into his and stepped back a pace. She followed. Still looking at her, still holding her hands, he swung her in a half circle and kicked the door shut.

Ken clasped his fingers tighter around Ingrid's hands. They felt icy to him. They trembled, too, or was that his own shaking? Her lips, soft, pale pink, and tremulous, parted enough for her top teeth to clench on her bottom lip. Her eyes, huge, deep brown, luminous, fixed on his face, filled with fear, with questions, and with despair. He wanted to ease her fear, answer her questions, and erase her despair, but still he could not speak as he gazed at her for the first time.

Hair the color of the richest, darkest coffee streamed over the shoulders of a salt-splattered denim jacket. Her skin was as pale as the heart of a rose, with two patches of color high on her cheeks, enhancing the beauty of her eyes.

He tried to speak. His throat locked up on him as he continued to stare at her, drinking her in. She was so damned far from being "ordinary," he couldn't believe she truly believed it herself. She made every blonde he'd ever seen look insipid, washed out, like an overexposed photograph. She was warm, alive, vibrant . . . Ingrid. He breathed in a gulp of her sweet scent.

"I'm . . . Ingrid," she whispered, and he blinked.

He dropped her hands and grabbed her elbows, shaking her lightly. "Lord! Did you think I wouldn't *know*?"

"I . . ." She shook her head. "The way—the way you're looking at me is . . ."

"I'm looking at you because you're the most . . ." His voice cracked. "The most beautiful thing I have ever seen," he continued in a soft, awestruck tone.

"I . . . am?"

"Yes. You're . . ." He let her go, took a pace away, cleared his throat. He couldn't tell her what it did to him, his first sight of her. She was so much more than he'd ever dreamed, so much more . . . everything. "You're—"

"Not a blonde."

"Good Lord!" He gaped at her, suddenly filled with fury that she could concern herself over something so utterly inane at a moment like this.

"Blond?" he bellowed. "Blond? What the hell does that have to do with anything? Do you think that matters to me? Do you believe I'm so shallow? Is that your opinion of me? Is that why you ran? Ingrid, I—" He broke off, rubbed his eyes, and turned from her to stride across the room. He spun back.

"I wanted you, you know." He tightened his hands into fists. "No. Let's get the words right. I *needed* you, Ingrid. I've never needed another human being the way I needed you when they locked me up in that little room to protect me from light, to protect my eyes from the shock of seeing again after all those months in darkness. But what they couldn't protect me from, what I had no defense against, was the desolation I felt when you refused to come to me. Do you know how close I came to saying to hell with it? How badly I wanted to run the risk of having to spend the rest of my life with a white cane in my hand? I'd have left that room, Ingrid, and gone after you, if Janet hadn't damned well sat on me for three days. You said you loved me! How could you do that to me? Why, for God's sake? That's all I want to know. *Why?*"

He watched her face grow paler, watched tears flood her eyes, spill down her cheeks. She lifted her chin and faced him, though, marched toward him and stood her ground three feet away. "I didn't come because I was afraid. At first, afraid for myself, then later, when I became more rational, I was afraid for you. I stayed away from you because I love you. Because I knew I was wrong for you."

"Wrong? How can you say that? You know what we had, what we planned. That night we talked about your getting pregnant. You said that if the time ever came that I could offer you the things I think are important, you'd choose me as the father of your children. That time was there, Ingrid, waiting for us to reach out and take it, take each other, and you left. When I needed you the most, you went out *sailing*!"

"No. You needed . . . thought you needed, you wanted a—a dream." Her voice was low, halting at first, then firmed. She wiped the tears from her face with the backs of her hands.

"You wanted what you thought I was." she continued. "What I'd let you believe I was. I'm sorry I misled you. That's why I'm here now, to tell you that, to tell you there's nothing for you to wait for, nothing I can offer. It's my fault you had a false impression of me. I knew all along I couldn't be what you really need. I can never be that."

"Dammit, you could have been *there* for me."

She pulled in a shaky breath. "Yes. As your friend I could have been and should have been. I'm sorry for that, too, sorry for letting you down."

"Not as my friend! As my lover. That's how I needed you. That's how I wanted you!" He waved a hand as she started to speak again. "No! Not what you're thinking. I'm not saying I wanted you to share my hospital bed. I needed you there to share the waiting, share the . . . fear. I needed you then for exactly the same reasons I need you now, will need you for the rest of my life: to share my darkness and make it light."

"No . . ." She backed away as he advanced. "I can't do that for you. Please, you have to understand. I didn't go away, didn't stay away to hurt you, but to protect you. I'm—"

He broke in impatiently as he caught her shoulders and held her in front of him. "Yes, you hurt me. Yes, you made me mad. But through it all, on a deep and basic level, I trusted you. That's all that kept me from going nuts. I knew you'd come through. I told Janet you would, and you have. You're here. You're home. And you're mine."

"Home?" Ingrid yelled, breaking free of him before she succumbed to the need to wrap herself around him, comfort him, be comforted by him. "This isn't your home, Ken! You should have left here long ago! You need to be back east, wheeling and dealing and making sure the powers that be buy your design! You shouldn't have hung around like this, waiting for me. It's futile anyway. I'm trying to tell you that. You have to listen!

"I can't help you, Ken. I'd hinder you. I'd be a detriment to your career. I stutter, dammit! I stutter really, really badly. I can't hold up my end of a conversation. I'm shy. I'm a dead loss at a party. I'm—"

Ken caught her gesturing hands and tugged on them, propelling her closer. Holding her by the shoulders, he shook her, just hard enough to get her attention. "You're the woman who, if she doesn't stop running off at the mouth, is going to find herself gagged so that I can get a chance to hold up *my* end of *this* conversation."

He wanted to laugh at her dumbfounded expression. "You're the woman I love," he went on when she blinked dazedly at him. "You're the woman I'm going to marry. You're the woman who's going to be the mother of my seven children.

"I know you stutter, you boob! I've heard you with other people, remember? Jennifer, Father Ralph, Maddie. That you didn't stutter with me made me love you all the more. It means you trust me, means you're comfortable with me. It means you love me the way you don't love anyone else. I love being that special to you."

Ingrid groaned in frustration. He still didn't get it. How could one man be so damned obtuse? Did she have to draw him a picture?

"It's not because I *trust* you that I don't stutter!" she shouted. "It's not because I love you. I do, both, but I didn't stutter with you because you were *blind*, Ken. You couldn't see me. It was the same as talking on the phone. That's what let me be so comfortable with you. You were no threat! You couldn't see me, so you couldn't judge me."

She sucked in a deep breath. "I hate that in myself, that fear of being judged, but I can't control it. I see myself reflected in other people's eyes and I grow smaller and smaller inside myself, until I can't function even halfway normally.

"It makes me feel shallow and stupid and inadequate. It also makes me nothing more than the rank coward Janet said I am. I know that, I know all of it, but I still can't change it, and the time since you regained your sight has proved it beyond any doubt. I ran the minute I knew you could see because I couldn't face you as a sighted man. I was too scared to have you hear me make a fool of myself."

"Ingrid, sweetheart," he said gently, "I can see you now."

She broke free of him, strode across the room, and bowed her head against the cool glass of a window. "I know, I know. That's what I'm trying to tell you. I could only function normally with you when you were blind. Now that you can see me, it'll never work!"

He followed her and turned her around, pinning her against his body. His heat burned her. She didn't think she could breathe through all that heat. Yet she shivered and squeezed her eyes closed.

"Ingrid, look at me."

Reluctantly, because she hated to have to stutter in front of him, hated the idea of seeing his eyes fill with impatience, or even pity, she obeyed. "Do I look any different?" he asked, those intense green eyes of his probing into her soul as they always had. "Do I seem like another man?"

She shook her head. "No. But you were never the problem. I was. I am."

"I've been looking at you—hell, I haven't been able to take my eyes off you," he said, "since I opened the door." He filled a hand with her hair, held it out and let it fall away in a sweeping, dark curtain to land on her shoulder. "Inky. So beautiful." He buried his face in it, then lifted his head and fixed her with that probing gaze again. "Inky hair, inky eyes. Lord, how I love you!

"And you've been yelling at me, giving me hell for hanging around here waiting for you, as if there was anything else I could do."

"You could have gone back to your real life," she said, pushing away from him before his heat melted her resolve to make him understand. "You could be taking care of your business. How many other hotshots are going to get in where you should be because you're not on the scene, doing whatever you have to do to get that contract?"

"You mean that new federal government complex in Regina? I've got it. I told you, my product sells itself."

She gaped. "But Janet said—"

He made an impatient gesture with his hand. "Janet believes I need her to fight my battles for me. She chose you for me, it seems, even before I did, and now she thinks she's honor bound to make it work. To her that means fighting my battles for me."

He smiled. "She's wrong of course. I knew you'd come through, Inky. I trusted you." He smoothed a hand over her hair. "Think you can stand living in Saskatchewan for a couple of years? The winters are cold, but we could sneak away to Hawaii for a month or two during the worst of it every year."

He grinned that sexy, devilish grin she loved and moved in closer, sliding his arms around her waist. "Failing that, I think I can manage to keep you from freezing."

"You aren't listening!" she shouted. "I can't be part of your life. I— You got the contract? And you never went back east?"

He nodded. "It was awarded today. They wanted me there for some kind of Parliament Hill ceremony, but I told them they'd hired me to build for them, not entertain politicians or media."

She swayed. "There'll be other contracts."

He steadied her. "Well, I hope so. A man with a wife and seven children to feed needs them."

"Ken, please listen to me. You need someone who's outgoing, congenial, someone who doesn't hate meeting strangers face-to-face, someone like Maddie, for instance, or—"

He shook her again. "Now, stop it! You've been telling me how bad a risk you are for me, telling me

I should trade you in and maybe try Maddie—*and never once did you stutter.*"

"I *never* said you should trade me in for Maddie," she said, breathing hard, her fists clenched at the front of his shirt.

"No? My mistake. You seemed perfectly willing to throw me to the other sharks all alone and lonely, so I figured why not her too?"

"Because . . ." She drew in a quick, ragged breath and said roughly, "Because you're *mine*." She glared at him. "Has she been hanging around? Dammit, Ken, she's a menace! She's blond. You know that. I'm sure you've seen her by now, and she's built like a— She's *blond*!"

He laughed. "She's a blonde, is built like a goddess, and is of utterly no account because she isn't you. And one more thing, Ingrid, you're still not stuttering."

"That's because I'm mad. I never stutter if I get mad enough."

"Then get mad, my love. Stay mad if that's what it takes to make you happy. I don't care. I only know I love to see you all fierce and possessive and— Oh, God, just shut up and come here."

Filling his hands with her hair, dragging her head back, he kissed her until every bit of fight, every ounce of mad had gone out of her.

He lifted her and carried her to the couch, sat and cradled her on his lap. Smoothing her hair back, he kissed her again. He pushed her jacket off and kissed her beautiful, tanned shoulders, exposed by her tank top. "I love you," he said, running his fingers through the glory that was her rich chocolate-colored hair. "And I'm not letting you go. I don't care what kind of barriers you throw across my path, we're together for the rest of our lives. Make no mistake, Ingrid, if I'm yours, then you're mine too."

She inhaled tremulously. "I love you," she said. "And I didn't—honestly, Ken—I didn't think of you as a lame duck. You were always just . . . you, and—*seven children*?"

He laughed. "That's negotiable. Your marrying me is not."

"Okay," she agreed. "Seven does sound excessive. Marriage sounds like . . . heaven."

He smiled at her. "Hey, you mad at me?"

She blinked. "No. Of course not."

"I hate to tell you this, sweet, but I'm looking right at you, you're not mad, and you're not stuttering. What do you make of that, hmm?"

Ingrid linked her hands behind his neck and laughed with joy. "Maybe I see you as a nonthreatening little child."

He stood, tossed her over his shoulder, and strode into his bedroom. Dropping her down on the blue spread, he straddled her. "If that's the case, I'll have to open your eyes to reality, Ingrid Bjornsen. This is no little child you're going to make love with. This is me, and I'm a man."

"Oh, yeah? Prove it."

To her satisfaction, he did.

"I, Ing-Ing-Ingrid, take yuh-yuh-yuh—"

Ken brushed her veil back and cradled her chin in his hand. "Look at me," he commanded softly. "Talk to *me*, love."

She fixed her gaze on his solemn green eyes. "I, Ingrid, take you, Kenneth, to be my lawful wedded husband . . ."

His smile encouraged her, his eyes praised her, and Ingrid smiled in triumph as she continued unfalteringly, repeating the ancient vows: " . . . to have and to hold . . . from this day forward, as long as we both shall live."

THE EDITOR'S
CORNER

Since the inception of LOVESWEPT in 1983, we've been known as the most innovative publisher of category romance. We were the first to publish authors under their real names and show their photographs in the books. We originated interconnected "series" books and established theme months. And now, after publishing over 700 books, we are once again changing the face of category romance.

Starting next month, we are introducing a brand-new LOVESWEPT look. We're sure you'll agree with us that it's distinctive and outstanding—nothing less than the perfect showcase for your favorite authors and the wonderful stories they write.

A second change is that we are now publishing four LOVESWEPTs a month instead of six. With so many romances on the market today, we want to provide you with only the very best in romantic fiction. We know that you want quality, not quantity, and we are as committed as ever to giving you love stories you'll never forget, by authors you'll always remember. We are especially proud to debut our new look with four sizzling romances from four of our most talented authors.

Starting off our new look is Mary Kay McComas with **WAIT FOR ME**, LOVESWEPT #702. Oliver Carey saves Holly Loftin's life during an earthquake with a split-second tackle, but only when their eyes meet does he feel the earth tremble and her compassionate soul reach out to his. He is intrigued by her need to help others, enchanted by her appetite for simple pleasures, but now he has to show her that their differences can be their strengths and that, more than anything, they belong together. Mary Kay will have you laughing and crying with this touching romance.

The ever-popular Kay Hooper is back with her unique blend of romantic mystery and spicy wit in **THE HAUNTING OF JOSIE**, LOVESWEPT #703. Josie Douglas decides that Marc Westbrook, her gorgeous landlord, would have made a good warlock, with his raven-dark hair, silver eyes, and even a black cat in his arms! She chose the isolated house as a refuge, a place to put the past to rest, but now Marc insists on fighting her demons . . . and why does he so resemble the ghostly figure who beckons to her from the head of the stairs? Kay once more demonstrates her talent for seduction and suspense in this wonderful romance.

Theresa Gladden proves that opposites attract in **PERFECT TIMING**, LOVESWEPT #704. Jenny Johnson isn't looking for a new husband, no matter how many hunks her sister sends her way, but Carter Dalton's cobalt-blue eyes mesmerize her into letting his daughter join her girls' club—and inviting him to dinner! The free-spirited rebel is all wrong for him: messy house, too many pets, wildly disorganized—but he can't resist a woman who promises to fill the empty spaces he didn't know he had. Theresa's spectacular romance will leave you breathless.

Last but certainly not least is **TAMING THE PIRATE**, LOVESWEPT #705, from the supertalented Ruth Owen. When investigator Gabe Ramirez sees Laurie Palmer, she stirs to life the appetites of his buccaneer ancestors and makes him long for the golden lure of her smile. She longs to trade her secrets for one kiss from his brigand's lips, but once he knows why she is on the run, will he betray the woman he's vowed will never escape his arms? You won't forget this wonderful story from Ruth.

Happy reading,

With warmest wishes,

Nita Taublib

Nita Taublib

Deputy Publisher

P.S. Don't miss the exciting women's novels from Bantam that are coming your way in August—**MIDNIGHT WARRIOR**, by *New York Times* bestselling author Iris Johansen, is a spellbinding tale of pursuit, possession, and passion that extends from the wilds of Normandy to untamed medieval England; **BLUE MOON** is a powerful and romantic novel of love and families by the exceptionally talented Luanne Rice. *The New York Times Book Review* calls it "a rare combination of realism and romance"; **VELVET**, by Jane Feather, is a spectacular novel of danger and deception in which a beautiful woman risks all for revenge and love; **THE WITCH DANCE**, by Peggy Webb, is a poignant story of two lovers whose passion breaks every rule. We'll be giving you a sneak peek at these terrific books in next month's LOVESWEPTs. And immediately following this page, look for a preview of the exciting romances from Bantam that are *available now!*

Don't miss these extraordinary books by
your favorite Bantam authors

On sale in June:

MISTRESS
by Amanda Quick

WILDEST DREAMS
by Rosanne Bittner

DANGEROUS TO LOVE
by Elizabeth Thornton

AMAZON LILY
by Theresa Weir

MISTRESS
Available in hardcover
by the *New York Times*
bestselling author

AMANDA QUICK

*With stories rife with wicked humor, daring
intrigue, and heart-stopping passion, Amanda
Quick has become a writer unmatched in the field
of romantic fiction. Now the author of fourteen
New York Times bestselling novels offers another unforgettable tale as a proper spinster embarks
on a delicious masquerade and a handsome earl
finds himself tangling with the most exotic and
captivating mistress London has ever known.*

"Power, passion, tragedy, and triumph are Rosanne Bittner's hallmarks. Again and again, she brings readers to tears."
—*Romantic Times*

WILDEST DREAMS
by

ROSANNE BITTNER

Against the glorious panorama of big sky country, award-winning Rosanne Bittner creates a sweeping saga of passion, excitement, and danger . . . as a beautiful young woman and a rugged ex-soldier struggle against all odds to carve out an empire—and to forge a magnificent love.

Here is a look at this powerful novel . . .

Lettie walked ahead of him into the shack, swallowing back an urge to retch. She gazed around the cabin, noticed a few cracks between the boards that were sure to let in cold drafts in the winter. A rat scurried across the floor, and she stepped back. The room was very small, perhaps fifteen feet square, with a potbellied stove in one corner, a few shelves built against one wall, and a crudely built table in the middle of the room, with two crates to serve as chairs. The bed was made from pine, with ropes for springs and no mattress on top. She was glad her mother had given her two feather mattresses before they parted. Never had she longed more fervently to be with her family back at the spacious home they had left behind in St.

Joseph, where people lived in reasonable numbers, and anything they needed was close at hand.

Silently, she untied and removed the wool hat she'd been wearing. She was shaken by her sense of doubt, not only over her choice to come to this lonely, desolate place, but also over her decision to marry. She loved Luke, and he had been attentive and caring and protective throughout their dangerous, trying journey to get here; but being his wife meant fulfilling other needs he had not yet demanded of her. This was the very first time they had been truly alone since marrying at Fort Laramie. When Luke had slept in the wagon with her, he had only held her. Was he waiting for her to make the first move; or had he patiently been waiting for this moment, when he had her alone? Between the realization that he would surely expect to consummate their marriage now, and the knowledge that she would spend the rest of the winter holed up in this tiny cabin, with rats running over her feet, she felt panic building.

"Lettie?"

She was startled by the touch of Luke's hand on her shoulder. She gasped and turned to look up at him, her eyes wide with fear and apprehension. "I . . . I don't know if I can stay here, Luke." Oh, why had she said that? She could see the hurt in his eyes. He should be angry. Maybe he would throw her down and have his way with her now, order her to submit to her husband, yell at her for being weak and selfish, tell her she would stay here whether she liked it or not.

He turned, looked around the tiny room, looked back at her with a smile of resignation on his face. "I can't blame you there. I don't know why I even considered this. I guess in all my excitement . . ." He sighed deeply. "I'll take you back to Billings in the morning. It's not much of a town, but maybe I can find a safe place for you and Nathan to stay while I make things more livable around here."

"But . . . you'd be out here all alone."

He shrugged, walking over to the stove and opening the door. "I knew before I ever came here there would be a lot of lonely living I'd have to put up with." He picked up some kindling from a small pile that lay near the stove and stacked it inside. "When you have a dream, you simply do what you have to do to realize it." He turned to face her. "I told you it won't be like this forever, Lettie, and it won't."

His eyes moved over her, and she knew what he wanted. He simply loved and respected her too much to ask for it. A wave of guilt rushed through her, and she felt like crying. "I'm sorry, Luke. I've disappointed you in so many ways already."

He frowned, coming closer. "I never said that. I don't blame you for not wanting to stay here. I'll take you back to town and you can come back here in the spring." He placed his hands on her shoulders. "I love you, Lettie. I never want you to be unhappy or wish you had never married me. I made you some promises, and I intend to keep them."

A lump seemed to rise in her throat. "You'd really take me to Billings? You wouldn't be angry about it?"

Luke studied her face. He wanted her so, but was not sure how to approach the situation because of what she had been through. He knew there was a part of her that wanted him that way, but he had not seen it in her eyes since leaving Fort Laramie. He had only seen doubt and fear. "I told you I'd take you. I wouldn't be angry."

She suddenly smiled, although there were tears in her eyes. "That's all I need to know. I . . . I thought you took it for granted, just because I was your wife . . . that you'd demand . . ."

She threw her arms around him, resting her face against his thick fur jacket. "Oh, Luke, forgive me. You don't have to take me back. As long as I know I *can* go back, that's all I need to know. Does that make any sense?"

He grinned. "I think so."

Somewhere in the distance they heard the cry of a bobcat. Combined with the groaning mountain wind, the sounds only accentuated how alone they really were, a good five miles from the only town, and no sign of civilization for hundreds of miles beyond that. "I can't let you stay out here alone. You're my husband. I belong here with you," Lettie said, still clinging to him.

Luke kissed her hair, her cheek. She found herself turning to meet his lips, and he explored her mouth savagely then. She felt lost in his powerful hold, buried in the fur jacket, suddenly weak. How well he fit this land, so tall and strong and rugged and determined. She loved him all the more for it.

He left her mouth, kissed her neck. "I'd better get a fire going, bring in—"

"Luke." She felt her heart racing as all her fears began to melt away. She didn't know how to tell him, what to do. She could only look into those handsome blue eyes and say his name. She met his lips again, astonished at the sudden hunger in her soul. How could she have considered letting this poor man stay out here alone, when he had a wife and child who could help him, love him? And how could she keep denying him the one thing he had every right to take for himself? Most of all, how could she deny her own sudden desires, this surprising awakening of woman that ached to be set free?

"Luke," she whispered. "I want to be your wife, Luke, in every way. I want to be one with you and know that it's all right. I don't want to be afraid any more."

DANGEROUS TO LOVE
by Elizabeth Thornton

"A major, major talent . . . a genre superstar."
—*Rave Reviews*

Dangerous. Wild. Reckless. Those were the words that passed through Serena Ward's mind the moment Julian Raynor entered the gaming hall. If anyone could penetrate Serena's disguise—and jeopardize the political fugitives she was delivering to freedom—surely it would be London's most notorious gamester. Yet when the militia storms the establishment in search of traitors, Raynor provides just the pretext Serena needs to escape. But Serena is playing with fire . . . and before the night is through she will find herself surrendering to the heat of unsuspected desires.

The following is a sneak preview of what transpires that evening in a private room above the gaming hall. . .

"Let's start over, shall we?" said Julian. He returned to the chair he had vacated. "And this time, I shall try to keep myself well in check. No, don't move. I rather like you kneeling at my feet in an attitude of submission."

He raised his wine glass and imbibed slowly. "Now you," he said. When she made to take it from him, he shook his head. "No, I shall hold it. Come closer."

Once again she found herself between his thighs. She didn't know what to do with her hands, but he knew.

"Place them on my thighs," he said, and Serena obeyed. Beneath her fingers, she could feel the hard masculine muscles bunch and strain. She was also acutely aware of the movements of the militia as they combed the building for Jacobites.

"Drink," he said, holding the rim of the glass to her lips, tipping it slightly.

Wine flooded her mouth and spilled over. Choking, she swallowed it.

"Allow me," he murmured. As one hand cupped her neck, his head descended and his tongue plunged into her mouth.

Shock held her rigid as his tongue thrust, and thrust again, circling, licking at the dregs of wine in her mouth, lapping it up with avid enjoyment. When she began to struggle, his powerful thighs tightened against her, holding her effortlessly. Her hands went to his chest to push him away, and slipped between the parted edges of his shirt. Warm masculine flesh quivered beneath the pads of her fingertips. Splaying her hands wide, with every ounce of strength, she shoved at him, trying to free herself.

He released her so abruptly that she tumbled to the floor. Scrambling away from him, she came up on her knees. They were both breathing heavily.

Frowning, he rose to his feet and came to tower over her. "What game are you playing now?"

"No game," she quickly got out. "You are going too fast for me." She carefully rose to her feet and began to inch away from him. "We have yet to settle on my . . . my remuneration."

"Remuneration?" He laughed softly. "Sweetheart, I have already made up my mind that for a woman of your unquestionable talents, no price is too high."

These were not the words that Serena wanted to hear, nor did she believe him. Men did not like greedy women. Although she wasn't supposed to know it, long before his marriage, her brother, Jeremy, had given his mistress her *congé* because the girl was too demanding. What was it the girl had wanted?

Her back came up against the door to the bedchamber. One hand curved around the door-knob in a reflexive movement, the other clutched the door-jamb for support.

Licking her lips, she said, "I . . . I shall want my own house."

He cocked his head to one side. As though musing to himself, he said, "I've never had a woman in my keeping. Do you know, for the first time, I can see the merit in it? Fine, you shall have your house."

He took a step closer, and she flattened herself against the door. "And . . . and my own carriage?" She could hardly breathe with him standing so close to her.

"Done." His eyes were glittering.

When he lunged for her, she cried out and flung herself into the bed-chamber, slamming the door quickly, bracing her shoulder against it as her fingers fumbled for the key.

One kick sent both door and Serena hurtling back. He stood framed in the doorway, the light behind him, and every sensible thought went out of her head. Dangerous. Reckless. Wild. This was all a game to him!

He feinted to the left, and she made a dash for the door, twisting away as his hands reached for her. His fingers caught on the back of her gown, ripping it to the waist. One hand curved around her arm, sending her sprawling against the bed.

There was no candle in the bed-chamber, but the lights from the tavern's courtyard filtered through the window casting a luminous glow. He was shedding the last of his clothes. Although everything in her revolted against it, she knew that the time had come to reveal her name.

Summoning the remnants of her dignity, she said, "You should know that I am no common doxy. I am a high-born lady."

He laughed in that way of his that she was coming to thoroughly detest. "I know," he said, "and I am to play the conqueror. Sweetheart, those games are all very well in their place. But the time for games is over. I want a real woman in my arms tonight, a willing one and not some character from a fantasy."

She turned his words over in her mind and

could make no sense of them. Seriously doubting the man's sanity, she cried out, "Touch me and you will regret it to your dying day. Don't you understand anything? I am a lady. I . . ."

He fell on her and rolled with her on the bed. Subduing her easily with the press of his body, he rose above her. "Have done with your games. I am Julian. You are Victoria. I am your protector. You are my mistress. Yield to me, sweeting."

Bought and paid for—that was what was in his mind. She was aware of something else. He didn't want to hurt or humiliate her. He wanted to have his way with her. He thought he had that right.

He wasn't moving, or forcing his caresses on her. He was simply holding her, watching her with an unfathomable expression. "Julian," she whispered, giving him his name in an attempt to soften him. "Victoria Noble is not my real name."

"I didn't think it was," he said, and kissed her.

His mouth was gentle; his tongue caressing, slipping between her teeth, not deeply, not threateningly, but inviting her to participate in the kiss. For a moment, curiosity held her spellbound. She had never been kissed like this before. It was like sinking into a bath of spiced wine. It was sweet and intoxicating, just like the taste of him.

Shivering, she pulled out of the embrace and stared up at him. His brows were raised, questioning her. All she need do was tell him her name and he would let her go.

Suddenly it was the last thing she wanted to do.

An All-Time Recommended Read in the
Romance Reader's Handbook

AMAZON LILY

by the spectacular

Theresa Weir

"Theresa Weir's writing is poignant, passionate and powerful . . . will capture the hearts of readers."—*New York Times* bestselling author Jayne Ann Krentz

Winner of Romantic Times *New Adventure Writer Award, Theresa Weir captures your heart with this truly irresistible story of two remarkable people who must battle terrifying danger even as they discover breathtaking love. Rave Reviews had praised it as "a splendid adventure . . . the perfect way to get away from it all," and Rendezvous insists that you "put it on your must-read list."*

"You must be the Lily-Libber who's going to San Reys."

The deep voice that came slicing through Corey's sleep-fogged brain was gravelly and rough-edged.

She dragged open heavy-lidded eyes to find herself contemplating a ragged pair of grubby blue tennis shoes. She allowed her gaze to pan slowly northward, leaving freeze-framed images etched in her mind's eye: long jeans faded to almost white except along the stitching; a copper waistband button with moldy lettering; a large expanse of chest-filled, sweat-soaked T-shirt; a stubbly field of several days growth of whiskers; dark aviator sunglasses that met the dusty, sweaty brim of a New York Yankees baseball cap.

Corey's head was bent back at an uncomfortable angle. Of course, Santarém, Brazil, wasn't Illinois, and this person certainly wasn't like any case she'd ever handled in her job as a social worker.

The squalid air-taxi building was really little more than a shed, and it had been crowded before, with just Corey and the files. But now, with this man in front of her giving off his angry aura . . . She couldn't see his eyes, but she could read enough of his expression to know that she was being regarded as a lower form of life or something he might have scraped off the bottom off his shoe.

She knew she wasn't an American beauty. Her skin was too pale, her brown eyes too large for her small face, giving her a fragile, old-world appearance that was a burden in these modern times. People had a tendency to either overlook her completely or coddle her. But his reaction was something totally new.

The man's attention shifted from her to the smashed red packet in his hand. He pulled out a flattened nonfilter cigarette, smoothed it until it was somewhat round, then stuck it in the corner of his mouth. One hand moved across the front of the faded green T-shirt that clung damply to his corded muscles. He slapped at the breast pocket. Not finding what he was searching for, both of his hands moved to the front pockets of the ancient jeans that covered those long, athletic legs. There was a frayed white horizontal rip across his right knee, tan skin and sun-bleached hair showing through. Change jingled as he rummaged around to finally pull out a damp, wadded-up book of matches.

"Damn," he muttered after the third match failed to light. "Gotta quit sweating so much." He tossed the bedraggled matchbook to the floor. Cigarette still in his mouth, his hands began a repeat search of his pockets.

Corey reached over to where her twill shoulder bag was lying on a stack of tattered *Mad* magazines. She unzipped a side pocket and pulled out the glossy black and gold matches she'd been saving to add to her matchbook collection.

He grabbed them without so much as a thank-you. "That's right—" he said, striking a match, "you girl scouts are always prepared." He shook out the match and tossed it to the floor.

"Are you Mike Jones?" She hoped to God he wasn't the pilot she was waiting for.

"No." He inhaled deeply, then exhaled, blowing a thick cloud of smoke her direction.

"Do you know when Mr. Jones will be here?" she asked, willing her eyes not to bat against the smoke.

"*Mister* Jones had a slight setback. He was unconscious last time I saw him." The man read the ornate advertisement for the Black Tie restaurant on the match cover, then tucked the matches into the breast pocket of his T-shirt. The knuckles of his hand were red and swollen, one finger joint cracked and covered with dried blood.

"I found Jones in a local cantina, drunk out of his mind and just itching to fly. Had a little trouble convincing him it would be in his best interest if he stayed on the ground. My name's Ash—Asher Adams, and it looks like I'll be flying you to the reserve. If you still want to go."

Corey pushed her earlier thoughts to the back of her mind. "Of course I still want to go." She hadn't come this far to back out now.

"You want my advice?" He pulled off the navy-blue cap and swiped at his sweating forehead before slapping the cap back over shaggy brown hair. "Go back home. Get married. Have babies. Why is it you women have to prove you're men? You come here thrill-seeking so you can go home and be some kind of small-town hero. So your whole puny story can be printed up in a little four-page county paper and you can travel around to all the local clubs and organizations with your slide presentation, and all your friends can ooh and aah over you."

Corey felt heated anger flushing her face. She pressed her lips together in a firm, stubborn line.

What an obnoxious boor! In her years as a social worker, she'd never, *never* come across anyone like him. And thank God for that, she fumed.

Asher Adams took another drag off his cigarette, then flopped down in the chair across from her, legs sticking out in front of him, crossed at the ankles. "Go back home," he said in a weary voice. "This is real. It isn't some Humphrey Bogart movie. This isn't Sleepyville, Iowa, or wherever the hell you're from—"

"Pleasant Grove, Illinois," she flatly informed him. "And I don't need your advice. I don't want it." Who did this overbearing man think he was? She hadn't taken vacation time to come here and be insulted by an ill-tempered woman-hater. And he talked as if she planned to settle in the jungles of Brazil. There was nothing further from her mind.

She zipped her bag and grabbed up her cream-colored wool jacket. "I'd like to leave now."

And don't miss these fabulous romances
from Bantam Books, on sale in July:

MIDNIGHT WARRIOR
by the *New York Times* bestselling author
Iris Johansen
"Iris Johansen is a master among
master stoytellers."
—*Affaire de Coeur*

BLUE MOON
by the nationally bestselling author
Luanne Rice
"Luanne Rice proves herself a
nimble virtuoso."
—*The Washington Post Book World*

VELVET
by the highly acclaimed
Jane Feather
"An author to treasure."
—*Romantic Times*

THE WITCH DANCE
by the incomparable
Peggy Webb
"Ms. Webb has an inventive mind
brimming with originality that makes
all of her books special reading."
—*Romantic Times*

OFFICIAL RULES

To enter the sweepstakes below carefully follow all instructions found elsewhere in this offer.

The **Winners Classic** will award prizes with the following approximate maximum values: 1 Grand Prize: $26,500 (or $25,000 cash alternate); 1 First Prize: $3,000; 5 Second Prizes: $400 each; 35 Third Prizes: $100 each; 1,000 Fourth Prizes: $7.50 each. Total maximum retail value of Winners Classic Sweepstakes is $42,500. Some presentations of this sweepstakes may contain individual entry numbers corresponding to one or more of the aforementioned prize levels. To determine the Winners, individual entry numbers will first be compared with the winning numbers preselected by computer. For winning numbers not returned, prizes will be awarded in random drawings from among all eligible entries received. Prize choices may be offered at various levels. If a winner chooses an automobile prize, all license and registration fees, taxes, destination charges and, other expenses not offered herein are the responsibility of the winner. If a winner chooses a trip, travel must be complete within one year from the time the prize is awarded. Minors must be accompanied by an adult. Travel companion(s) must also sign release of liability. Trips are subject to space and departure availability. Certain black-out dates may apply.

The following applies to the sweepstakes named above:

No purchase necessary. You can also enter the sweepstakes by sending your name and address to: P.O. Box 508, Gibbstown, N.J. 08027. Mail each entry separately. Sweepstakes begins 6/1/93. Entries must be received by 12/30/94. Not responsible for lost, late, damaged, misdirected, illegible or postage due mail. Mechanically reproduced entries are not eligible. All entries become property of the sponsor and will not be returned.

Prize Selection/Validations: Selection of winners will be conducted no later than 5:00 PM on January 28, 1995, by an independent judging organization whose decisions are final. Random drawings will be held at 1211 Avenue of the Americas, New York, N.Y. 10036. Entrants need not be present to win. Odds of winning are determined by total number of entries received. Circulation of this sweepstakes is estimated not to exceed 200 million. All prizes are guaranteed to be awarded and delivered to winners. Winners will be notified by mail and may be required to complete an affidavit of eligibility and release of liability which must be returned within 14 days of date on notification or alternate winners will be selected in a random drawing. Any prize notification letter or any prize returned to a participating sponsor, Bantam Doubleday Dell Publishing Group, Inc., its participating divisions or subsidiaries, or the independent judging organization as undeliverable will be awarded to an alternate winner. Prizes are not transferable. No substitution for prizes except as offered or as may be necessary due to unavailability, in which case a prize of equal or greater value will be awarded. Prizes will be awarded approximately 90 days after the drawing. All taxes are the sole responsibility of the winners. Entry constitutes permission (except where prohibited by law) to use winners' names, hometowns, and likenesses for publicity purposes without further or other compensation. Prizes won by minors will be awarded in the name of parent or legal guardian.

Participation: Sweepstakes open to residents of the United States and Canada, except for the province of Quebec. Sweepstakes sponsored by Bantam Doubleday Dell Publishing Group, Inc., (BDD), 1540 Broadway, New York, NY 10036. Versions of this sweepstakes with different graphics and prize choices will be offered in conjunction with various solicitations or promotions by different subsidiaries and divisions of BDD. Where applicable, winners will have their choice of any prize offered at level won. Employees of BDD, its divisions, subsidiaries, advertising agencies, independent judging organization, and their immediate family members are not eligible.

Canadian residents, in order to win, must first correctly answer a time limited arithmetical skill testing question. Void in Puerto Rico, Quebec and wherever prohibited or restricted by law. Subject to all federal, state, local and provincial laws and regulations. For a list of major prize winners (available after 1/29/95): send a self-addressed, stamped envelope entirely separate from your entry to: Sweepstakes Winners, P.O. Box 517, Gibbstown, NJ 08027. Requests must be received by 12/30/94. DO NOT SEND ANY OTHER CORRESPONDENCE TO THIS P.O. BOX.

Don't miss these fabulous Bantam women's fiction titles

Now On Sale

WILDEST DREAMS
by Rosanne Bittner

Against the glorious panorama of Big Sky country, award-winning author Rosanne Bittner creates a sweeping saga of passion, excitement, and danger... as a beautiful young woman and a rugged ex-soldier struggle against all odds to carve out an empire—and to forge a magnificent love.

"Power, passion, tragedy, and trumph are Rosanne Bittner's hallmarks. Again and again, she brings readers to tears."—Romantic Times

____56472-2 $5.99/6.99 in Canada

DANGEROUS TO LOVE
by Elizabeth Thornton

"A major, major talent...a genre superstar."—Rave Reviews
"I consider Elizabeth Thornton a major find."
—Bestselling author Mary Balogh

____56787-X $5.99/$6.99 in Canada

AMAZON LILY
by Theresa Weir

Winner of Romantic Times's New Adventure Writer Award, Theresa Weir captures your heart with this truly irresistible story of two remarkable people who must battle terrifying danger even as they discover breathtaking love....
"Romantic adventure has no finer writer than the spectacular Theresa Weir."—Romantic Times

____56463-3 $4.99/$5.99 in Canada

Ask for these books at your local bookstore or use this page to order.

❏ Please send me the books I have checked above. I am enclosing $ _____ (add $2.50 to cover postage and handling). Send check or money order, no cash or C. O. D.'s please.

Name _____

Address _____

City/ State/ Zip _____

Send order to: Bantam Books, Dept. FN142, 2451 S. Wolf Rd., Des Plaines, IL 60018
Allow four to six weeks for delivery.
Prices and availability subject to change without notice.

FN 142 7/94

Bestselling Women's Fiction

Sandra Brown

_____	28951-9 TEXAS! LUCKY	$5.99/6.99 in Canada
_____	28990-X TEXAS! CHASE	$5.99/6.99
_____	29500-4 TEXAS! SAGE	$5.99/6.99
_____	29085-1 22 INDIGO PLACE	$5.99/6.99
_____	29783-X A WHOLE NEW LIGHT	$5.99/6.99
_____	56045-X TEMPERATURES RISING	$5.99/6.99
_____	56274-6 FANTA C	$4.99/5.99
_____	56278-9 LONG TIME COMING	$4.99/5.99

Amanda Quick

_____	28354-5 SEDUCTION	$5.99/6.99
_____	28932-2 SCANDAL	$5.99/6.99
_____	28594-7 SURRENDER	$5.99/6.99
_____	29325-7 RENDEZVOUS	$5.99/6.99
_____	29316-8 RECKLESS	$5.99/6.99
_____	29316-8 RAVISHED	$4.99/5.99
_____	29317-6 DANGEROUS	$5.99/6.99
_____	56506-0 DECEPTION	$5.99/7.50

Nora Roberts

_____	29078-9 GENUINE LIES	$5.99/6.99
_____	28578-5 PUBLIC SECRETS	$5.99/6.99
_____	26461-3 HOT ICE	$5.99/6.99
_____	26574-1 SACRED SINS	$5.99/6.99
_____	27859-2 SWEET REVENGE	$5.99/6.99
_____	27283-7 BRAZEN VIRTUE	$5.99/6.99
_____	29597-7 CARNAL INNOCENCE	$5.50/6.50
_____	29490-3 DIVINE EVIL	$5.99/6.99

Iris Johansen

_____	29871-2 LAST BRIDGE HOME	$4.50/5.50
_____	29604-3 THE GOLDEN BARBARIAN	$4.99/5.99
_____	29244-7 REAP THE WIND	$4.99/5.99
_____	29032-0 STORM WINDS	$4.99/5.99
_____	28855-5 THE WIND DANCER	$4.95/5.95
_____	29968-9 THE TIGER PRINCE	$5.50/6.50
_____	29944-1 THE MAGNIFICENT ROGUE	$5.99/6.99
_____	29945-X BELOVED SCOUNDREL	$5.99/6.99